BLACKSTONE AND
THE WOLF OF WALL STREET

Recent Titles by Sally Spencer from Severn House

THE BUTCHER BEYOND
DANGEROUS GAMES
THE DARK LADY
THE DEAD HAND OF HISTORY
DEATH OF A CAVE DWELLER
DEATH OF AN INNOCENT
A DEATH LEFT HANGING
DEATH WATCH
DYING IN THE DARK
A DYING FALL
THE ENEMY WITHIN
FATAL QUEST
GOLDEN MILE TO MURDER
A LONG TIME DEAD
MURDER AT SWANN'S LAKE
THE PARADISE JOB
THE RED HERRING
THE RING OF DEATH
THE SALTON KILLINGS
SINS OF THE FATHERS
STONE KILLER
THE WITCH MAKER

The Inspector Sam Blackstone Series

RENDEZVOUS WITH DEATH
BLACKSTONE AND THE TIGER
BLACKSTONE AND THE GOLDEN EGG
BLACKSTONE AND THE FIRE BUG
BLACKSTONE AND THE BALLOON OF DEATH
BLACKSTONE AND THE HEART OF DARKNESS
BLACKSTONE AND THE NEW WORLD
BLACKSTONE AND THE WOLF OF WALL STREET

BLACKSTONE AND THE WOLF OF WALL STREET

Sally Spencer

This first world edition published 2010
in Great Britain and in the USA by
SEVERN HOUSE PUBLISHERS LTD of
9–15 High Street, Sutton, Surrey, England, SM1 1DF.
Trade paperback edition first published
in Great Britain and the USA 2011 by
SEVERN HOUSE PUBLISHERS LTD.

British Library Cataloguing in Publication Data

Spencer, Sally.
  Blackstone and the Wolf of Wall Street. – (The Inspector
  Sam Blackstone series)
  1. Blackstone, Sam (Fictitious character) – Fiction.
  2. Police – New York (State) – New York – Fiction.
  3. Millionaires – Crimes against – Fiction. 4. Kidnapping
  victims – Fiction. 5. Coney Island (New York, N.Y.) –
  Social conditions – Fiction. 6. Detective and mystery
  stories.
  I. Title II. Series
  823.9'14-dc22

ISBN-13: 978-0-7278-6916-6   (cased)
ISBN-13: 978-1-84751-262-8   (trade paper)

All Severn House titles are printed on acid-free paper.

Severn House Publishers support The Forest Stewardship Council [FSC],
the leading international forest certification organisation. All our titles that
are printed on Greenpeace-approved FSC-certified paper carry the FSC logo.

Mixed Sources
Product group from well-managed
forests and other controlled sources
www.fsc.org Cert no. SA-COC-1565
© 1996 Forest Stewardship Council

Typeset by Palimpsest Book Production Ltd.,
Falkirk, Stirlingshire, Scotland.
Printed and bound in Great Britain by
MPG Books Ltd., Bodmin, Cornwall.

PROLOGUE

Though he was desperate to complete his mission before he lost his nerve, Knox forced himself to take only small, careful steps as he made his way slowly along Fifth Avenue.

There was good reason for this caution. The weak sun had struggled to bring a little cheer into the shivering city during the day, but the second it had been vanquished over the horizon, the pitiless winter had returned with a vengeance.

Now, the sun's pale warmth seemed no more than a distant memory – a rumour that, once, times had been better. Now, frost clung mockingly to the lamp posts and patches of black ice began to form across the sidewalk.

Black ice!

Damn it to hell.

You couldn't see it, because it was almost transparent.

You couldn't guess where it might be, because it did not spread itself evenly, but instead chose to lurk in isolated spots, waiting with malevolent patience for the unsuspecting foot to fall on it.

And there was black ice lurking, too, on the journey that is our lives, Knox thought bitterly. Take a wrong step on *that* journey – make just one little misjudgement – and instead of advancing, you were lying on the ground, bruised and battered.

He himself had stepped on black ice, and that particular sheet of it had been called William Holt, who hadn't looked dangerous and had given no warning of what he might do.

It just didn't seem fair!

Knox reached into his overcoat pocket, and felt the reassuring handle of the revolver he had bought earlier that day.

'It's going to happen,' he reassured himself. 'I'm going to do it!'

But he mustn't slip and fall, because, if he did, he knew that it would probably be enough to shake his resolve – to convince him that men like him simply did not take their revenge in this way.

He was still finding it hard to believe that everything had collapsed so quickly around him.

Only two months earlier – as recently as *Christmas*! – he had been regarded by almost everyone who mattered in New York as one of the city's great successes.

He had noticed people pointing him out in expensive restaurants, and had found it easy enough to imagine what they were saying.

'That's Edward Knox. You'd never think it to look at him, but he's worth millions of dollars.'

And now?

Now, it was all over. His house had been foreclosed. He could no longer afford to pay for his sons to attend their expensive college. His wife had left him.

He was finished.

He was resigned to that.

He accepted he would never be able to dredge up the energy to start again from scratch, and though he was still walking – albeit timidly – he was already as good as dead.

But before he finally lay down, he'd promised himself, he would make one last attempt to see that justice was done.

He had reached his destination, a large house close to St Patrick's Cathedral, which – like all the other houses around it – was in complete darkness. He walked around the side of the building to the tradesman's entrance, and tapped softly on the door.

Though the Holt mansion had electric light throughout, unlike most of the private dwellings in the city, the woman who opened the door was carrying a small kerosene lantern in her hand.

'It's safer this way,' she whispered.

She led him into the kitchen, and placed the lantern on the table.

He examined her in the flickering light. She was in her late twenties – he knew that for a fact – and a few years earlier she had been a very pretty little thing. But time had not been kind to her. Now she could have been taken for at least ten years older than her actual age.

'Have you got the money?' she hissed urgently.

He nodded. 'Right here,' he said, reaching into his pocket and taking out a brown envelope.

She grabbed the envelope from him, ripped it open without ceremony, and began counting the bills on the table.

'It's all there,' he promised her.

And so it was. Some people might have considered him foolish to hand over the last of his savings to this woman, but he had no doubts on the matter. As far as he was concerned, it was the best thousand dollars he had ever spent.

The woman had finished counting.

'I'm not doing this for the money,' she said.

'Then give it back to me!' he said harshly – and instantly felt guilty.

'I can't give it back,' the woman said. 'I need it to get away from here – *but that's not why I'm doing this.*'

'I know, Margaret,' he told her.

'I was only supposed to be his secretary,' the woman said. 'I was supposed to do no more than take shorthand and typewrite his letters. I was good at it. That should have been enough for him. But it wasn't.'

'I know,' Knox said for a second time.

'He didn't use physical force to get me into his bed—' Margaret Wilkins continued.

'I don't really need to know the details,' Knox said, uncomfortably.

'. . . but if it wasn't rape, it was certainly as good as.'

'There's no point in dwelling on the past,' advised Knox, who found himself doing little else now.

'But even though I didn't ever *want* him to sleep with me, it still hurt that he'd only make use of me when there wasn't some other woman within easy reach.'

'He's a bastard,' Knox said, though he never usually swore in the presence of ladies. 'We both know that. That's why I'm here and why you're letting me into the house.'

'Yes, that's why you're here and why I'm letting you into the house,' Margaret Wilkins repeated dully.

'Where is he?'

'In his study. He always works late into the night.'

'And is there anyone else around?'

'No, the rest of them went to bed at least an hour ago.'

'Then let's get it over with,' Knox suggested.

Carrying her lantern in front of her, Margaret Wilkins led him through a maze of corridors to the servants' stairs, and then up to the first floor. Here, the corridors – designed for use by family and friends, rather than just as a passageway for mere domestics – were wider and more impressive.

The woman came to a stop in front of a solid teak door.

'He's in there,' she whispered.

'Will the door be locked?'

'No, it's never locked. He wouldn't even dream that anyone would dare to enter without his permission.'

Knox let his fingers brush against the butt of his revolver.

'You'd better go now.'

Margaret Wilkins shook her head. 'I want to stay. I want to see it happen.'

'Don't be a fool,' Knox hissed back. 'Go now, and you can say you knew nothing of what went on. Stay, and you'll be as guilty as I am.'

'I don't care,' the woman said stubbornly.

'Take the money I've given you and start a new life,' he urged her.

For a second, it looked as if she would refuse again. Then she gave a brief nod, turned, and hurried down the corridor. Soon, she was no more than a faint island of retreating light, and he was left in the darkness.

With one hand he reached into his pocket and grasped his revolver. With the other he groped for the door handle, and – once he had found it – gave it a sharp turn and pushed the door open.

The electric light inside the room blinded him, but only for a moment, then his eyes adjusted and he saw Big Bill Holt sitting at his desk. Holt was still wearing the tuxedo he must have put on for dinner, and there was a faraway – almost ecstatic – look in his eyes. At first, he did not even seem to notice that someone had entered the room, but when that fact registered, the eyes blazed with anger.

'What the hell are you doing here?' he demanded.

Knox advanced further into the centre of the room. 'You cheated me,' he said. 'You took all my money – and you *cheated* me.'

Holt shrugged his massive shoulders. 'Nobody cheated you. You went into a business where you could either have made or lost money – and you lost it.'

'But *you* didn't lose, did you?' Knox demanded, aware that a hysterical note was creeping into his voice.

'No, I didn't lose,' Holt agreed. 'I had the sense to get out in time.'

'And you didn't tell me.'

Another shrug. 'Since when have I been your nursemaid?'

This was something very wrong about all this, Knox thought. When he had played out the scene in his mind – and he must have done that a hundred times – things had been quite different.

In the Knox mind-version, Holt jumps to his feet and rushes around the desk. And this is what Knox wants. Because it is not enough that the other man must die – he must know humiliation before that death.

Holt's anger has swollen him to almost twice his normal size. He is like a raging bull that has sighted the red cape – like a ravenous lion springing at its prey. He knows that he can snap the puny intruder

in two – as if he were no more than a twig – and that is just what
he intends to do.

Knox waits until his enemy is halfway across the room – then
produces the gun from his pocket.

Holt sees the revolver, and comes to an abrupt stop.

He is still like a raging bull, but now one that has the smell of its
own death in its nostrils – still the ravaging lion, but now a lion
which realizes it is no match for its intended victim. His arms drop
uselessly to his sides and his eyes are suddenly filled with fear.

'What's that?' this fantasy Holt says in a trembling voice, as his
eyes fix on the gun.

'You know what it is,' the fantasy Knox replies, his own voice as
firm and steady as the hand in which he is holding the weapon.

Holt sinks to his knees, his hands clenched in prayer.

'Please don't kill me!' he sobs. 'Please!'

And that is the moment at which Knox pulls the trigger.

That was what *should have* happened – but it *hadn't*!

Holt was continuing to sit behind his desk.

Angry – yes.

Frightened – possibly.

But still sitting there!

Knox pulled out the revolver and pointed it at his enemy.

'Put the gun away, before you hurt yourself,' Holt said.

But the fear was in his eyes now – just as Knox had dreamed it
would be.

'Stand up!' the man with the revolver said.

'Why should I?' Holt demanded.

Why indeed, Knox wondered.

Because, he supposed, that was how he had scripted it to be –
how it was *meant* to be.

'Stand up, and you may just live,' he said. 'Stay where you are,
and I'll kill you right now.'

Holt still made no move. 'I'll pay you back all the money you
lost. I'll pay you back *double* what you lost.'

For an instant, Knox almost gave way.

But *only* for an instant – because he knew that the moment he
lost the upper hand, Holt would crush him.

'I'm going to count to three, and if you're not standing up by
"three", I *will* kill you!'

Slowly and reluctantly, Holt rose to his feet – to reveal that he
was naked from the waist down.

'What the . . .' Knox gasped.

And then he understood.

'You got a *whore* under your desk,' he said. 'You've spent the money you stole from me on a *whore!*'

Holt forced a smile to his face.

'Oh, not all of it,' he said. 'Even the best prostitutes are nowhere near as expensive as that.'

He was trying to make a joke of the whole situation, Knox realized. Because he knew it would make him seem more human – make him more difficult to kill.

But that wouldn't work. In fact, it only made matters worse, because only a monster would rob two fine young men of their college education and then squander the money on a common prostitute.

'If you still believe in God, then pray to Him now,' Knox said, his finger already tightening on the trigger.

It was the woman's scream which made his hand jerk – made the bullet he fired strike Holt not in his black heart, but only in the shoulder.

Big Bill rocked, but somehow managed to hold his ground.

And then the woman herself appeared – rising up suddenly from behind the desk and burying her head in Holt's massive chest.

As if that would protect her!

As if she would have been worse off staying where she was!

Knox looked down at the gun in his hand, almost as if he were wondering how it had ever got there.

He couldn't shoot again, he told himself, because the woman was in the way.

But even if she hadn't been, he understood – deep down – he would not have fired a second time, because he had only ever been brave enough to loose off one shot, and that shot had already gone.

Despite his wound, Holt was struggling to get from behind the desk – to come at him just as he had done in the fantasy – but the woman was clinging on to him with all the strength that her fear had given her.

And suddenly, there was a fourth person in the room – a stocky young man in a nightshirt.

That's George, Holt's eldest son, Knox thought in the detached way of someone who has withdrawn from the drama and is now only part of the audience.

George Holt looked at his father and the woman, then at Knox, then at his father and the woman again.

'Oh my God!' he said in a voice which was almost a moan. 'Oh my God, oh my God, oh my God . . .'

'For Christ's sake, be a man for once!' his father said harshly. 'You see what the problem is. Deal with it.'

But George stood rooted to the spot – as if he couldn't have moved even if he wanted to.

'Deal with it!' his father repeated.

And slowly – almost like a sleepwalker – George Holt turned to face the man with the gun.

There were still five bullets left in the chamber of the revolver, Knox thought. And at this range, he couldn't miss. But he had no argument with *George* Holt. Besides, he was feeling very, very tired, and pulling the trigger seemed like just too much of an effort.

And so he stood there.

Watching as George crossed the room towards him.

Watching as George came to a stop and bent his elbow back to give the blow he was about to deliver more force.

Watching as the big fist came towards him – growing ever larger until it filled his whole world.

And then everything went black.

ONE

Seven years later

There were barmen who would have been uncomfortable about working in a saloon that was only a short step from Sing Sing Prison, but this particular one – Jack O'Toole – considered himself a student of human nature in all its manifestations, and saw the location almost as a bonus. He liked the fact that his customers were not the run-of-the-mill carpenters and plumbers who patronized most saloons, and prided himself on being able to spot which side of the law each of them had been drawn from.

The saloon had been busy that morning – it always was on execution days – but the rush had eased off somewhat by the time the two men came in, and as they walked across the room to the counter, O'Toole made one of his famously rapid assessments of them.

They were an odd pair, and that was for sure, the barman thought.

The older of the two looked around forty. He was over six feet tall, and thin as a rake, but there was a hardness emanating from his wiry frame which would make even the beefiest troublemaker think twice about tangling with him. He had a large nose which – the barman thought whimsically – he could almost have borrowed from the Old Testament, and dark eyes which were not actually blazing with righteousness and anger at that moment, but looked as if they could manage the trick quite easily. He was dressed in a brown suit that had seen better days and had a decidedly un-American cut.

The other man was younger – possibly only twenty-three or twenty-four – and though he looked fit enough and manly enough, there was still evidence on his face of the boy he had so recently been. His disposition seemed sunnier – more overtly optimistic – than his companion's, and *his* suit had a sharpness and style about it that made the barman green with envy.

'What can I do for you, gentlemen?' O'Toole asked.

'I'd kill for a beer,' said the shorter man.

'So would I,' the taller man agreed. 'Kill for it – and damn the consequences.' He paused, and smiled down at his companion. 'But if I was to be executed for the crime, I still think I'd prefer the rope to the electric chair.'

'What do you *really* think of the way we dispatch our murderers over here?' the shorter man, Alex Meade, asked, as the barman was filling a jug for them.

'It was . . . interesting,' replied the taller man, Sam Blackstone.

'You mean, *impressive.*'

'I mean *interesting.*'

Meade chuckled. 'You just can't bring yourself to say that we've got the edge on you in this matter, can you, Sam?' he asked. 'You just can't admit that while you Brits are still stuck in the fifteenth century with your executions, we Yanks have embraced living in the twentieth.'

Strictly speaking, it wasn't the twentieth century until next year – 1901 – Blackstone thought, but there seemed little point in getting into a pedantic debate with the American colleague who had been kind enough to take the trouble to bring him to Cayuga County to witness the execution.

'To tell you the truth, the whole process seemed rather slow and ponderous,' Blackstone admitted.

'Slow and ponderous?' Meade repeated. 'The guy was dead within fifteen seconds of pulling the switch.'

'Maybe he was,' Blackstone conceded. 'But, dear me, it seemed to take for ever to get him into a position where the switch *could* be pulled.'

'And how long would it take in Limeyland?' Meade asked, sounding a little aggrieved.

'If everything goes smoothly, there's never more than twelve seconds between the condemned man leaving his cell and taking the drop which breaks his neck.'

Meade shook his head in wonder. 'You guys,' he said. 'England must be the only country in the world that makes a positive *virtue* out of being old-fashioned. It's a miracle to me that you ever gave up bows and arrows.'

'Being old-fashioned is not just one of our greatest strengths,' Blackstone replied, as the barman handed him the jug of frothing beer. 'It's also an important part of our charm.'

'Is that right?' Meade asked, as he turned and headed for a free table. 'I must admit, I never knew Englishmen *had* charm.'

There were many things about America that Blackstone found strange and disconcerting, and the saloon culture was one of them. Back in England, each pub was a series of small rooms, only vaguely connected to one another. Here, on the other side of the pond, intimacy seemed to have been sacrificed in the interest of ostentatious democracy, and most drinking establishments were like this one, consisting of one vast, almost prairie-like room.

The beer was different, too. It had none of the gravity of a pint of London bitter. It was lighter and more frivolous – a sign, as he saw it, that Americans had still not come to appreciate what a serious matter drinking was.

'You're drawing comparisons again, aren't you?' Alex Meade asked him, from across the table.

'Yes, I suppose I am,' Blackstone admitted.

But then, wasn't it only natural that he would?

It was less than a month since he had disembarked from the second class deck of the liner that had brought him to New York, and been met on the quayside by the fresh-faced detective sergeant in the straw boater.

His mission had been simple – to identify a prisoner and take him back to England, where the man was under sentence of death. But things had not worked out quite as intended. Within a few hours of first setting foot on American soil – or rather, on American concrete – Blackstone had found himself involved in an investigation into the murder of a police inspector.

Nor had the successful conclusion of that case done anything to speed his return home. His prisoner had escaped – been *allowed* to escape, bribed his way *into* an escape – and until he was recaptured, Blackstone was seconded to the NYPD.

'Did I ever tell you how the invention of the electric chair came about?' Alex Meade asked innocently.

But there was nothing really innocent about it – Meade had an almost missionary zeal when it came to explaining his country to his English friend, a zeal which Blackstone found fascinating and irritating in almost equal measure, and often both at the same time.

The Englishman smiled again. 'No, you never did tell me,' he confessed.

Meade took a long sip of his beer, which Blackstone guessed meant that this would be one of his longer anecdotes.

'As with so many other things in this great country of ours, it was driven by commerce,' Meade began. 'Specifically, it was driven by the War of Currents.'

'The War of Currents?' Blackstone repeated, as he knew he was supposed to.

'Indeed,' Alex Meade replied. 'See, the first person to start supplying power in America was Thomas Edison.' He paused. 'You'll have heard of him?'

Blackstone nodded. 'Invented the light bulb, didn't he?'

'Among other things,' Meade agreed. 'At any rate, Edison's power system used direct current, which was fine and dandy in a way, but had the drawback that the power generator could never be more than a mile and a half from the place that was using the power. That didn't matter at first, because direct current was the only show in town, so everybody used it. Then along came Nikola Tesla and George Westinghouse with their alternating current.'

He paused again, in case there was anything Blackstone wished to say.

'I'm not much of a scientist,' the Englishman admitted.

'Tesla invented AC while he was working for Edison, but Tom wasn't interested in the idea. Westinghouse was quite another matter. He could see the potential of a power source that could be created many miles away from where it was being used, and went into compe tition with Edison.'

'And part of that competition was to see who could produce the first electric chair?' Blackstone guessed.

Meade chuckled. 'You couldn't be further from the truth. What actually happened was that it soon became obvious to Edison that Westinghouse's system was vastly superior, but – Tom being Tom – he couldn't bring himself to admit it publicly and change over to it himself. So what he did do was to start spreading the story that alternating current was much more *dangerous* than direct.'

'I believe that's what you Americans would call "dirty pool",' Blackstone said.

'Yeah, but, at the same time, we can't help admiring the guy for being so smart,' Meade replied. 'Where was I?'

'Dangerous,' Blackstone prompted.

'That's right. Now, at just that time, the authorities were looking for a more humane way of executing people than hanging them,' Meade continued. 'A dentist called Southwick had already come up with the idea of an electric chair, and Edison secretly financed a guy called Brown to develop it.'

'Because of his *own* interest in finding a more humane way?'

Meade shook his head. 'Edison was against capital punishment on principle – totally against it,' he shrugged, 'but, when all's said and done, business is business.'

'Ah, now I understand,' Blackstone exclaimed. 'The chair was to be powered by alternating current!'

'Exactly! The message he was sending out was, "If AC can fry a man to death, do you really want it in your home?" So Brown developed the chair, and Edison held a number of public demonstrations to show just how dangerous it was. It was mostly stray cats and dogs he electrocuted – kids were paid fifty cents to collect them for him – but he would sometimes use it on unwanted cattle or horses. Course, he didn't want the process to be called "electrocution" – that would give *all* electricity a bad name. What he was pushing for was for it to be known as being "Westinghoused".'

'Clever,' Blackstone said, grudgingly.

'It sure was,' Meade agreed. 'Anyway, New York State bought the idea of the electric chair, and was all set for its first execution. Then it hit a snag.'

'And what was that?'

'Westinghouse didn't want alternating current associated with the electric chair, and so he refused to sell the prison the generator. So what Edison did was to set up a fake company in South America, and buy a generator for a university down there. Then, once he had his hands on it, he shipped it right back to New York, where it was used for the execution of a man called Kemmler.'

'And it was a great success, was it?' Blackstone asked.

Meade suddenly looked slightly cagey. 'Not immediately,' he admitted.

'So what went wrong?'

'It took a little longer than expected.'

'*How* much longer?'

'Well, the first seventeen second burst didn't kill him, and the doctors in attendance said he should been given a second dose, straight away. But they *couldn't* do it straight away, because the generator needed to be recharged.'

'But when it *was* recharged, it *did* work?' Blackstone asked.

'Sure,' Meade agreed – much too quickly.

'Immediately?' Blackstone pressed.

'Well, no,' Meade conceded. 'Not until the blood vessels under his skin had burst and he'd caught fire.'

'Very humane,' Blackstone said drily.

'Yeah, it was a botched job,' Meade admitted. 'George Westinghouse said, with some glee, that they could have done a better job with an axe – but we've improved since then, as you've just seen for yourself.'

A uniformed prison guard entered the saloon, looked around him, and then walked over to the table where the two men were sitting.

'Detective Sergeant Meade?' he asked tentatively.

'That's right,' Meade agreed.

The prison officer held out a telegram. 'This just arrived. They said it was urgent.'

Meade slit the cable open, quickly scanned the words, and then whistled softly.

'Ever heard of William "Big Bill" Holt?' he asked Blackstone.

Blackstone shook his head. 'Is he important?'

'He's about the most important reclusive millionaire in the whole of the USA.'

'And just how many reclusive millionaires *are* there?' Blackstone asked, with a smile.

'Must be hundreds of them,' Meade said. 'Well,' he corrected himself, 'ten or fifteen, anyway. But like I said, Big Bill's the most important.'

'And I take it something's happened to him – or someone close to him,' Blackstone guessed.

'To him,' Meade confirmed.

'Robbed?' Blackstone speculated. 'Murdered?'

'Possibly both,' Meade said. 'But all we actually know at the moment is that he's been *kidnapped*.'

TWO

The first stage of the streetcar journey from Manhattan to Coney Island took them along the canyons which ran between brown and crumbling tenement blocks, but soon they had left the City of Brooklyn behind them, and were out in open country, where the only buildings they now saw were white clapperboard farmhouses.

'Strictly speaking, this case is outside our jurisdiction,' Alex Meade said, as the streetcar rattled noisily along. 'If we were playing it by the book, the whole thing would be handled by the local boys on Coney Island.'

'So why *isn't* it being handled by them?'

'My guess is that the powers-that-be in Albany – the Governor and the Attorney General – think that the kidnapping of a man like Holt is far too important a matter to be left in the hands of hayseeds.'

'So if it's *that* important, why has the case been given to a detective sergeant and a Limey who's just passing through?' Blackstone pondered.

'Because we're good?' Meade asked.

'Or could it be that if things go wrong, there'll be a lot of shit flying about, and none of the higher-ups want any of that shit sticking to them?' Blackstone countered.

'Maybe,' Meade conceded. 'But with two guys like us on the case, nothing *is* going to go wrong, is it?'

Blackstone shook his head in wonderment. There really was no limit to Alex Meade's optimism, he thought. Place the man in front of a thousand angry tribesmen who were waving spears at him, and he would be still be planning what he was going to do the next day.

Nothing *is* going to go wrong!

There were a hundred things which could go wrong with *any* investigation – and in a kidnapping, you could multiply that by ten.

The streetcar rattled on, taking them ever closer to the place where nothing could go wrong.

'So what can you tell me about this Big Bill Holt?' Blackstone said.

'Very little,' Meade told him, almost shamefacedly.

Blackstone raised a surprised eyebrow. If this case had been on his own patch, back in London, then *he* would have known very little, too, because, as a boy brought up in an orphanage and a man mainly used to dealing with common criminals, Holt would have moved in circles far above him.

But Alex Meade was different. His father was a very successful lawyer, he himself was Harvard-educated – and, before he had chosen to disgrace himself by becoming a policeman, he had been very much a part of fashionable and prosperous New York society. Besides, Alex was an incorrigible gossip who collected information in much the same way as other men collected stamps or grievances, and it was almost inconceivable that he didn't have a full tale to tell.

'Big Bill dropped out of the limelight when I was little more than a kid,' Meade said, as if he felt the need to defend his ignorance. 'Nobody says much about him any more – because there's not much to say.'

'But he *is* still in business, is he?'

'Oh hell, yes, he's never *off* the financial pages. When William Holt catches a cold, the whole of Wall Street shivers.'

The streetcar crossed a bridge over a muddy creek, and suddenly they were in another world, as distinct from the countryside they had recently travelled through as that countryside itself had been from grim industrial Brooklyn. Immediately ahead were lines of single-storied brick buildings, but beyond them – beyond *them* – lay some of the most fantastic structures Blackstone had ever seen in his life.

There were Chinese towers and Moorish domes, castles painted in gaudy colours, swings which hung from a fulcrum dizzily high in the air, and a huge wheel which turned with majestic slowness while its passengers jabbered and pointed excitedly into the distance.

'Welcome to Coney Island, the entertainment capital of America,' Alex Meade said complacently. 'Bet you ain't got anything like this over in old England, Sam.'

No, they hadn't, Blackstone admitted to himself. It would never have occurred to the English to indiscriminately borrow bits of half the cultures of the world and lump them in all together on one garish site. And yet, he had to concede, it somehow worked.

'Don't worry, Sam, you'll soon catch up with us,' Meade said, in a kindly tone.

And they probably would, Blackstone thought. Give it a few years, and staid Southend-on-Sea would probably look *just* like Coney Island.

The streetcar juddered to a halt, and the conductor announced they had reached the terminus.

'There's our ride,' Meade said, and pointed to a black police department carriage which had a white-haired uniformed police sergeant standing next to it.

The sergeant said his name was Walter Jones. He immediately reminded Blackstone of the wise old sergeants he had known back in London, and when Jones informed him, as they were getting into the carriage, that he'd been policing Coney Island for a long, long time, the Englishman was not in the least surprised.

'It was no more than a village when I started out,' Jones said, as the carriage left the shops, the bars, the vaudeville houses and the amusement parks behind it. 'Kinda peaceful and slow.'

'And then the railroad and the streetcars arrived,' Meade said.

Jones nodded. 'And everything changed for ever,' he said, with just a hint of sadness in his voice. 'The railroad came in '89, the first amusement park – Captain Paul Boyton's Sea Lion Park – opened in '95, and now it seems like the whole world wants to spend its money on Coney Island.'

'When did William Holt buy his house here?' Blackstone asked.

'Must have been 1893,' Jones answered.

Blackstone and Meade exchanged a knowing glance – that was the same year Holt decided to became a hermit, the glance said.

'Tell us about it,' Meade suggested.

'Well, Mr Holt bought the house – it's called Ocean Heights – from the van Ryans. They were a real old Coney Island family, and very well-liked. But, it has to be said, they'd let the place go to rack and ruin. So the first thing Mr Holt did was to have it ripped apart.'

'Ripped apart?'

'Yeah, more or less. He pretty much rebuilt it from scratch, which made him real popular round here.'

'How so?' Meade asked.

'Well, he didn't bring all his workers in from the city, you see, which is what the high muckety-mucks usually do. No, sir, he employed local men. And when the house was finished and ready to move into, he employed local folk to run it for him, too. Matter of fact, the only people who work there that ain't from Coney Island are that butler of his, and – of course – the Pinkertons.'

'Of course,' Blackstone agreed.

But he was thinking, who – or what – are the *Pinkertons*?

A number of improbable possibilities flashed fancifully through his mind:

Fred and Lily Pinkerton, a famous music hall act he personally had never heard of, but who were now exclusively employed to entertain the Holt family.

Members of an obscure North American Indian tribe.

A sect which had broken away from the Dutch Reform Church.

'Any time you're ready, Sam, I'm more than willing to help you,' Meade said, with barely concealed amusement.

Blackstone sighed. 'All right, who *are* the Pinkertons?' he asked dutifully.

'Members of the Pinkerton Detective Agency, which was founded by Allan Pinkerton in 1850.'

'And I take it that they're well-known to most Americans,' Blackstone said, resignedly.

'Hell, yes,' Meade agreed. 'They acted as President Lincoln's bodyguards during the Civil War, and were employed to help track down Jesse James and the Wild Bunch. At one point, there were more Pinkerton agents than there were men serving in the US Army. They've done all kinds of work – including strike-breaking. And until Congress passed a law in '93 to make it illegal for them to work for government agencies, they practically ran the investigative branch of the Department of Justice. Isn't that right, Sergeant Jones?'

'It is,' the sergeant agreed. 'There sure is a lot of stuff about this country that you don't know, ain't there, Mr Blackstone?'

'There sure is,' Blackstone agreed.

And even with Alex Meade to guide him, that ignorance still had a fair chance of tripping him up at some point in this investigation, he cautioned himself.

'It was a couple of the Pinkerton agents who were killed,' Jones said.

'Killed?' Meade repeated incredulously, as if he suspected he might have misheard.

'Had their throats slit,' Jones told him.

'But the cable we got in Sing Sing never said anything about that!' Meade protested.

Of course it hadn't, Blackstone thought. Big Bill Holt was important, and Big Bill Holt had been kidnapped. What had happened to the hired help was neither here nor there.

'There's Ocean Heights now,' Sergeant Jones said, pointing out of the open carriage window.

Blackstone looked out at the house. In England, he thought, a dwelling like that would have been surrounded by a long high wall, but walls did not seem to be the American way.

The house was on a small hillock, three stories tall and – unlike most of the other dwellings they had passed en route – was made of stone. It was large and impressive enough to be called a 'grand' house, Blackstone decided, but it fell well short of the size – and ostentation – of the Fifth Avenue chateaux which many of William Holt's fellow millionaires had built for themselves.

He turned his attention from the building itself to its surroundings. There were formal gardens – fifty yards wide – running along the front and sides of the house. Beyond them was woodland, which was the ideal hiding place for kidnappers waiting for the right moment to swoop. The back of the house presumably – given its name – faced out on to the ocean, which, if these same kidnappers had chosen to avail themselves of it, would have presented a perfect escape route.

'Holt must have put all his faith in security *inside* the house,' said Alex Meade, who was developing an uncanny knack for reading his new partner's thoughts.

'Yes – and *that* seems to have worked out very well indeed,' Blackstone said sourly.

'Just dandy,' Meade agreed.

Sergeant Jones banged on the roof of the carriage, as a signal for the driver to stop.

'Better go and see how my boys are doing,' he said.

There were plenty of his 'boys' in evidence. At least half a dozen uniformed policemen were wandering around in a purposeful-looking – yet clearly disorganized – manner.

It wouldn't do any good, of course, Blackstone told himself. Searches required patience, not energy, and in their attempt to show their sergeant how enthusiastic they were, they'd probably already destroyed any clues the kidnappers had thoughtfully left for them.

'See what I mean about hayseeds?' Meade asked, as the carriage began to move again. 'These guys don't have a clue about how to handle a case as big as this one.'

That was probably true, Blackstone agreed, though he doubted if the New York City Police Department – which seemed to spend very little time on police work, and a great deal of time on lining its own pockets – knew how to handle it either.

'This is your big chance to show the department what you're made of, Sam,' Meade said with his characteristic bubbling enthusiasm. 'This is your opportunity to demonstrate to the stuffed-shirts and time-servers how a *real* policeman – a *Scotland Yard* policeman – handles a tough investigation.'

Maybe it was, Blackstone agreed. Or maybe it was his opportunity to demonstrate just how much out of his depth he was in this young country with its strange ways.

It was as the carriage drew to a halt a second time that they noticed the man in the tweed suit. He was in his late thirties, or perhaps a little older, with sandy hair and the sort of bland, unexceptional features that even a police artist would struggle to make look distinctive. He was watching the arrival of the carriage, and though the expression on his face said it was really of very little interest to him, the intensity of his stance told quite a different story.

The man remained fixed to the spot until they had climbed down from the carriage, then ambled across to them as if he had all the time in the world.

'I'm Inspector Flynn,' he said, in a lilting Irish accent. '*You'll* be them fellers from New York.'

He made it sound a thousand miles away, instead of just across the water. In fact, he made it sound as if it were a completely different world – and one he didn't want intruding on his own.

'I'm Detective Sergeant Meade, sir,' Alex said.

'Are you indeed?' Flynn asked, as if he had reason to doubt it.

'Yes, sir,' Meade affirmed.

'Well now, there's no need to call me "sir",' Flynn told him. 'You're not one of *my* men.'

And what he means, by extension, is, 'And *I'm* not one of *yours*, either,' Blackstone thought.

'And this is Inspector Blackstone of New Scotland Yard,' Meade continued, with nothing in his tone revealing that he'd even noticed how frosty the atmosphere was.

'Blackstone,' Flynn repeated reflectively. 'You'll be that Englishman who solved Inspector O'Brien's murder, will you?'

'I was certainly involved in the investigation,' Blackstone agreed.

'He was a good man, Inspector O'Brien – a credit to the Old Country,' Flynn said musingly. 'But tell me, Mr Blackstone,' he continued, his voice losing its wistful edge, 'have you ever, during your time at New Scotland Yard, served in the Irish Special Branch?'

'No,' Blackstone replied.

'From what I've heard from my cousins across the water, they're real bastards in that Special Branch,' Flynn said. He removed his derby and scratched his head lightly. 'And you're *sure* you never belonged to it?'

'You don't know me, Mr Flynn, so I'll excuse you for suggesting I lied the first time you asked me the question,' Blackstone said. 'But, if I was you, I wouldn't make a habit of doing that.'

Flynn smiled, though – like most of his expressions – it hardly seemed to change his face at all. 'I think there's just a possibility we might get on, Mr Blackstone,' he said.

'Let's hope so,' Blackstone agreed. 'Where was Holt when the kidnapping took place?'

'In his private suite,' Flynn replied.

'And where were his guards – the ones who were killed?'

'Right there with him – guarding him.'

So how had the kidnappers found it so easy to get the drop on two trained agents, Blackstone wondered.

'Have you heard from the kidnappers yet?' he asked.

'Not a word. But we will – eventually. They wouldn't have gone to all the trouble of snatching Big Bill if they hadn't expected to make a profit out of it.' Flynn replaced the derby on his head. 'Right then,' he continued, 'we'll go and see where it all happened, shall we?'

The house had an entrance hall – laid with shining hardwood and partially covered with expensive oriental carpets – in which there was enough room to have held a dance. There was a sweeping spiral staircase which led to the upper rooms. There were portraits on the walls, and a large stone fireplace which either pre-dated the house itself or was an excellent imitation of one that did. All-in-all, Blackstone thought, it was just what he might have expected.

What he had *not* expected was that they would soon leave the opulence of the hallway far behind them, and be walking down a set of narrow steps that were accessed by a discreet door under the staircase.

'Why are we going down here?' Meade asked.

'You want to see the scene of the crime, don't you?' Flynn replied, over his shoulder.

'Yes, but I thought Big Bill was in his suite when he was kidnapped,' Meade said.

'And so he was,' Flynn agreed.

There was a narrow corridor at the foot of the steps, which led to a solid steel door with a peephole in the centre of it.

'It feels as if we're underground,' Meade said, puzzled.

'That's because we are,' Flynn replied. He pushed the metal door open. 'Won't you step into my parlour, said the spider to the fly?'

THREE

The room on the other side of the steel door was small and square. The cement walls were whitewashed, and the only furniture it contained was an old table and two battered straight-back chairs.

'So this is the guard room, is it?' Blackstone asked.

'They said you fellers from Scotland Yard were as sharp as razors, and so you are,' Flynn answered.

'But they weren't killed here,' Blackstone continued.

'Brilliant!' Flynn said with mock awe. 'And what exactly was it that tipped you off, Inspector? Could it have been the absence of blood stains?'

'You're just what we need on this case – a cop who'd rather be a comedian,' said Meade, in a voice which was almost an angry growl.

'So if they weren't killed here, it must have happened in Holt's suite,' Blackstone said hastily.

'Correct,' Flynn said, and taking two steps forward, he placed his hand on a door which faced the door through which they entered, and pushed.

The heavy steel door swung open, revealing the apartment which lay beyond it.

Blackstone just had time to take in the massive mahogany desk close to the far wall before he heard Flynn say, 'I expect it'll be the floor that you'll be wanting to look at first,' and lowered his eyes accordingly.

The space between the door and the desk was largely occupied by a rug which had once been the property of a gigantic polar bear. The bear's head – still attached – faced towards the entrance to the room. Its mouth was open, and its powerful teeth – which could crunch through human bones in an instant – were menacingly on display.

But it was the fur itself which drew the eye. It wasn't the dirty white it would have been in the wild, nor yet the sanitized white attained through conscientious bleaching. It was, instead, almost entirely covered in an obscene rusty-brown stain.

'If you'd like to know what sixteen pints of blood look like, *that's* what they look like,' Flynn said grimly. '*That's* what it's like to be slaughtered like a pig.'

'Jesus!' Meade said shakily.

'What position were the Pinkerton agents in when they were discovered?' Blackstone asked. 'Were they on their fronts or on their backs? And were their heads closest to the door, or was it their feet?'

Flynn closed his eyes for a second. 'They were lying on their backs, and their heads were closest to the door,' he said. 'Cody, the senior one, was to the right, and Turner, his partner, was to the left.'

'Which means they were standing facing the desk when they had their throats slashed,' Blackstone mused. 'Their killers stood behind them.'

But just what kind of security guards *were* they that they allowed that to happen, he wondered.

He raised his head and took in the rest of the scene. The room was dominated by the large mahogany desk, which was stacked high with documents at both ends. In the middle of the desk was a large rosewood tray, which held a knife, a fork and the remains of what appeared to be an evening meal.

There was an ottoman running along one wall, and a bank of filing cabinets running along another.

But for the lack of windows – and the blood-soaked rug – it could have been any successful businessman's office, Blackstone thought.

'Not a very hospitable man, your Mr Holt,' he said aloud.

'He's not *my* Mr Holt,' Flynn replied, with a sudden sharp edge to his tone. 'And just what leads you to make assumptions about his hospitality?' Then he paused for a second, before adding, 'Ah, I see! It's the lack of any chairs *in front of* the desk that you've noted.'

Blackstone said nothing.

'You're quite right, of course,' Flynn conceded. 'Only four people ever came down here.' He counted them off on his fingers. 'The two sons – who are known in this household as Mr George and Mr Harold – the butler, and one of the maids who does the cleaning.'

'So apart from when he left the suite, they were the only people he saw,' Meade said.

'They were the only people he saw *period*,' Flynn replied.

'I beg your pardon?'

'According to the information I've been given, he *didn't* leave the suite.'

'Ever?'

'Ever!'

So he'd been down there for seven years, Blackstone thought, and in that time he had only seen four people. Well, if he hadn't been mad when he decided to bury himself in this vault, he was probably pretty close to it now.

'Can we see the rest of the suite, now?' he asked.

Flynn shrugged. 'Why not?'

The bedroom was entered through a door at the back of the study. There was a low, persistent hum in this room, almost as if it had a life of its own, and when Blackstone placed the back of his hand against the wall, he felt a slight vibration.

'That's the generator,' Flynn said. 'Its installation was personally supervised by Thomas Edison himself. I'm told it powers both the electric light and the extractor fans.'

Extractor fans! That would explain why the air down there was both fresh and cool, Blackstone thought.

'If there are fans, there must be ventilation shafts,' he said aloud.

'That'd be your sharp mind working again,' Flynn replied.

'And how wide are the shafts?'

'Not wide enough for a man to crawl down, if that's the direction your thoughts are moving in, Mr-Scotland-Yard-Man.'

Blackstone looked around the room. All it contained was a bed, a dressing table and a wardrobe.

He opened the wardrobe. There were at least a dozen suits hanging from the rail. He ran the edge of one of the jackets between his thumb and finger. The material felt expensive to him – but then, what did he know?

'Would you say this is a good quality suit, Alex?' he asked his partner.

Meade gave the jacket a cursory glance. 'From the cut, I'd say that it comes from Jackson Brothers,' he said. 'Which means that it's not just *good* quality, it's the *best*.'

Blackstone took the suit out of the wardrobe, and held it up in front of himself.

Big Bill hadn't acquired his nickname just because he was important in the business world, he decided. The man these suits had been made for had to be at least six feet three tall and with a barrel of a chest.

'If he really never left this place, as you say, why did he need so many clothes?' Alex Meade asked Flynn suspiciously.

'Now you wouldn't be accusing me of purveying you untruths, would you?' the local inspector replied, deceptively lightly.

'Wouldn't I?' Meade challenged. 'Well, what makes you think—?'

'No, *of course* he's not accusing you of anything like that,'

Blackstone interrupted. He turned to Meade. 'We used to have district officers in British India who, even when they were alone and in the middle of the jungle, would still dress formally before they sat down to dinner. Maybe Mr Holt is cast in the same mould.'

'Maybe he is,' Meade admitted, reluctantly.

Another half-smile flitted across Flynn's face. 'You're a great one for the diplomacy, aren't you, Mr Blackstone?' he asked.

'Whenever possible,' Blackstone agreed.

He took hold of the wardrobe and heaved it to one side.

'What are you looking for now?' Flynn asked. 'The entrance to a secret tunnel?'

'That's right,' Blackstone replied.

Not that he expected to find one, any more than he had expected the ventilation shafts to be wide enough to accommodate a man. The position of the Pinkertons' bodies had pretty much ruled out any method of entry other than the obvious one – but he had learned from experience that the point at which the solution looked *so* obvious that there was absolutely no need to check it out, was *precisely* the point at which it *should* be checked out.

There was nothing behind the wardrobe but a blank wall, and a single tap with his knuckles was enough to reassure Blackstone that the wall had not been recently disturbed.

There was one more room – the bathroom.

'I expect, coming from England, you'll be a stranger to inside plumbing,' Flynn said.

'Now just hold on there a minute!' Meade protested angrily. 'Inspector Blackstone is a guest in our country, and—'

'It's all right, Alex,' Blackstone said soothingly. He turned to Flynn. 'You're quite right, Inspector. In London, the house I board in has a single tap in the back yard and an outside privy which it shares with several other houses.'

'Worse than I thought,' Flynn mused, then continued, in an obvious attempt to bait the Englishman. 'Do they pay you so badly in New Scotland Yard that that's the best you can afford?'

'No, they don't. But I use most of my salary for other purposes.'

'And what purposes might they be?'

To help keep the orphanage running, Blackstone thought.

'That's really none of your business, now is it, Inspector Flynn?' he said aloud.

Flynn gave him another half-smile.

'As hard as I'm trying, you're making it difficult for me to dislike you, Mr Blackstone,' he said. 'Is that deliberate?'

'Yes,' Blackstone told him. 'I'm a graduate of a charm school.'

Flynn's smile widened, and then was gone. 'Well, I imagine that before I leave you alone to root around like pigs in the forest, there'll be some questions you'll be after asking me,' he said.

'A few,' Blackstone agreed. 'Did the Pinkerton Detective Agency have the *sole* responsibility for guarding Mr Holt?'

'It did.'

'And who chose which guards would be assigned here?'

'Pinkerton's New York City office.'

'So Holt himself had nothing to do with it?'

'Nothing at all. The Pinkertons don't work like that. You tell them the job you want doing, but you don't tell them *how* to do it.'

'Do the agents live somewhere on Coney Island, or do they travel in from the city every day?'

'They live on Coney Island – in the grounds of this very house. Holt had a row of cottages specially built to accommodate them.'

'And how many agents are there?'

'Six.'

'So they worked three eight-hour shifts?'

Flynn shook his head. 'They worked twelve-hour shifts, with one pair resting. And before you say anything else on the subject, I'd agree with you that, *under normal circumstances*, twelve hours *is* far too long for any man to remain vigilant.'

'But not in *these* circumstances?'

'Exactly. Think about it – the only way to get into the suite is through the guard room, and the only way to get into the guard room is through that steel door. A trained monkey could have done the job them Pinkertons were doing.'

'So what went wrong *last* night?'

'Ah, there you have me,' Flynn admitted. 'I think I'd have to say that if Cody and Turner let the kidnappers in, it could only be because they were working hand in glove with them.'

'And the moment the kidnappers were inside, they murdered Cody and Turner because they were the weak link in the chain?'

'Well, exactly. You'd agree with that, would you?'

'It's a possibility,' Blackstone said.

But, in truth, he'd already decided it was more than that – because Flynn was right and there was *no way* that the kidnappers could have got in without the cooperation of the guards.

'What time did Cody and Turner report for duty last night?' he asked.

'Eight o'clock.'

'And the bodies were found by the next shift, when they reported for duty at eight in the morning?'

'No, they were discovered by Fanshawe, the butler, when he brought Holt's breakfast tray down at seven o'clock.'

'Did the next shift turn up for duty at the usual time?'

'Yes, they did.' Yet another half-smile from Flynn. 'Now why would you ask that question? Are you wondering how deep the conspiracy runs? Has it started to cross your mind that the other guards might have been involved in it as well?'

'No,' Blackstone said firmly.

'No?' Flynn sounded surprised. 'And why hasn't it? It's a reasonable assumption.'

'No, it isn't – and you *know* it isn't. If all the guards were involved in the conspiracy, then all the guards would be dead.'

Flynn stroked his chin. 'Your mind seems to run on the same lines as mine, Mr Blackstone,' he said. 'And since I happen to have a very *good* mind, that means you'll probably do as well on this case as anybody could – myself included.' He paused for a moment. 'But I wouldn't like you to take that as meaning that I don't still resent you robbing me of my investigation.'

'Understood,' Blackstone said.

'So would you now like to have a word with the two guards yourself?' Flynn asked.

'Indeed I would,' Blackstone agreed.

The two Pinkertons who had reported for duty at eight o'clock were waiting for Blackstone and Meade in the butler's parlour. Both men were in their mid-thirties, and exuded an air of competence which suggested that, should trouble arise, they would know how to deal with it.

Their names, they said, were Brown and White.

'People think we're playing some kind of joke when we tell them that – but we're not,' the man who had introduced himself as White said. 'They really are our names.'

'Tell me about Cody and Turner,' Blackstone said.

'Cody was a pretty regular guy – one of the boys,' White said. 'We're gonna miss working with him.'

There was an awkward pause, then Brown added, 'Turner did his job.'

'But you didn't like him?'

'We didn't really *know* him,' Brown said. 'He was a Holy Joe. Belonged to the Salvation Army.'

'No, he didn't,' White corrected his partner. 'He belonged to *some kind* of religious army, but it wasn't the *Salvation* Army.'

'Anyhow,' Brown said, brushing aside the correction as an irrelevance, 'Holy Joe didn't drink, didn't smoke, didn't gamble, never looked at a woman apart from his wife . . .'

'He was a royal pain in the ass,' White said. Then he looked guilty, and added, 'Sorry, shouldn't speak ill of the dead.'

'But even if Turner *was* a royal pain in the ass, were he and Cody, in your opinion, both good Pinkerton men?' Meade asked.

'Hell, yes, two of the best,' White said. 'They'd never have been given an important job like this one if they hadn't been.'

'Did Cody and Turner get on well with Mr Holt?' Blackstone asked.

White looked puzzled, and Brown said, 'Get on well with him?' as if the phrase had no meaning for him.

'Get on well with him,' Blackstone repeated patiently. 'Did they, for example, ever complain about the way he spoke to them?'

'Spoke to them?' Brown echoed.

'They didn't *speak* to Mr Holt,' White said. 'And neither do we. Mr Holt's the guy on the other side of the door. We maybe get a glimpse of him when we're admitting one of the PPEs—'

'PPEs?' Meade interrupted

'People Permitted to Enter. But a glimpse was as much as we got.'

'So you've never been inside the study?'

'Hell, no!'

'And yet that's precisely where Cody and Turner were murdered.'

'You've gotta be wrong about that,' White said. 'Maybe that's where their bodies were found, but my guess is that they were killed in the guard room and dragged in there later.'

'If they'd had their throats cut in the guard room, there'd have been blood all over the floor – and there isn't,' Blackstone said grimly. 'But there *is* blood on the polar bear rug in front of the desk.'

'I don't believe it,' White said stubbornly.

'Maybe their killers got the drop on them, and forced them into the study at gunpoint,' said the more pragmatic Brown.

'And how were their killers ever *allowed* to get the drop on them?' Blackstone asked. 'How do you think they even managed to get through the steel door and into the guard room?'

'Hey, just what are you suggesting?' Brown demanded.

'You know what I'm suggesting,' Blackstone countered.

Brown shook his head emphatically. 'It can't be true,' he said.

'What can't be true?' White asked, the slower of the pair, obviously perplexed.

'He thinks Ben Cody and Holy Joe Turner were in on the kidnapping,' Brown explained.

White's hands bunched up into fists. 'If you weren't a cop, I'd take you outside and beat the living shit out of you,' he growled.

'But he *is* a cop,' Brown said, placing a restraining hand on his partner's shoulder. 'Listen, Mr Blackstone, there's bad apples in every barrel, so I'm not going to try and tell you that there've never been any in the Pinkertons. But Ben Cody's not one of them. My kid got sick last year, and when I ran out of money for medicine, Ben lent me some. Lent me some! Hell, there was no *lending* about it – he refused to let me pay him back!'

'And I may not like him much, but I'd trust Holy Joe Turner with everything I own,' White said. 'Jesus, the guy don't care about money – he gives most of his wages to this religious army of his.'

'So how *did* the kidnappers get past the steel door, and into the guard room?' Blackstone persisted.

'There's gotta be some way you ain't thought of yet,' White said in what was almost a mumble. 'Some way that didn't involve Ben and Holy Joe.'

But Brown said nothing. Instead, he fixed his eyes intently on the floor – as if he were watching the drama of his own crumbling faith in human nature being played out there.

FOUR

There were two carriages coming up the approach to Ocean Heights, and though it was unlikely they *were* actually racing each other, the speed at which they were moving certainly gave that impression.

'That'll be *Mr* George and *Mr* Harold,' Inspector Flynn said.

'You know them, do you?' Blackstone asked.

'There's not an official or businessman on Coney Island who *doesn't* know them,' Flynn replied. 'They're important people round these parts – and you'd better not forget it.'

'*Know* them, but don't *like* them,' Blackstone guessed.

'I was scarcely more than a babe-in-arms when my family left Ireland,' Flynn said, almost reflectively. 'I've got uncles and aunts back there who I don't even remember, but there's two figures that are burnt into my brain. One of them was the landlord – the *English* landlord.'

He's waiting for me to ask what this has to do with my question, Blackstone thought.

'The English landlord,' he repeated, non-committally.

'He used to ride around on his fine white horse, with a fat smirk on his face, and watch the peasants, breaking their backs in the fields. And why were they out there breaking their backs, Mr Blackstone?'

'So that the landlord could live in luxury, while they could earn just enough to not actually starve to death?'

'Just so. The other man I remember is the parish priest. He was a well-meaning sort of feller, in his own way – maybe even kind. But he watched those poor peasants suffering – and he did nothing about it.'

'And when you look at Mr George and Mr Harold, you're reminded of the landlord and the parish priest?' Blackstone asked.

'When I look at *most* men with any kind of authority, I'm reminded of either the landlord or the parish priest,' Flynn replied.

'So which of the two is which?' Blackstone asked.

The corner of Flynn's mouth twitched slightly. 'You're the big man from Scotland Yard. You work it out for yourself.'

The carriages came to a halt in front of the house, and the two passengers climbed out. One of them was a solid chunk of a man, with a square, block-like body and a round head balanced on top of it like a watermelon on a gatepost. The other had a thin sensitive face and a frame which looked as if it might well blow away in a strong wind.

'I'll wager I can pick out the one who reminds you of your landlord,' Blackstone said to Flynn.

'And if I was inclined to throw my money away, I'd take you up on that wager,' Flynn replied.

The chunky brother stood still and looked around him. The expression on his face seemed to suggest that he was expecting a larger reception committee – and was offended there wasn't one.

The skinny brother, in contrast, made a beeline for Inspector Flynn.

'Have the kidnappers been in contact with you yet, Inspector?' he asked breathlessly, as if he'd been running.

'I'm afraid they haven't, Mr Holt,' Flynn said.

'Mr Harold,' the skinny brother said automatically. 'Mr *Holt* is my father.'

The other brother – Mr George – had clearly given up waiting to be fêted, and joined them.

'Have the newspapers been informed of the kidnapping yet, Flynn?' he demanded.

'Not by me, nor by anybody in my department, sir,' the inspector said. 'And we'd prefer it if you didn't . . .'

'The board will have to be briefed – and so will the brokers,' Mr George said, 'Otherwise, God alone knows what effect the news will have on our stock position when it gets out. And it *will* get out – make no mistake about that.'

'This is Inspector Blackstone, from Scotland Yard, sir,' Flynn said evenly. 'He and Sergeant Meade will be in charge of the investigation.'

Mr George nodded vaguely, as if he'd heard the words but had not yet had time to process them.

'Thank heavens we closed that deal with the Furness Trust this morning,' he said to his brother, 'because if we'd left it even a little later, they'd certainly have found out that Father had gone missing – and then they'd *never* have signed.'

'Is there somewhere we could have a private conversation, sir?' Blackstone asked.

'A private conversation?' George repeated, as though he had no idea what the other man was talking about.

'That's right,' Blackstone agreed.

'But why would we —?'

'Inspector Blackstone needs to ask us some questions about Father,' Harold said quietly.

'Ah, yes, of course he does,' George agreed. He took his pocket watch out of his waistcoat pocket. 'No doubt you'd like this meeting right away, Inspector . . . er . . .'

'Yes, sir, I would.'

'And so would we – but there are few important business calls we still need to make, so could we postpone it for half an hour, do you think?'

'I'm sure that would be fine, sir,' Blackstone agreed, because it seemed pointless to say anything else.

George nodded. 'Good,' Then he turned towards his brother. 'Well, for God's sake, don't just stand there like a tailor's dummy, Harry. If we've only got thirty minutes to make those calls, it will need both of us.'

The two men headed for the house, George striding ahead, Harold scampering after him like a puppy which was finding it difficult to keep up.

'There are some people who maintain that money has an almost magical effect – and they're not wrong,' Flynn murmured, almost to himself. 'Sweet Jesus, how else could you explain the fact that a few bits of paper can turn a man into a walking heap of shit?'

Though the SS *Star* of Liverpool was close enough to port for the travellers to stand on deck and admire the New York skyline, the first class passengers – having partaken of a sumptuous banquet the previous evening and, anyway, regarding sightseeing as slightly *passé* – felt under no obligation to take advantage of the opportunity. As a result, the two women walking up and down the first class deck had it all to themselves.

They were an odd pair.

One of the women was well into middle age and had the kind of thick squat body and sturdy legs which suggested she came from peasant stock stretching back over generations. She was dressed in a skirt made of rough fabric and had a hand-knitted shawl over her broad shoulders.

The second woman was still young enough to regard middle age as nothing but a distant threat. Her face had none of the natural ruddiness of her companion's, but instead displayed the slightly pinched features of those born into urban poverty. *Her* body was wiry and muscular, though there was nothing boyish about it, as the rounded bosom straining against the confinement of her inexpensive blouse more than proved.

They had been promenading up and down the deck for some time, the older woman leaning heavily on her companion, when the younger woman – Ellie Carr – noticed that one of the stewards was approaching them. His very gait told her instantly that he was the sort of man who confused 'official' and 'officious' – the sort who considered that having been handed a key made him automatically superior to anyone who hadn't.

Easy, girl, she told herself. Play it straight.

But even as the words passed through her mind, she knew she wasn't going to – knew that, though she guiltily considered it somewhat childish, she still got considerable pleasure from blowing the wind out of the sails of people who *deserved* to have the wind blown out.

The steward came to a sharp halt directly in front of them, rudely blocking their way.

Well, he was asking for it, wasn't he, Ellie thought.

'Do you know that this is the first class deck?' the steward demanded.

'Yeah, as a matter o' fact, I do,' Ellie replied. 'There's lots of fings to suggest that's what it is, but it was the big sign sayin' "First Class Deck" wot really tipped me off.'

'And that means it is reserved for first class passengers,' the steward said stonily.

'Well, that's all right, darlin', 'cos that's what I am,' Ellie replied.

'You! A first class passenger?' the steward repeated, disbelievingly.

'Me! A first class passenger,' Ellie confirmed.

'And *I'm* one of the first class stewards,' the man said. 'So why is this the first time I've seen you on the entire voyage?'

'Ah, well, that's easily explained,' Ellie replied. 'See, I've been spendin' a lot of me time in steerage.'

It was no mean feat to produce an expression which conveyed both a contempt for steerage and a look of arrogant self-congratulation at having his suspicions confirmed, but the steward managed it.

'In steerage!' he repeated.

'That's right. See, there's bin a bit of a stomach bug goin' round, an' since the ship's official doctor has bin spendin' most of 'is time wiv the first class passengers – it bein' a well-known fact that the rich suffer much more from their illnesses than the poor do – I fort I might as well 'elp out wiv some of the patients in cattle class.'

The steward sneered. 'So you're a doctor, now, are you?'

'As a matter of fact, I am,' the woman said. 'The name's Dr Ellie Carr.'

There had been a Dr E. Carr on the passenger manifest, the steward remembered, but he had automatically assumed – who wouldn't? – that the 'E' stood for something like Edward or Eustace.

There *were* women doctors, of course – the steward was not so far behind the times as not to know that – but he was still far from convinced that this woman was one of them.

'So why are you travelling to New York, *Doctor*?' he asked, cunningly. 'I'd have thought that there were probably more than enough physicians already in the new world.'

'There probably are, in general terms,' Ellie agreed. 'But the very fact that I'm making this journey would suggest there's a distinct lack of forensic pathologists, don't you think?'

'For . . . forensic pathologists?' the steward said, struggling with the words. 'I'm not sure I know exactly what that means.'

'And I'm sure you have absolutely *no idea* what it means,' Ellie countered, 'but the City Hospital and the New York Police Department obviously do, or they'd never have clubbed together to buy me my ticket, now would they?'

Her accent, which had started out as broad cockney, was growing more refined by the minute, the steward thought. And there was a real authority in her voice now – the sort of authority which he would expect in someone who actually was what she claimed. So maybe – and as incredible as it might seem – she really *was* the genuine article.

In which case, he thought, he was in big trouble, and his mind was filled with the nightmare image of him being pulled up in front of the captain for treating an eminent physician as if she were no more than a common washerwoman.

He cleared his throat. 'Well, since we're almost in New York, there's not much more I can do for you on this trip, ma'am,' he said.

'Not much more?' Ellie repeated quizzically. 'Have you done *anything at all* for me?'

'Well, no, ma'am,' the steward admitted. 'What with you attending to the sick and all, I haven't really had the opportunity. But if there's anything I *can* do before we land . . .'

'As a matter of the fact, there is,' Ellie interrupted. 'This lady next to me is Mrs Gruber. Would you like to say "hello" to her?'

The steward looked down at the woman. Her face was weather-beaten, and as he leaned closer to her his nostrils filled with the smell of boiled cabbage.

'Hello, Mrs Gruber,' he said, forcing himself to smile.

'Hello,' the woman replied, in a thick foreign accent.

'Mrs Gruber's been rather under the weather,' Ellie Carr said, 'which is why I've brought her up here from steerage for a breath of fresh air.'

'I see,' the steward said.

'The fing is,' Ellie continued, lapsing mockingly back into cockney, 'it's a bit of a strain for a bag o' bones like me to keep 'olding her up, so I was wonderin' if you wouldn't mind walkin' 'er around for a bit yerself.'

The steward swallowed. 'I'd be delighted to,' he said.

Ellie smiled. 'Do you know,' she replied, 'I was almost certain you'd say that.'

With a poor attempt at graciousness, the steward offered the peasant woman his arm, and the two of them began to walk away along the deck.

Left alone, Ellie turned her gaze towards the skyscrapers, which were becoming commonplace in New York, but were still strangers to the London landscape.

'Well, 'ooever would have thought it, Mum?' she said softly to the woman who had been dead for ever ten years. ''Ooever would 'ave imagined that your little Ellie would end up travellin' first class to America?'

She needed no ghost to respond, because she already knew the answer.

Nobody would have thought it. *Nobody* would ever have imagined that a snotty-nosed kid from the slums would end up not only being a doctor, but a doctor who the Yanks were eager to consult.

It was largely a matter of luck, she told herself. She was lucky she had been born with a good brain. She had been lucky that her own interest in forensic pathology had developed just before the science really started to get off the ground, and thus made her a pioneer almost by default.

'But you're right, Mum,' she said into the wind. 'It wasn't *just* luck – I've worked damned hard for it as well.'

And paid the price, she thought – in all sorts of ways.

She was flattered the Americans had invited her to visit them. She was as excited as only a true evangelist – eager to impart her knowledge to the world – can be.

But she was nervous, too.

Not about defending her views and discoveries – she was on solid ground there.

Not about meeting new people and finding herself in new

situations – you didn't claw your way out of the East End unless you had the ability to take that kind of thing in your stride.

She was nervous because she knew that in New York was a man who she was desperate to see, and yet both afraid and embarrassed to meet; a man who sometimes seemed like *the* man her destiny had always intended for her, and at others seemed more like the instrument that fate had specifically designed to destroy the life she had worked so hard to build up.

'Do you think we can we make it work this time, Sam?' she asked.

Overhead, a seagull screeched loudly, then opened its bowels and deposited their load on the deck, only a few feet away from her.

She sighed. 'You're probably right, seagull,' she said wistfully.

FIVE

George Holt's study was on the first floor of the house, and its corner location meant that it had views of both the sea and the woods.

The room had a far less businesslike atmosphere than his father's office, Blackstone thought, looking around him. True, it contained a large, impressive desk and several tall filing cabinets, but there were personal touches, too – stuffed animal heads mounted on the wall and a billiard table in the corner.

Blackstone and Meade stood facing the brothers, across George's desk. They had not been invited to sit down, so, in this way at least, the new world seemed very much like the old.

'You told me that you had some questions you wanted to ask us,' George said crisply.

'I did,' Blackstone agreed. 'Am I correct in assuming that your father has been living in his underground suite for seven years?'

'You are.'

'And that, until last night, he hadn't left it – not even for an hour?'

'Not even for a *moment*,' George said.

'So what happened to make him retreat to this place – to turn himself into a virtual prisoner?'

'That's an easy question to answer,' said George, with a hint of contempt seeping into his voice. 'He lost his nerve.'

'What do you mean?'

George shook his head, wonderingly. 'I'd have thought what I just said was straightforward enough for even a *Limey* to understand, but if you want me to repeat it, I will.' He took a deeply theatrical breath, and then continued, 'He . . . lost . . . his . . . nerve.'

'There was an attempt on his life,' Harold said.

'An attempt on his life!' George repeated, with a snort of disgust. 'Do you call what Edward Knox did *an attempt on his life?*'

'He fired a gun at Father,' Harold said. 'He *shot* him.'

'It was no more than a flesh wound,' George said dismissively.

'That was just a matter of luck,' Harold persisted.

'No, it wasn't,' George countered. 'Knox would never have had the nerve to actually *kill* him. It's my belief that the pathetic wretch only intended to fire into the wall, and the fact that he hit Father *at all* is principally down to his incompetence.'

'Do you think we could start this particular story at the beginning?' Blackstone asked.

'Father had been involved in several business deals which had gone bad,' Harold said. 'Holt and Co managed to emerge with a decent profit, but several of our partners in those businesses – including Edward Knox – ended up in the bankruptcy court.'

'Their own fault entirely,' George said. 'In the business world, you need to learn to be a strong swimmer pretty damn quickly, especially when the current keeps changing. Those men didn't learn – and so they went under.'

'Father received several anonymous death threats after the companies collapsed, and Inspector Manson said—'

'Manson was our pet policeman,' George interrupted. 'We paid him a retainer of a thousand dollars a year not that I could see he ever did anything to earn even a single cent of it!'

'. . . Inspector Manson said that as the threats seemed to have come from more than one source, Father might be wise to stay away from the office until everybody had cooled down a little.'

'And your father agreed to do that?' Blackstone asked.

'Yes, he did, but Knox came to our house on Fifth Avenue, late one night. The doors were all locked, but he'd bribed Father's secretary, Margaret Wilkins, to let him in.'

George laughed. 'Father trusted her, you see, even if she *was* little more than a servant. Well, he's never made *that* kind of mistake again!'

'He was too rigid about how he reacted to the whole incident – at least in that way,' Harold said.

'Would you mind explaining that, sir?' Blackstone asked.

'Just because one person has let you down, that doesn't mean everyone else will – and by refusing to see anyone other than us and a couple of servants, he's only been punishing himself.'

'Anyway, as I said earlier,' George continued, 'it was a botched attempt at murder by a weedy little man who was in police custody half an hour later – but it was still enough to make Father lose his nerve.'

'I don't think that *was* when Father lost his nerve,' Harold said firmly. 'The experience *unnerved* him, certainly. It would have unnerved anyone . . .'

'Unnerved anyone,' George echoed, contemptuously.

'. . . but I think it was what happened to Arthur Rudge which really frightened him.'

'Who's Arthur Rudge?' Meade asked.

'He was Father's head bookkeeper,' Harold replied darkly. 'He was murdered a few days after Knox tried to kill Father.'

'He *wasn't* murdered,' George said, again dismissively. He turned to Meade. 'Rudge died in a fire at his apartment. It started in his bedroom, and, if you ask me, what caused it was one of those cheap cigars he was always smoking.'

'The police never ruled out murder,' Harold said.

'Well, of course they didn't!' George replied exasperatedly. 'Crime is their business – no crime, no jobs – so they're always going to find suspicious circumstances, aren't they?'

'Father didn't rule it out either,' Harold said firmly. 'He's never openly admitted it, but I'm convinced he truly believes that Rudge was murdered – and that's what tipped him over the edge.'

'Tipped him over the edge!' said his brother.

George seemed to believe that the best way to counter any statement was not to argue against it but to repeat it in an incredulous voice, Blackstone thought.

Well, perhaps he was right – it certainly seemed to work for a lot of politicians he had heard speak.

'It had always been Father's belief, up to that point, that everyone he did business with was absolutely terrified of him,' Harold explained to Blackstone. 'What Knox did shook his faith in that belief a little, but I think he convinced himself that it was no more than an aberration.'

'A what?' George asked.

'But he couldn't continue to convince himself of that once his bookkeeper was killed,' Harold ploughed on. 'If his enemies were brave enough to murder someone as important to the company as Rudge—'

'He *wasn't* important to the company!' George interrupted. 'Hell, we've managed well enough without him, haven't we?'

'We've certainly *managed*,' Harold agreed cautiously. 'But it wasn't that easy at first. We made mistakes which cost us hundreds of thousands of dollars – mistakes which we'd never have made if we'd had Rudge to advise us.'

'Poppycock!'

'Do you see what I'm getting at, Inspector?' Harold asked.

'I think so,' Blackstone said. 'It wasn't so much that Rudge was important in *himself*, as that he was important as a symbol of your father's *power*. He was under your father's protection – and if he was killed, then that protection didn't seem to be worth much. In other words, if they dared kill Rudge, they'd find it just as easy to kill his boss.'

'Hogwash!' George said.

'So you don't think your father *should* have been worried, sir?' Blackstone asked.

'Of course he shouldn't! The pathetic little men he ruined – and who he was hiding from – aren't responsible for the kidnapping. *That* was the work of professional criminals.'

'How *can* you say that Father was cowardly to take the precautions he did?' Harold demanded angrily. 'And that's what you're doing, isn't it – calling him a coward?'

George's expression softened. 'I never used that word, little brother,' he said, in a much gentler voice. 'What he did was weak, rather than cowardly. But whatever you call it, he must take part of the responsibility for the events of last night – because if he *hadn't* acted as he did, it would never have happened.'

'You know nothing about him!' Harold protested.

'And *you* know nothing about hunting,' George countered.

'What are you talking about?' Harold asked.

'It's almost unheard of for the leader of a wolf pack to be challenged,' George said. 'If other members of that pack start to find his leadership unbearable, they go off and form new packs of their own, and—'

'So now you're calling Father a wolf?'

'Well, of course I am! Up until Arthur Rudge's death, he was one of the biggest wolves on Wall Street – and you know it.'

'But he . . .' Harold began.

And then he fell silent, as if he had realized that he had nothing with which to counter his brother's argument.

'Go on with your point, sir,' Blackstone said.

'As I said, challenges to the leader of the pack are rare. But if something happens to that leader – if his leg is damaged in a trap, or he's wounded by a hunter – the other wolves will have no hesitation in killing him. And that's what happened to Father – he showed himself to be weak in the eyes of the criminal fraternity – and now he's paying the price.'

'You're being unspeakable!' Harold said hotly.

'I'm being *realistic*,' George replied. 'But what's happened in the past is neither here nor there. Father has been kidnapped, and soon his kidnappers will contact us and demand a ransom.' He turned to Meade again. 'The New York Police Department will not try to stop us paying it, will they?'

'No, sir, but we would request that you allow one of our men to deliver it,' Meade said.

George nodded. 'Of course. I'd be more than happy to leave it in the hands of the professionals. But there is something we must decide before we get the ransom demand, Harry,' he continued, speaking to his brother, 'and that is how much we're prepared to pay.'

'We'll pay whatever they ask,' Harold said.

George shook his head, pityingly. 'And if they ask for a billion dollars? Do we agree to pay them that?'

'Of course we don't. We don't have anything *like* a billion dollars. I doubt if anyone in the world is that rich, but—'

'So we must discuss the price we can *afford* to pay.'

'Whatever we have, we'll give to them.'

'You'd sell all the stock?'

'Yes.'

'And all the real estate?'

'If necessary.'

'In other words, you're prepared to bankrupt us?'

'If that's what it takes.'

George shook his head again. 'Father wouldn't thank you for doing that,' he said. 'He'd rather be dead than poor – and you know it.'

'It's highly unlikely that the kidnappers will demand a bigger ransom than they think you can lay your hands on easily, sir,' Blackstone said. 'The longer they hold your father, the more risk they're running, which is why they'll want the whole business over with as quickly as possible.'

'What are the chances they've already killed him?' George asked Blackstone. Then he turned to his brother again, and said, 'I have to ask, Harry.'

'It's unlikely they'll kill him before they get their hands on the money,' Blackstone told him.

'And once we've paid them?'

They've already killed two men, so there's no reason on earth why they should let their victim live, Blackstone thought.

'It's impossible to guess *what* they'll do,' he said aloud. 'That's why our best hope is to find him before the ransom is paid – and why I want you to delay paying it for as long as possible.'

'I thought you said they'll want it paid quickly,' Harold said.

'They will,' Blackstone agreed. 'But if the amount they're demanding is large enough, they'll probably already have accepted that they'll have to wait *two or three* days.'

The phone on the desk rang. Both Harold and George grabbed for it, but George got there first.

'Yes, it is,' he said. 'No, I . . . Now look here, my man, that's a lot of money . . . Yes, of course we can raise it – we're not paupers, and you must already know that, or you'd never have kidnapped my father – but we can't raise it in less than four days . . .. Why not? Because we don't *have* that amount of cash around the house, you bloody idiot!'

It might have been better if Harold had reached the phone first, Blackstone thought. Then again, it might not have been.

'Say you can raise it in *three* days,' he mouthed at the older brother.

'All right, we'll try and get it together in three days,' George said into the phone.

Harold had been writing something on a piece of paper, and now he slid it across to his brother. Looking at it upside down, Blackstone read, 'SAY YOU WANT TO SPEAK TO HIM.'

'I demand to speak to my father,' George said. 'Why? Why do you think, you imbecile? Because I need to be convinced he's still alive.'

There was a pause, then George continued, 'Listen, you bastard, if you don't bring him to the phone, I'm hanging up.'

Another pause.

'No, you won't kill him – because if you do that, you'll never get your hands on the money.'

A third pause.

'Yes, I understand,' George said. 'I give you my word that I won't ask where he is, or anything about you – but I *will* speak to him.'

George covered the mouthpiece with his hand. 'He says they're bringing him to the phone. He must be in another room.'

'Keep him talking as long as you can,' Blackstone said. 'And try to remember everything he says.'

George removed his hand from the mouthpiece. 'How are you, Father?' he asked. 'How are they treating you? . . . You don't sound like yourself. Are you sure you *are* my father? . . . Then tell me this – what was the name of the dog I had when I was a boy? . . . Yes, that's right.'

He covered the mouthpiece again. 'They've taken him away again. I . . . I couldn't stop them.'

'You're doing well,' Blackstone told him.

And, after a shaky start, so he was.

'Yes,' George said, when the kidnapper came back on the line. 'Yes . . . I'll get one of my people to deliver . . . Why not? . . . All right, in that case, I suppose it had better be me who . . .' A sudden look of horror came to his face. 'You want *what*?' he spluttered.

Blackstone noticed that, despite the cool of the room, beads of sweat had begun to form on George's forehead.

'I can't have that,' George said, and now he was starting to sound worried. 'I will simply *not* allow it . . . Listen to me, *please* . . .'

What the hell was the kidnapper saying, Blackstone wondered. What *could he* have said that would turn George so quickly from the bumptious gentleman addressing an underling into a desperate supplicant?

'You have to understand,' George pleaded. 'He's not strong . . . the strain will be far too much for him . . .'

So that was what the kidnappers wanted, Blackstone thought. Well, he supposed he should have expected it.

'But, but . . .' George protested. 'I . . . all right, I agree. I *have to* agree, don't I?'

He hung up the earpiece. His face had lost colour, and there was a slight tremble in his hand, but it was clear he was doing his very best to pull himself together again.

'That went better than it might have done,' he said, in a voice which was unnaturally even. 'They want half a million dollars, but if we can get Father back safely, the stocks will go up by at least that much. And they've given us three days to raise the money – which is more than *I'd* have allowed if I'd been in their shoes.'

'You're sure that really was your father you spoke to?' Blackstone asked.

'Oh yes, it was him, all right. I asked him the name of my dog.'

'I heard that, but if the kidnappers had done their research . . .'

'He didn't call her Topsie, which was what everyone else knew her as – he used the name *he'd* christened her.'

'Which was what?'

'Shithead,' George replied. He shrugged. 'My father doesn't like animals much. He only let me have a dog because our late mother insisted on it.' He took a deep breath. 'They'll ring again in two days' time, to say where they want the money delivering to and . . . and I'm sorry, Harry.'

'Sorry?' Harold repeated.

'I said I'd get someone from the company to hand over the money, and when he wouldn't agree to that, I said I'd do it myself. But he wouldn't agree to that, either. He said . . . he said it had to be you.'

SIX

The two detectives had asked for – and been given – a room from which to conduct their enquiries. That this room was in the family's part of the house, rather than a cubby hole somewhere in the bowels of the servants' quarters, was, Blackstone suspected, more Harold's doing than George's.

It was, all things considered, a very pleasant room, for though it was minimally furnished – containing no more than two armchairs and a coffee table – it was light and airy, and afforded them an excellent view of the boat dock at the back of the house.

Looking down on that boat dock, Blackstone tried to picture the kidnappers hustling their victim to a waiting boat, under the cover of darkness.

What state would Big Bill have been in, if that was what had happened, he wondered.

Would he have walked there under his own steam – reluctantly, yet more than conscious that there was a gun pressed into his back, and that the man holding it had already ordered the murder of his bodyguards?

Would he, having observed the two violent deaths – and probably spattered with the Pinkerton men's blood himself – have been in such a state of shock that he merely needed to be guided like a lost child?

Or would he have been unconscious – a dead-weight carried, not without considerable effort, between two of his kidnappers?

'However they got him away from here, this wasn't where the crime originated,' he said aloud.

'What was that, Sam?' Alex Meade asked.

'There may be people on Coney Island who were *involved* in the kidnapping, but it was *planned* in New York.'

'So who's behind it?' Meade wondered. 'Is it professional criminals, with no connection to Holt, as George seems to believe? Or was it done under the orders of some of the disgruntled businessmen who Big Bill had bankrupted?'

'It could be either of those,' Blackstone admitted. 'Or then again, it could be George himself. Or even Harold. After all, who knew more about Holt's security arrangements than they did themselves?'

'Do you *really* think one of them might have been involved in the kidnapping?'

'Stranger things have been known.'

'But why would either of the two sons want to steal *his own* money?' Meade wondered.

'Perhaps because it *isn't* his money – it's Big Bill's.'

'But it *will be* his, eventually.'

'Unless William Holt has been planning to disinherit him, in favour of his brother.'

'I don't see it,' Meade said. 'If either of them wanted to steal money from their father, it would be much easier – and a lot less bloody – for him to have embezzled it.'

'You're right,' Blackstone conceded.

Meade smiled with pleasure. 'Do you know, I think I'm turning into quite a good detective – under your excellent guidance, *of course!*'

Blackstone smiled back at him. 'Of course,' he agreed.

'So how do we approach this investigation?' Meade asked, growing serious again.

'By trying to find out *how* it was done here on Coney Island, and *who* planned it back in New York,' Blackstone said.

'And we only have three days,' Meade pointed out.

'And we only have three days,' Blackstone echoed.

'Do you think we'll find Holt alive?'

'If we get a lead on the kidnappers *before* the ransom's handed over – or if we can capture one of the kidnappers in the *act* of taking the money, and make him talk – then there's a chance we can save Holt,' Blackstone said. He frowned. 'But I wouldn't bank on either of those two things happening.'

There was a discreet knock on the parlour door, and then the door swung open to reveal a middle-aged man in full butler's livery.

'I was wondering if you two gentlemen required any kind of refreshment,' he said.

'You're Fanshawe, aren't you?' Meade asked.

'I am, indeed, sir,' the butler replied, in a plummy voice.

'And you're English!' Blackstone said, surprised.

'That, too, is correct,' the butler agreed.

'There was a fashion in New York, a few years back, for employing English butlers,' Meade explained to Blackstone. 'It was generally felt that they added a certain touch of class to any establishment.'

'And so we do, sir,' said Fanshawe, with the slightest of smiles playing on his lips.

'You seem very calm about the fact that your master's gone missing,' Meade said suspiciously.

'One of the reasons we English butlers are so valued is our sang-froid,' Fanshawe told him. 'For all you know, sir, there may well be a torrent of doubt and confusion raging in my bosom, but I consider it beneath me to have it on public display.'

'Nice,' Meade said appreciatively. 'I don't know what they pay you, but you're worth every cent of it. You *are* paid well, aren't you?'

'Extraordinarily well,' the butler admitted. 'My old master, the Earl of . . . well, let's just call him the Earl . . . was most generous, by English standards, but he would positively blanch if he knew what I was earning now.'

Blackstone stood up. 'If you can spare me the time, Mr Fanshawe, I'd like you to show me the boat dock,' he said.

'I would be delighted to, sir,' Fanshawe said, 'but since I am no expert on such matters – and since I have many other household duties to attend to – I think it might perhaps be more appropriate if I arranged for someone else to—'

'I want *you* to show it to me,' Blackstone said firmly. 'And as for your other duties, I'm sure Mr George will excuse you for neglecting them when he learns that you have been assisting me in my enquiries into his father's disappearance.'

For a moment it looked as if Fanshawe was about to protest, then he sighed and said, 'Very well, sir.'

Alex Meade made a move to stand up, but was prevented by Blackstone putting a restraining hand on his shoulder.

'I don't need you, Alex,' Blackstone said. 'You'd be much more useful staying here and carrying on the work we've already begun.'

'The work we've already begun?' Meade repeated, puzzled. Then realization dawned. 'Oh yes, of course,' he added. '*That* work.'

Fanshawe led Blackstone out of the house to the steps which ran down to the boat dock.

'It was kind of you to ask if we required refreshments,' Blackstone said, as they walked.

'I see it as no more than part of my duties, sir,' the butler replied.

'Of course, in most houses in England, the butler would have considered it below his dignity to serve mere policemen, and would have sent one of his underlings to do the job,' Blackstone continued. 'But if you'd done that, you'd never have been able to get a closer look at us, would you, Fanshawe?'

'What's this about?' the butler asked, his sangfroid – and some of his plummy accent – temporarily deserting him.

Blackstone shrugged. 'It's about the fact that if you're to be of any use to me in this investigation, there are a few things we need to get clear first – and I thought you might be happier doing it when there was no one else listening.'

'What kind of things?'

'Well, for a start, there's the fact that you're an impostor,' Blackstone said mildly.

'An impostor? What do you mean?'

'You do a good job of playing the part of the butler, but you don't *quite* carry it off. And do you know what lets you down?'

'No, what?' Fanshawe asked sullenly.

'Your sense of humour,' Blackstone told him.

'What's wrong with my sense of humour?' Fanshawe asked.

'Nothing at all. But I've never known a butler who had one – or, at least, who showed it to the people he was serving. So my guess is that while you've probably studied a couple of butlers from a distance, you were never one yourself while you were in England.'

Fanshawe held out his hands, as if inviting Blackstone to clap handcuffs on them.

'It's a fair cop,' he admitted. 'I was never more than an under-footman in the old days. But, you see, the Yanks don't want under-footmen – what they require is what they call the *genuine article.*'

'So you forged your references?'

'I prefer to think of it as enhancing them slightly,' Fanshawe said, with a sheepish grin.

They had reached the dock, and Blackstone looked down at the ocean. This same water would be washing against the shores of his homeland in a few days, he thought – and there was at least a part of him that wished he could be there to greet it.

'The Holts haven't lost out by taking me into their service, you know,' Fanshawe said. 'My references might be slightly question-able, but I'm a bloody good butler.'

Blackstone grinned. 'I'm sure you are, Mr Fanshawe.'

'So you won't blow my cover with Mr George and Mr Harold?' Fanshawe asked, trying his best to make what was a desperate plea sound like a straightforward question.

'Not if, in return for my silence, you'll help me with my investi-gation.'

'In any way I can.'

'Then your secret's safe with me.'

Fanshawe straightened his spine and brushed a speck of imaginary dust off his impeccable jacket – and as he did so, Blackstone noticed that the tip of his right index finger was missing.

'How did that happen?' the inspector asked.

'How did what happen?' the butler countered.

'How did you lose part of your finger?'

'Oh, that!' Fanshawe said. 'I lost it in an accident, years ago. I never even think about it any more – apart from when I'm serving at table.'

'What's so special about serving at table?' Blackstone asked, intrigued.

'Ah, you see, the Quality wouldn't like to be served by a muti-lated man. Being so obviously perfect themselves, they expect perfec-tion in everything else – even in their lackeys. So *when* I'm serving at table – which is always a white glove job – I put on a *special white glove with padding in the right index finger.*'

'You don't sound as if you *like* the Quality much,' Blackstone said.

'They serve God's purpose, just as I serve mine,' Fanshawe said, enigmatically. 'But you said I might be able to help you with your investigation,' he added, in his best butler voice, 'In what particular manner, if I may enquire, sir?'

'How long have you worked for Mr Holt?'

'Nine years, though, strictly speaking, before we moved to Coney Island I was Mr George's butler-valet.'

'And what was Big Bill like before he decided to retreat under-ground?' Blackstone asked.

Fanshawe laughed. 'Before he became a badger, he was a bit of a ram.'

So, Big Bill was a wolf to George, while to his butler he was a ram who'd become a badger.

'Bill had an eye for the ladies, did he?' Blackstone asked.

'A little more than an eye,' Fanshawe said. 'His preference was for high class prostitutes – they tend to be much more adventurous than the average woman, you know.'

'So I've heard,' Blackstone replied.

'But he's never been a man to restrict himself unnecessarily, and, generally speaking, if it moved, he usually wanted to mount it – a common prostitute, a society lady, a scullery maid, the wife of one his numerous business partners, he's had them all, in his time.'

'And then, suddenly, he gave it all up.'

'That's right, he did – right after Arthur Rudge was killed.'

'You said *killed*, rather than *died*,' Blackstone pointed out.

'Yes, I did,' the butler agreed. 'I'm inclined to go along with Mr Harold on that one.'

'What's his life been like since he became a badger, Mr Fanshawe?'

'Highly predictable,' the butler said. 'I take him his breakfast and the morning newspaper at seven thirty in the morning. Once he's eaten, he studies the reports that Mr George and Mr Harold have prepared for him. Sometimes they come to see him to hear what he thinks about the reports – sometimes he writes his own report, and I pass it on to them.'

'So even though he's a badger, he's still running the business?'

'Not really. Mr George and Mr Harold make most of the decisions since he signed the company over to—'

Fanshawe stopped, suddenly, as if he realized he'd said something he shouldn't have.

'Since he signed the company over *to them*,' Blackstone prodded.

'For God's sake, don't tell anybody I told you, or I'll lose my job,' Fanshawe said, and this time he didn't even *pretend* not to be begging.

'Why is it such a secret?' Blackstone wondered.

'Because Wall Street has confidence in Big Bill,' Fanshawe said, 'and there'd be a real panic if they thought he wasn't running the company any more.'

'Even though George and Harold have been running it successfully for some time?'

'Yes. It might not make sense to folk like you and me – but that's the way they think on Wall Street.'

'What happens when he's finished with the reports?'

'I take him his lunch, and he has his afternoon nap.'

'And then?'

'Sometimes he does a little more work in the afternoon, and sometimes he just sits there. At nine o'clock, I take him his dinner, and then he goes to bed.'

'I've known other prisoners like him,' Blackstone said reflectively. 'Men who have lost everything that they enjoyed in life, and now pass their days in a sort of semi-trance. What an existence!'

'Oh, you mustn't feel sorry for him,' Fanshawe said. 'It's the existence he has chosen for himself – and, most of the time, he seems perfectly content with it.'

And maybe that contentment came mainly from the fact that he'd cheated his enemies and was still alive, Blackstone thought – though after the previous evening, it was perfectly possible that his luck had finally run out.

'Tell me about his visitors,' he said.

'There's Mr George, Mr Harold, the chambermaid and me – though I don't know if you'd count me and the chambermaid as visitors.'

'Nobody else?'

'Haven't Mr George and Mr Harold already told you about this?' Fanshawe asked.

'Yes, they have,' Blackstone said. 'And now I'm asking you.'

'He has no other visitors,' Fanshawe said – and it was obvious that he was lying.

'Tell me what happened last night,' Blackstone said.

'I took him his tray at nine o'clock, asked if there was anything else he wanted, then retired for the night.'

'What about the rest of the staff?'

'They went to bed, too.'

'Does this house *always* turn in so early?'

'No. When Mr George and Mr Harold and their wives are here, there's often a great deal of socializing, and it can be well after midnight before we get to bed. But when they're away – as they were last night – I make it my business to see that the domestic staff has an opportunity to catch up on its sleep.'

'Meaning, you *order* the staff to bed.'

The butler grinned. 'That's right. Who would ever have thought that an under-footman, who could never have aspired to be being a butler in the old world, would end up *ordering* twenty-odd people to go their beds in the new one?'

'You heard nothing unusual in the night?'

'I heard nothing *at all*. And neither did any of my staff.'

'Are you certain about that?' Blackstone asked sceptically.

'Oh yes, sir, I took it on myself to question each and every one of them this morning.'

Blackstone nodded. 'You've been very helpful, Mr Fanshawe,' he said, 'and I won't detain you from your duties any longer.'

'That's very kind of you, sir,' the butler said. 'And I'm delighted to have obliged.'

As they turned and walked back to the steps that led up to the house, Blackstone said, 'Oh, by the way, Mr Fanshawe, was it you, or one of the brothers, who had the job of providing the women for Mr Holt?'

It was a shot in the dark, but from the way Fanshawe hesitated before saying, 'Women? I don't know what you're talking about, Inspector,' it was clear that it had hit its target.

SEVEN

The row of six cottages in which the guards were quartered lay about a third of a mile from the main building. The cottages themselves were neat, modest structures, and they reminded Blackstone of the dwellings which the English aristocracy graciously bestowed on its stewards, head gardeners, retired nannies and other especially favoured servants.

'Holt treats his guards well,' Meade said, as they approached the cottage at the end of the row.

'Wouldn't you – when they were all that stood between you and danger?' Blackstone asked.

But treating them well hadn't – apparently – done him any good, he thought, because the kidnappers had somehow managed to get through two steel doors before they snatched him, and it was hard to see how they had done that without the collusion of the guards.

Meade knocked on the cottage door. His knock was answered by a pleasant-looking woman in her thirties. She was wearing a black dress, and a black scarf covered her hair.

'Mrs Turner?' Meade asked solicitously. 'We're from the police department – Sergeant Meade and Inspector Blackstone. I know this must be a very difficult time for you, but I was hoping you'd be feeling strong enough to answer a few questions about some of the things your late husband did before he passed on.'

'You mean, before he was *murdered*,' Mrs Turner said, in a remarkably firm voice.

'Well, yes,' Meade replied, awkwardly.

'Calling it by another name won't take the horror away from the act, you know,' Mrs Turner said. 'Nor will it do anything to diminish my grief.'

'No, of course not,' Meade agreed, stumbling slightly over his words. 'If you'd rather we came back later . . .'

'It must be faced,' Mrs Turner said. 'Like all other crosses we must bear in this vale of tears, it must be faced. Please come inside, gentlemen.'

She led them into a sitting room which was so plainly furnished that it was almost Spartan, and invited them to sit down.

'If you wish, I could make you a cup of coffee,' she said.

'No . . . no . . . that's fine,' Meade said. 'Are you sure you wouldn't prefer to talk to us later?'

Blackstone ran a professional eye over the woman. There was no need for Meade to worry, he decided, for though it was plain from her face that she had been crying heavily, she was very much in control of herself now.

'You are quite right, Mr Blackstone,' Mrs Turner said.

'Right?' he repeated.

'I noticed the way you looked at me. You do not think – as Mr Meade does – that it would be cruel to continue with your questioning. And you are correct. Though my husband died in a terrible manner, I am at peace – for the Lord's love has sustained me in my times of trouble. You see that, don't you?'

'Yes, of course I do,' lied Blackstone, who had lost his faith in a *loving* god while still in childhood, and now was finding belief in even a *vengeful* god a bit of a stretch.

Mrs Turner sat down and folded her hands demurely on her lap. 'I am ready to begin,' she said.

Alex Meade coughed. 'Forgive me for asking this,' he began, 'but isn't it rather unusual for a person of a religious persuasion, like your husband, to find work as a bodyguard?'

'Yes, I suppose it is,' Mrs Turner agreed. 'But it was what the good Lord intended.'

'Could you explain?'

'My husband is – was – a Soldier of God,' Mary Turner said simply.

'Ah – so that's the organization the other guards were talking about!' Meade said. 'In many ways, the Soldiers are a bit like the Salvation Army,' he explained to Blackstone.

'And in many ways they are *not*,' Mrs Turner said sharply. 'In the Salvation Army, the women go into the dens of iniquity alongside the men. The Soldiers keep their wives well away from the battle front. Our duty is to keep the fire burning in the hearth, and to soothe our men when they come home battered and bleeding from their struggle.'

'I still don't see . . .' Meade began.

'Joseph was commanded, by the Vicar General of our movement himself, to make a request to be posted here,' Mrs Turner said.

Perhaps so, but it was strange that the Pinkerton Detective Agency had agreed to the request, Blackstone thought.

Come to think of it, it was strange that the Pinkertons had employed a deeply religious man like Joseph Turner in the first place.

'And what are you thinking now, Mr Blackstone?' Mrs Turner asked. 'That Joseph was unsuited to be a bodyguard?'

'As a matter of fact, Mrs Turner, that's *just* what I was thinking,' Blackstone admitted.

'My husband was not always a man of peace and a man of God,' the woman said. 'Before he saw the light, he was a lost sheep – a sinner.'

'But I still don't see—'

'He was *also* a United States Marine.'

And that explained everything, Blackstone thought, because the Pinkertons wouldn't see him as Holy Joe – they'd see him as a man who knew how to take care of himself in even the most difficult circumstances.

'Why did the Vicar General want your husband to work for William Holt?' Meade asked.

'He didn't, especially,' Mrs Holt replied. 'What he desired was that Joseph should find employment on Coney Island.'

'Why?'

'Is that not obvious? The place is awash with sin. It has vaude-ville houses and concert saloons which would not have been out of place in Sodom and Gomorrah. Every day, on Coney Island, there are women who commit the act of fornication – for money!'

'Shocking!' Blackstone said.

'Not to a man like my husband,' Mary Turner replied, with a sincerity and simplicity that almost made him feel ashamed of himself. 'The Soldiers of God *cannot* be shocked. They have descended into the pit in which the sinners dwell and have been charged by the Lord to drag those sinners from it with the rope of repentance and cords of forgiveness.'

'So you're saying that it didn't matter what kind of job he had, as long as it paid enough to feed the family and left him time to follow his true vocation?' Blackstone asked.

'Exactly,' Mrs Turner agreed.

'But just a minute,' Meade said. 'Don't the fleshpots . . .' He paused and blushed. 'I'm sorry, Mrs Turner, I didn't mean to . . .'

'You may call them fleshpots, Mr Meade,' the woman said, 'for is that not what they are?'

'Don't the fleshpots open mainly at night?'

'They do.'

'Which was precisely when your husband would be on duty in the guard room.'

'Not at first,' Mrs Turner said. 'At first, he only worked for Mr

Holt in the daytime, and his nights were devoted to the gamblers and drinkers, the fallen women and the criminals. And then, one evening a few weeks ago, another of the guards was taken sick, and Joseph was told to replace him. Our first thought was that Satan had made the man sick, in order to keep Joseph from his holy work. But we were wrong. It was God's doing – God's *will* – that Joseph be there!'

'And why would God *want* Joseph to be there?'

'To bear witness.'

'To what?'

'To the sin of the world.'

'Would you care to be a little more specific?'

'When Joseph returned home the following morning, he was pale and trembling. I asked what was wrong, and he said that the Lord had given him a new mission – right here at Ocean Heights. And that very day, he asked to be transferred to the night shift.'

'So what was his new mission?'

'I don't know. He would not tell me.'

'Did he say *why* he wouldn't tell you?'

'He said that there are some abominations in this world that I should be sheltered from. He hoped he could deal with them without being sullied himself – he would pray for the strength to do so – but he was not willing to imperil my soul.'

'But you already knew all about the fallen women on Coney Island,' Meade said, puzzled.

'Yes, I did,' Mrs Turner agreed.

'So what could be worse than that?'

'I do not know – and it was not my place to press him.'

'Apart from giving up his work in the vaudeville halls, did you notice any other changes in your husband's behaviour after that first time on the night shift?' Blackstone asked.

'Yes, I did,' Mrs Turner said. 'He began to travel into the city at least once a week.'

'And he'd never done that before?'

'No, he did not like cities. He said – and I agree with him – that they were nothing more than cauldrons of vice.'

'Did he seem to have any money worries in the last few weeks?' Meade asked.

'Why should he worry about money?' Mrs Turner wondered. 'We live very simply here, as you can see. And Joseph sends – sent – most of his wages to the Soldiers of God in New York.'

'Did he have any enemies?'

'None. His past was far behind him, and he was now a man of

peace – a man of righteousness.' Mrs Turner paused. 'Why must you continue to search for motives for my husband's death?' she continued.

'Well, because—' Meade began.

'He was killed not because of *who* he was,' Mrs Turner interrupted firmly, 'he was killed because of *where* he was.'

'You're convinced that what Turner saw, that first night on duty, was a woman entering Holt's suite?' Meade asked, as he and Blackstone walked back towards Ocean Heights.

'Yes, I am,' Blackstone replied. 'Fanshawe all but admitted that Holt had women visit him.'

'And you also believe that the woman who Turner saw that night was probably a prostitute?'

'It's likely. Most respectable ladies would baulk at the idea of meeting their gentlemen friends in an underground bunker, late at night. Besides, Fanshawe also said that William Holt *preferred* prostitutes because they had less inhibitions.'

'So what was so different about this *particular* prostitute?' Meade worried. 'What set her apart from all the other prostitutes on Coney Island?'

'The price, for a start,' Blackstone said. 'I would imagine that a wealthy man like Holt wouldn't settle for the kind of common whore who can be picked up on Surf Avenue. His "ladies" are probably provided by one of the better class of brothels in New York.'

'You're missing the point,' Meade said.

Blackstone chuckled. Just a month earlier, Alex would never have dreamed of saying anything like that, because, as far as he was concerned, the man from New Scotland Yard was the absolute expert on everything. Now, working together on their second case, Meade was acting less like a disciple and more like a partner – which was all to the good.

'So just *what* point am I missing?' he asked.

'That Turner regarded her – or what she did – as an abomination. That he was prepared to give up the work he was doing with all the other prostitutes and concentrate just on saving her.'

'Or saving William Holt *from* her,' Blackstone said.

'So what did she *do* that was so abominable?' Meade continued. 'Did she submit to some particularly disgusting desire of Holt's? And even if she did, how would Turner – on the other side of the steel door – even *know* about it?'

'Those are all good questions,' Blackstone said. He smiled. 'What a pity we don't have answers to *any* of them.'

They had reached Ocean Heights. There was no sign of any of the uniformed policemen who had been milling around earlier. Now, the only local police officer left on the scene was Inspector Flynn, who was sitting on a bench in the garden, smoking a cigarette, and looking up at the house with casual indifference.

'Well, if it isn't Inspector Blackstone and Sergeant Meade,' Flynn said, by way of greeting. 'And just what's going through your minds at the moment, gentlemen? Are you asking yourselves why the local hayseed has sent all his boys away?'

Blackstone smiled.

'Perhaps,' he said. 'Or perhaps I'm wondering if they're hidden in bushes, waiting to pounce when the murderer makes his proverbial return to the scene of the crime.'

'Ah, now *there's* a thing I'd never thought of doing,' Flynn said, with mock chagrin. 'Maybe I'll try that the *next* time I get a crack at a sensational murder – assuming, of course, that that one isn't taken off me as well.' He took a pull on his cigarette. 'The simple truth of it is that I sent them away because they'd done the job they had to do.'

'And what job might that be?' Blackstone asked.

'Looking busy,' Flynn said. 'Acting as window dressing.'

'Window dressing?' Meade repeated.

'Whenever there's a serious crime, people expect us to run around like blue-arsed flies,' Flynn explained. 'So Mr George and Mr Harold will have looked out of their window and thought, "Yes, the police are doing a good job down there", despite the fact that we all know that my boys wouldn't recognize a clue if it jumped up and hit them on the arse.'

'If I ever get that cynical, I'll shoot myself,' Meade said – and then realized he had not said the words *quite* as much under his breath as he might have wished.

'If you *don't* get that cynical, then shooting yourself might be a good idea,' Flynn said lightly.

'You haven't really sent your boys *home*, have you?' Blackstone asked.

Flynn smiled. 'No, I haven't,' he admitted.

'So what *did* you send them to do?'

'It occurred to me that there are two parts to any kidnapping,' Flynn said. 'The first part is actually snatching your victim. The second part is taking him somewhere he can't be found. Now, Holt is a big man, and – conscious or unconscious – it won't have been easy to get him off Coney Island.' He took another drag on his cigarette. 'So, bearing that in mind, I've dispatched my boys to traverse the highways and byways in search of any unusual traffic late last night.'

'That was a good move,' Blackstone said.

'Why, thank you!' Flynn replied. 'The approval of the English police has always been my fervent desire.'

'But suppose they didn't move him by road at all?'

'Ah, it'll be the water you're thinking of. And even though I may be a poor, dumb, potato-filled Mick, that *did* occur to me, too, and some of my boys are out talking to the local fishermen.'

Blackstone grinned. 'I look forward to the day when you're Commissioner of Police, Mr Flynn,' he said.

'Then you'll be waiting a long time,' Flynn told him. 'I'm too good a cop to get promoted much further.'

He was probably right about that, Blackstone thought.

'We're going to take another look at the bunker,' he said aloud.

'And why would you want to be doing that?' Flynn wondered. 'Do you think there was something you missed the first time round?'

Yes, Blackstone admitted, he did.

And that thought had been nagging at his brain for over an hour.

But it was not something obvious – like a bloody footprint or torn-off button – that he had missed, he told himself. In fact, he had the distinct feeling that rather than it being something that he *might* find, it was something that *should have* been there – and wasn't.

'Would you care to join us, Inspector Flynn?' he asked.

The Irishman shook his head. 'It's tempting,' he admitted, 'but I'll only be in Sergeant Meade's way – and I'd just hate for *that* to happen.'

EIGHT

The footman who answered the door looked at the two detectives as if they were something unpleasant that the cat had dragged in.

'Neither Mr George nor Mr Harold is at home,' he said.

'Is that right?' Alex Meade asked, in a deceptively mild voice, quite unlike his own. 'How strange! They were both here half an hour ago, and I haven't seen them leave.'

The footman's look of contempt only deepened. 'What I meant was that they are not at home *to receive visitors*,' he explained slowly, as if speaking to a simpleton. 'However, should you wish me to escort you to the room which has been assigned for your usage—'

'You'll be gracious enough to give my request your consideration – and might even decide to grant it?' Meade interrupted, all mildness gone, and his tone now reminiscent of a buzz saw.

'I'm afraid—' the footman began.

'And so you should be,' Meade told him, bunching his hands into tight fists. 'So should any man who is about three seconds away from losing his teeth.'

'I don't—' the footman said.

'Your safest course of action would be to shut up and listen,' Meade advised him. 'Do you think you can manage that?'

The footman did no more than nod.

'There's been a couple of murders in this house, and that means all the old rules – all the old ways of doing things – have flown right out the door,' Alex Meade said. 'So here are the *new* rules. One: you don't treat us like you treat the guys who've come to empty the septic tank – though you shouldn't treat the guys who've come to empty the septic tank like that, either. Two: we go wherever we want to in this house, without having a flunkey in a penguin suit hovering over us as if we were about to steal something.'

Listening to Meade speak, Blackstone felt a mixture of feelings. There was pride that his protégé had grown up so much in only a month. There was amusement at the look on the stuffed-shirt of a footman's face. And there was perhaps a little envy too – because, in England, the only person who was allowed to talk to an important man's servant like this was the important man himself, and any policeman who ignored that was more than likely to find himself out a job.

Meade had not finished yet. 'Three: we don't need permission *from* anybody to talk *to* anybody – and that includes the almighty Holts. And four: if you break any of the first three rules, I *will* smash your teeth and swear you did it falling over. Are we clear on that?'

'We're clear,' the footman said sullenly.

'Try again,' Meade advised him.

'We're clear, *sir*,' the footman said.

Meade nodded. 'Good. We're going down to the basement now. Make sure nobody disturbs us.'

'Yes, sir,' the footman said.

'So tell me, is there anyone else you're planning to reduce to a quivering wreck today?' Blackstone said, as he and Alex Meade descended the steep stairs to the basement.

'Depends if anybody else crosses me,' Meade growled.

'You were already angry, even before that footman got snotty with you, weren't you?'

'Damn straight!'

'With Flynn?'

'Hell, yes. This is all a *game* to him, isn't it?'

'No, I don't think it is,' Blackstone said. 'He might *appear* frivolous, but he's as serious about the case as you or me – possibly even more so, since it happened on his patch.'

They had reached the first of the steel doors.

Meade tapped on it experimentally with his knuckles, then said, 'I believe what Mrs Turner told us – and I don't just mean I believe that *she* believes it, I mean I believe it's *true*.'

'You believe it's true that her husband was an honest man who could never have been bribed to let the kidnappers into the guard room?'

'Yes. And, by all accounts, the other murdered guard was almost as saintly as Turner.'

'He would seem to have been,' Blackstone agreed.

'So how *did* the kidnappers get beyond this door?' Meade asked, exasperatedly.

'I don't know. It might have been through trickery.'

'But what *kind* of trickery would be likely to work?' Meade asked, his frustration bubbling over. 'What could have persuaded the guards to go against all their training and allow strangers to pass through the door in the middle of the night?'

'Nothing,' Blackstone admitted. 'Someone – a person they knew and trusted – must have told them it would be all right.'

'And who could that person be?' Meade demanded. 'I can only think of three – Fanshawe, Mr George or Mr Harold.'

'Or Big Bill himself,' Blackstone pointed out.

'You think he'd let his own kidnappers in?'

'He won't have known that's what they were – he will have thought they were there for some completely different reason.'

'So after seven years of refusing to see anybody but his sons, his butler and the parlour maid—' Meade said sceptically

'And one – or a number of – prostitutes,' Blackstone amended.

'. . . after seven years of that, he suddenly changes his attitude to visitors completely?'

'Circumstances may have changed. He may not have *wanted* to see them, but he could have thought it *necessary*.'

Meade sighed dispiritedly. 'This is getting us nowhere,' he said. 'We can speculate and deduce for forever and a day – and it all still ends with us disappearing in a cloud of smoke up our own assholes. It's solid facts – not fancy theories – that we need.'

'Then let's see if there are any solid facts on the other side of that door,' Blackstone suggested.

They opened the second steel door, and William Holt's study – the room in which he had spent every day for the previous seven years – lay before them.

Blackstone ran his eyes over the whole area: the filing cabinets; the bearskin rug, soaked with the blood of the men who had been hired to protect Big Bill; the desk, with its towers of paper and its dinner tray.

'There's something missing,' he told himself.

But what?

He wished he had Ellie Carr with him at that moment, he thought – but then, he wished he had her with him *most* of the time, both when he was investigating a crime and when he wasn't.

He had never experienced love for a woman until his thirties, and then – as if to make up for lost time – he fallen in love three times in as many years. Each time, it had been a disaster. His first two loves had betrayed him for a cause. His third, Dr Ellie Carr, had not so much betrayed him as deserted him for the work that she loved – the work that consumed her.

'We could use a forensic criminologist right now,' he said.

'I didn't know there *was* such a thing as forensic criminologist,' Meade replied.

And maybe there wasn't, Blackstone conceded – yet.

Maybe most people – in both the police and the scientific community – still refused to accept that science and crime detection could work hand in glove. But Ellie would change all that – even if it killed her.

He looked around the study again.

What *was* missing?

What *should have* been there – and wasn't?

'Where's the tray?' he asked.

'The dinner tray?' Meade said. 'It's right over there on the desk.'

'Not the *dinner* tray – the *breakfast* tray!'

'You've lost me,' Meade admitted.

'Put yourself in Fanshawe's shoes,' Blackstone said. 'You're taking your master his breakfast. You knock on the door to the guard room, and find that not only is it open, but there's no sign of the guards. You open the door to the study, and see the guards – drenched in blood – lying on the rug.'

'And you still have the breakfast tray in your hands!' Meade said, getting the picture.

'So what do you do with the tray?'

'Chances are, you're so shocked that you drop it on the floor.'

'Or maybe, if you've got more nerve and self-control than most people, you put it down somewhere.'

'But what you don't do is run off to raise the alarm with the tray still in your hands.'

'So what's your conclusion from all that?' Blackstone asked.

'That when Fanshawe came down here this morning, he didn't bring a tray with him. Because he knew it wouldn't be necessary! Because he knew what he was going to find!'

'I think we've just discovered who told the guards to let the kidnappers in,' Blackstone said grimly.

Blackstone stood at the back of the house, looking at the black clouds over the ocean. Some of them, it might have seemed to any *other* observer, were intent on buffeting their rivals out of the way. Others adopted a more placatory approach and tried to meld into the bigger neighbours. And there were yet others which, having recently formed a union, soon found that union unsatisfactory, and began to drift away.

None of this great natural drama registered with the inspector. Though he was looking, he was not *seeing*. All he actually *saw* – in whatever direction he looked – was his own stupidity.

'You should never have allowed it to happen, Sam Blackstone,' he told himself angrily.

When he'd suspected that he'd caught Fanshawe out in a lie, he should have begun a deeper interrogation of the butler immediately. Instead, he'd made the decision to let the man stew in his own juice for a while.

And that had been the *wrong* decision!

Meade appeared round the corner of the house. 'The servants have completed the search of the building,' he said.

'And they haven't found him?'

'No.'

Of course they hadn't found him! Fanshawe had realized what danger he was in – and had made a run for it.

'We haven't lost him yet,' Alex Meade said, with forced cheerfulness. 'I've just been on the phone to the police in Brooklyn, and they're going to watch both the railroad station and the streetcar terminal. If he's used either of those to make his escape, we'll have him.'

Unless he's donned some sort of disguise, Blackstone thought.

Unless the policemen assigned to watch out for him happen to be looking the other way when he walks past.

Unless he hasn't used the streetcar or the railroad at all, but instead has found some other way to get off Coney Island.

Unless . . . unless . . . unless . . .

There were too many imponderables – *far* too bloody many!

Inspector Flynn was still on the bench in the garden. He seemed not to have moved an inch since the last time Blackstone and Meade had seen him.

'There's a storm brewing,' he called out. 'I can feel it in the air. An hour from now, it'll be raining cats and dogs.'

'Thank you for the weather forecast, sir,' Meade said, with barely concealed animosity.

'Just what is it that bothers you about me, Sergeant?' Flynn asked, as if he were genuinely curious.

'Nothing, sir,' Meade replied.

'Is it the fact I've been sitting here on my big fat Irish arse for the last hour?' Flynn wondered.

'Frankly, sir, yes,' Meade admitted.

'And what would you have preferred me to do? Walk behind you like a conjuror's assistant, hoping you'd find some menial – meaningless – task to keep me busy? Or walk *ahead* of you, with a swagger to my step, as if this case hadn't been snatched out of my grasp and given to two fellers who know nothing about Coney Island or the people who live here?'

'I'm sorry, sir, I haven't been fair with you,' Meade said contritely. 'I know that if I'd had a case taken away from me—'

'Besides, you can learn a great deal by just sitting and looking,' Flynn interrupted him. 'I know, for example, that the two ladies of the house – Mr George's wife and Mr Harold's wife – are on their way here, because I've seen their personal maids arrive with their luggage. I know that one of the maids employed in the kitchen not only steals food, but is stupid enough to do it while I'm here. And I know that Mr Fanshawe isn't attending to his duties at the moment, because I saw him slip into the woods half an hour ago.'

'You saw *what*!' Blackstone exploded.

Their first instinct was to run towards the woods, and that – without even consulting each other – was exactly what they did. But even as they approached the closest trees, Blackstone was beginning to realize that instinct was not enough – that what they needed was a plan.

'Wait a minute, Alex,' he called out to the younger man, who had already pulled ahead of him by several yards.

Meade came to skidding halt which tore up the immaculate lawn, and waited for his partner to catch up.

'This may be just what Fanshawe *wanted* us to do,' Blackstone said. 'He may have planned all along for us to blunder around in the woods looking for him, when, in fact, he was already gone.'

'True,' Meade agreed. 'But what do we lose by looking anyway?'

He was right, Blackstone thought. It was possible that, instead of running, Fanshawe had retreated into the woods like a wounded bear, and that they'd find him huddled up pitifully at the base of a tree.

The sudden rumbling sound overhead made Blackstone look up.

Flynn had been wrong about the timing of the coming storm, he thought. The heavy clouds, picked up by a vigorous wind, had advanced from the sea with the speed of a crack cavalry division, and were now engaged in the work of darkening the sky above them.

'We'll split up,' he decided. 'You skirt around the left side of the wood, and I'll do the same to the right. Then we'll both head towards the middle.'

There was more thunder above them, and a bolt of lightning seared its way across the sky.

Meade grinned. 'Don't they say the worst place to be in a thunderstorm is in a wood?' he asked.

'Yes, I believe they do,' Blackstone said.

And then they both set off in their search for Fanshawe the butler.

The rain, which the thunder and lightning had promised, came two or three minutes later. At first, only a few drops managed to find their way through the dense foliage overhead. Then, as the drenching con-tinued, the smaller branches bent under the weight of the downpour, and tiny waterfalls trickled their way down to the floor of the wood.

Blackstone searched slowly and methodically. Charles the First of England had escaped the pursuing Roundheads by hiding in the branches of an oak tree, but Fanshawe the butler would not be allowed to pull the same trick, and *his* pursuer spent almost as much time looking up as he did looking ahead.

The rain was even heavier now, and the dusty soil beneath Blackstone's feet was acquiring a springy sponginess. His second best suit was taking some punishment, too, and he could feel drops of water trickling down his neck. Soon, the approaching dusk would combine with the heavy grey clouds to make the tops of the trees almost invisible. Then, as night fell, even the bases of the trees would become nothing more than vague black shapes ahead of him.

But he would not give up his search. He had been a hunter of men for a long time – first in India and then in London – and his instinct told him that while there was no reason for Fanshawe to still be in the woods, in the woods was exactly where he was.

Yes, he was still there. Cold and shivering – perhaps afraid – but *still there*.

Another flash of lightning cut its way through the sky – lighting up the woods in a ghostly yellow light, making the very trees them-selves seem to tremble at its power.

'I'm not going to give up, Mr Fanshawe, so you might as well come out!' Blackstone shouted.

Now *that* was a pointless exercise, he told himself. Even if Fanshawe had been likely to be swayed by the words, it was improb-able, given the wind which had started to howl and the rain which continued to crash down, that he would even have heard them.

Small dips in the floor of the wood, hardly visible to the naked eye, had now become tiny bubbling rivers. Trees sighed and creaked. The wind, gaining confidence, searched for holes in Blackstone's defences at which to hurl its chill and the rain it carried with it.

'You might as well give yourself up, Mr Fanshawe!' he called out.

And then, in a new flash of lightning, he saw a pair of legs suspended in mid-air.

NINE

If a body had been discovered hanging from a tree in Central Park, the New York City Police Department would already have flooded the whole area around the 'incident' in the garish glow of hastily erected arc lights. But this *wasn't* New York – it was Coney Island (part of the city, *in theory*, since 1st of January 1898 – yet still going very much its own way), and the officers at the scene had to make do with hand-held kerosene lanterns.

Inspector Flynn stood watching, as one of his men climbed the tree and then shimmied along to the branch around which the rope had been looped.

'Well, looking on the bright side, at least it's stopped raining,' he said to Blackstone.

It had indeed. The storm had departed with the same sudden speed with which it had arrived, and now there was only the dank smell in the air, and the squelching of soil underfoot, to indicate that it had even occurred.

Blackstone looked up at the dangling corpse.

Fanshawe had probably hoped for a quick, painless death, he thought. That was what most people who hanged themselves anticipated – but it didn't usually work out like that.

Hanging was both an art and a science. A good hangman would take into account the weight of the condemned man, and calculate the length of the rope – and hence the length of the drop – accordingly. He would place the noose in just the right position for the sudden impact to snap the man's spine and send his brain into a state of unconsciousness. The amateur attempting suicide, on the other hand, knew none of this, and would invariably get it wrong.

And so it would have been with Fanshawe. When he jumped from the tree, he had probably been expecting instant oblivion.

And what had he found instead?

That he was dangling a few feet from the ground, fighting for breath!

Perhaps he had clawed up at the rope, in a desperate attempt to save himself, while, all the time, he was growing weaker and weaker through lack of oxygen.

Or perhaps he had decided simply – as many had done before him

– that though he'd got it wrong, his death would still be just as inevitable, and merely take longer than he had anticipated.

'Shall I cut him down, sir?' the policeman in the tree called.

'I suppose you might as well, now you've gone to all the trouble of climbing up there,' Flynn replied. He turned to Blackstone. 'They're good boys that I've got working for me, Inspector. Very good boys! But they wouldn't even think of taking a crap without asking my permission first.'

The policeman on the branch produced a knife and began to saw through the rope.

'Hold on a second,' Flynn said. 'You two – Johnson and Taylor!' he called out to a couple of young officers who were standing a few feet away from him. 'Have you signed off duty for the night?'

The two men looked perplexed.

'No, sir,' one of them said.

'Ah, so you are still *on* duty, but you thought you'd leave the donkey work to me and Inspector Blackstone here, did you?'

'Is there something that you'd like us to do, sir?' the young policeman asked.

'Could be,' Flynn mused. 'You see the body hanging from that tree, Officer Johnson?'

'Yes, sir.'

'And you see your man up there – Officer Polk – cutting through the rope with his knife?'

'Yes, sir.'

'So tell me, Officer Johnson, what do you think is going to happen to it when he's finished the job?'

'The body will fall to the ground, sir,' Johnson said.

'Yes, it will,' Flynn agreed. 'It will fall like a sack of flour. But it isn't a sack of flour, is it?'

'No, sir.'

'No, sir! It's a man! And the way I see it, even if the poor bastard's already lost most of his dignity, we should at least do all we can to try to preserve what little is left.'

'You want us to take hold of him?' Johnson said.

'Now you're getting the picture,' Flynn agreed.

'So there's a soft side to your nature, after all,' Blackstone said, as he watched Johnson and Taylor step forward, and grab hold of the swinging corpse.

Flynn's stance stiffened slightly. 'There's nothing soft about maintaining a man's dignity,' he said. 'The Irish have been fighting for it – and dying for it – for five hundred years.'

The rope went slack, and the two officers strained against the sudden weight. 'Shall we put him on the stretcher, sir?' Johnson asked.

'Now that *is* a good idea you've just come up with,' Flynn said. 'You'll go far in your chosen career, my boy.'

'Yes, sir,' the young policeman said, clearly confused. 'Thank you, sir.'

'See what I mean, Inspector Blackstone?' Flynn asked in a lower voice. 'Without me, they'd be as lost as babes in the woods.'

Johnson and Taylor laid the body on the stretcher, and then reached for the handles.

'One more thing, Officer Johnson,' Flynn said softly.

'Yes, sir?'

'I couldn't help thinking – and I'm quite prepared to accept that I may be wrong on this – I couldn't help thinking that Mr Fanshawe might look a *little more* at peace if you took the bloody noose from around his neck. What do *you* think, Officer Johnson?'

'I . . . I think we should take off the bloody noose, sir.'

'Good lad,' Flynn said approvingly.

Johnson held the dead man's head, while Taylor tugged at the slip knot and slackened the noose enough for it to be removed.

'And don't go throwing that bit of rope away,' Flynn said. 'The coroner will want to see it.'

Taylor placed the noose on the dead man's chest, and then the two officers picked the stretcher up and began walking towards the edge of the woods.

'It's not much of a cortège, Inspector Blackstone,' Flynn said, 'but it is what we have, and I suppose, out of respect, that we'd better follow it.'

The horse-drawn police ambulance was parked, waiting, in front of the house.

'Would it be all right to put the body inside, sir?' Taylor asked.

'It would be an excellent idea,' Flynn told him.

Johnson and Taylor slid the stretcher into the ambulance, and once the doors were closed, the driver tugged lightly on the reins and his horse obediently clip-clopped away.

'Are they taking him into town?' Blackstone asked.

Flynn laughed. 'Now why would they want to go and do that?' he wondered. 'Why let our local sawbones – who's considered good enough, by the people who live around here, to cut the legs off *living* men – get his hands on the *dead* Mr Fanshawe? Far better, I would have thought, to take him to the big city, where he can be sliced open by a real *expert*.'

The words, if written down on paper, would seem bitter, but the way Flynn delivered them, they were not, Blackstone thought.

He had still not quite got Flynn worked out. Alex Meade had said that the man was playing a *game*, yet it wasn't a game he was playing at all. It was a *role* – the role of aggrieved local policeman. But if that wasn't what he really was, then who the hell *was* he?

'Do you think Fanshawe *was* involved in the kidnapping?' he asked – not so much because he had any doubts himself as to see what Flynn thought.

'It does seem likely he was involved,' Flynn said. 'A man doesn't top himself without a powerful motive – and the thought of going to the electric chair for his part in two murders would certainly have provided him with that. On the other hand . . .' he paused.

'Yes?'

'On the other hand, it's perfectly possible that he was totally innocent in this affair, and that what drove him to desperation was the thought of his past wrongdoings catching up with him.'

'*What* past wrongdoings?'

'Someone who closely resembles the description of Fanshawe has been wanted by the English police for a number of years.'

'Go on,' Blackstone encouraged.

'It's possible – and bear in mind it's a hayseed policeman who's telling you this – that Fanshawe's real name was Ernest Hoddle, and that he used to belong to a gang which specialized in breaking into the houses of the British aristocracy. Would I be right to call those places "stately homes"?'

'You know you would.'

'At any rate, one of these burglaries – must have been about twelve years ago now – went wrong. The son and heir of the noble family in question heard a noise, went to investigate, and caught the burglars in the act. He'd thoughtfully taken his pistol with him, and fired at Hoddle. Fortunately for our hero, the young man wasn't a very good shot – he was probably drunk, as, I believe, your decadent English aristocrats are *most* of the time. Hoddle received a wound which, though it must have been very painful at the time, wasn't serious, and before the young lord could fire again, one of the other burglars had the presence of mind to smash his skull in. It was never suggested that the robbers *intended* to kill this flower of English youth, but he did die, and so it was murder. Three of the gang were hanged – but the police never did get their hands on Hoddle.'

'You said that Hoddle was slightly wounded.'

'That's right, I did.'

'What was the nature of the wound?'

Flynn smiled. 'Didn't I say? I must be getting forgetful in my old age.'

'You *still* haven't said,' Blackstone pointed out.

'No more I have,' Flynn agreed. 'It seems that the young buck shot off the tip of Hoddle's right index finger.'

'Where did you get all this information from?' Blackstone asked.

'Why, from your very own little precinct station.'

'From my *what*?'

'From New Scotland Yard. And I must say, Mr Blackstone, that the Yard's efficiency would put the New York Police Department to shame.'

'You were first called to investigate this case at what time?' Blackstone demanded.

'Can't remember, exactly.'

'Eight o'clock this morning?'

'Maybe a little later than that.'

'And you're seriously asking me to believe that, since then, there's been enough time for you to cable New Scotland Yard, for New Scotland Yard to go through its records, and for another cable to be sent back to you in reply to your questions?'

'As I said, they were very efficient.'

'I don't believe it,' Blackstone said.

'Now isn't that just the trouble with you English?' Flynn asked. 'You're a nation of clerks that sees itself as a nation of heroes. You think nobody could rule the world better than you – and you couldn't be wronger. Yet when it comes to something you *are* good at – the paperwork, the crossing of the "t"s and dotting of the "i"s – you won't even take credit where credit's due.'

'You have a way with words – I'll give you that,' Blackstone conceded. 'But however many flowers you decorate a piece of bullshit with, it *is* still bullshit.'

'You're not so bad with the words yourself – and I'm sure we could sustain this merry banter for hours if we wanted to,' Flynn replied. 'Unfortunately, we're about to be denied the opportunity, because here comes your sergeant – and he looks to me like he's got a lot on his mind.'

Blackstone turned and saw that Meade was, in fact, approaching them – and that he *did* look as if he had a lot on his mind.

The sergeant drew level with the other two men. 'The family want to see us,' he said.

'The "family", is it?' Flynn said. 'The whole clan. Now you should find that a *very* interesting experience.'

'They want to see all three of us,' Meade told him.

'Maybe they do, Sergeant,' Flynn replied. 'But, you see, one of the few advantages of having my investigation snatched from under me is that I don't have to jump whenever the "family" clicks its fingers.' He reached up with his right hand and tipped the brim of his hat in a casual salute. 'I'll probably see you in the morning, gentlemen,' he concluded

And then he turned, and followed the ambulance down the drive.

TEN

From the moment he entered the salon on the second floor of Ocean Heights, it was obvious to Blackstone that the furniture had recently been rearranged – and the *way* it had been rearranged said equally clearly that this was intended to be not so much a meeting as an interrogation.

George Holt was sitting with his wife, who he introduced as 'Mrs Elizabeth Holt', on a sofa just to the left of the main window. Harold Holt was sitting with *his* wife – Mrs Virginia Holt – on an identical sofa to the right of the main window. Facing the sofas – though some distance apart from them – were the two upright chairs on which Blackstone and Meade were bidden to sit.

The room itself was very much the kind of *nouveau riche* salon that Blackstone might have expected to find – the mirrors were in the grand and ostentatious Second Empire style, and the furniture was elaborate enough to proclaim 'handmade by master craftsmen' (which was just another way of screaming 'very expensive').

No surprises there, then, he thought.

But what *did* surprise him – to such an extent that he considered, for some moments, the possibility that this might all be part of some elaborate practical joke – was the complete mismatch between each of the sons and his wife.

Bumptious George's wife, Elizabeth, was thin and pale. Her features in general were pinched and her mouth little more than a slit, but her eyes, in complete contrast, were big and wide, rather like those of a frightened deer.

Sensitive Harold's wife, Virginia, on the other hand, had the generous bosom of a music hall singer, eyes which seemed to offer dark erotic pleasure, and the lips of a courtesan. Even though she was sitting down, it was possible to see that she was at least three inches taller than her husband, and she exuded a strength which suggested that – should she choose to – she could easily break him in two.

Once the two detectives were seated, George cleared his throat self-importantly. 'I am rather displeased—' he began.

'Tell me, Sergeant Meade, are you, by any chance, one of the *Connecticut* Meades?' Virginia asked, cutting in.

'I was certainly raised in Connecticut,' Alex Meade replied.

'And are you any relation – however distant – to Mr Robert Meade, the brilliant attorney and ruthless politician?'

'My father would revel in that description,' Meade said with a smile. 'Your opinion of him coincides perfectly with his own – though, in my view, you're both rather far from the mark.'

Virginia Holt laughed. 'How deliciously you phrase your thoughts,' she said. 'Robert Meade's son! Well, well, well.' She paused for a moment. 'I must admit though, Alex . . . I may call you Alex, mayn't I?'

'Of course.'

'I must admit that I find it extraordinary, given your background, that you are a policeman.'

Meade smiled again. 'A lot of people do.'

'Extraordinary, but not necessarily reprehensible,' Virginia said. 'I have the greatest respect for any man who is prepared to throw off his heritage and make his own way in the world.'

'For goodness sake, Virginia, this isn't one of your afternoon tea parties,' George said exasperatedly. 'We're not here to make polite social chit-chat. Meade and his assistant have come to report their findings to us.'

'I'm afraid you're wrong on two counts,' Alex Meade said. 'The first is your assumption that Inspector Blackstone is my assistant. In actual fact, I am his.'

George ran his eyes up and down Blackstone's second-hand brown suit, which had not been improved in appearance by the soaking it had received out in the woods.

'Really!' he said.

'Really,' Meade agreed. 'I'd have thought, for most people, that the fact he's an inspector, while I'm only a sergeant, would have given that away.'

'I'd assumed, since Blackstone is a foreigner, that *you* would be in charge,' George said huffily. 'But that's all by the way. As I'd started to say earlier, I'm rather displeased that—'

'Don't you want to know the other count on which you were wrong?' Virginia interrupted.

George sighed. 'Very well. On what other count do I appear to be wrong, Sergeant?'

'You're wrong about us being here to *report* to you,' Meade said. 'We report to the Commissioners of Police as a matter of course, and to the governor if requested to do so.'

Elizabeth Holt looked down at her hands, as if she felt the conversation was taking rather an unpleasant turn.

Virginia, in contrast, released a positive roar of laughter and said, 'That's put you in *your* place, George.'

'I might remind you that I have some influence with the government in Albany, Sergeant Meade,' George said stiffly, reddening.

'And so, I can well imagine, does Sergeant Meade's father,' Virginia countered.

What a cosy group they were, Blackstone thought – and how jolly their family meals must be.

'Would it be all right with you if I now said what I have *already* attempted to say twice before?' George asked his sister-in-law.

'Of course, my dear George,' Virginia said airily. 'I wouldn't *dream* of stopping you.'

'I am rather displeased that you have allowed Fanshawe, who was clearly involved in the kidnapping of my father, to escape the consequences of his actions,' George told the detectives.

'Yes, I suppose you could call hanging himself "escaping the consequences of his actions",' Blackstone said, to Virginia's obvious amusement. 'Could I ask who employed him originally?'

'He was engaged by my father, as all the servants were,' George said. 'He came with excellent recommendations.'

Of course he did, Blackstone thought. When a man is forging his own recommendations, he very rarely resorts to modesty.

'Does the name Ernest Hoddle mean anything to you, Mr Holt?' he asked.

George frowned. 'No. Should it?'

'Probably not,' Blackstone said. 'We'll need you to give us a list of Fanshawe's friends and acquaintances.'

'Friends and acquaintances?' George repeated.

Virginia laughed again. 'It's something of a revelation to my brother-in-law that servants *have* friends and acquaintances. As far as he's concerned, they only really exist when they're serving him.'

'Really, Virginia, must you?' the mouse-like Elizabeth asked, in squeaky defiance.

'Yes, I must,' Virginia countered. 'Speak the truth and shame the devil. That's my motto! Not that I'm suggesting – even for a moment – that there's anything diabolical about my dear brother-in-law.'

'That's enough, Virginia,' Harold said quietly.

'Oh, my lord and master has spoken, and I must, perforce, fall silent,' Virginia said.

She said the words with mock horror, but even so, fall silent was exactly what she did.

George cleared his throat again. 'To return to your question,

Inspector, I'm not sure Fanshawe *had* any friends. He hardly ever left the estate. He was devoted – he *seemed* devoted – to the service of my father.'

'No friends and hardly ever left the estate,' Blackstone mused. 'And yet he somehow seems to have established contact with a gang of vicious kidnappers who are probably based in New York City.'

'Yes,' George conceded. 'That *does* appear to have been the case.'

Assuming that Flynn was right, and Fanshawe and Hoddle *were* the same man, had that man been playing an *incredibly long* game? Blackstone wondered.

Could the former burglar of stately homes have been content to wait for *nine years* before committing his next criminal act?

No, that didn't seem at all likely.

So perhaps, before being contacted by the kidnappers, Fanshawe had been using Ocean Heights as a base from which to operate some entirely different criminal operation – though it was hard to imagine what the nature of that operation might be.

It was even possible, he supposed, that Fanshawe really *had* gone straight for those nine long years, and had only recently, after being contacted by the New York criminals, been tempted to return to his old ways.

But if he *had* been involved in the kidnapping, why had he stayed around once it had been pulled off?

Perhaps because the other members of the gang had *told him* to stay around, so he could watch the police investigation and gauge what progress it was making.

But then why, when he'd realized that the police were on to him, had he given no thought to escape – in which, the chances were, he would have succeeded – but had instead chosen to hang himself in the woods?

Thinking about this case wasn't just like banging your head against a brick wall . . .

'Sam?' said a dreamy voice from somewhere in the ether.

. . . it was like banging your head against a *series* of brick walls, none of which stayed in one place long enough for you to have any effect on it.

'Sam?' said the voice again, and this time it seemed closer and much more immediate.

Blackstone glanced around him, and realized that Meade and the entire Holt family were looking at him expectantly.

'Sorry,' he said, 'I was just following a line of thought.'

George – to whom *any* thoughts seemed to be no more than distant acquaintances – allowed his lip to curl with disdain.

'Following a line of thought,' he repeated. 'And was it leading you anywhere interesting?'

Why don't you take a long walk along a short pier, you bastard! Blackstone wondered silently.

And aloud, he said, 'We shall need to question the servants – especially the ones who worked mostly closely with Mr Fanshawe.'

'That could be arranged. Shall we say – tomorrow morning?' George suggested.

'Shall we say – now!' Blackstone countered.

'Ah, but that would be rather difficult,' George told him.

'And why might that be?'

'Well, you see, the staff who worked closest with Fanshawe are what I believe you people in England call the *upstairs* staff – that is to say, the ones who have direct contact with the family.'

'So?'

'They are precisely the ones who will be most involved in the process of serving dinner, a process which, I need not remind you, has already been made difficult enough by the loss of our butler, and would be almost impossible if any other servants were withdrawn from it.'

'You haven't, by any chance, forgotten that your father's been kidnapped, have you?' Blackstone said.

'No, I haven't forgotten that. How could I?'

'And it has occurred to you, hasn't it, that our questioning your servants could play an important part in our search for him?'

'Of course.'

'And yet you're content to leave questioning them until tomorrow?'

'Look, Inspector, I do appreciate your difficulties,' George said, suddenly full of sweet reasonableness, 'and, by the same token, I would expect you to appreciate ours. This has been a tragic day, I'll grant you that, but whatever has happened, the life of the house must go on as normal.'

'Why?' Blackstone asked.

'Because the routine of the house is of great importance. The staff expect things to run in a certain way, and would lose some of their respect for us if we allowed even Father's kidnapping to hamper that.'

'So you're all slaves to your servants' expectations, are you?' Blackstone asked.

George scowled. 'I would not put it in quite that manner, but suffice it to say that dinner must be served at the same time as it always is, in the same way as it always is.'

'Besides,' Virginia said, 'how *can* you question them, Mr Blackstone, when you'll be at dinner yourself?'

'I'm not sure—' George began.

'You *are* inviting Inspector Blackstone and Sergeant Meade to dinner, aren't you, my dear George?' Virginia asked.

'They . . . they probably don't have their tuxedos with them,' George mumbled.

'*Probably* don't? Since they came here to investigate the kidnapping, I'd be very surprised if they *did* have their tuxedos with them,' Virginia said.

They made a lot of assumptions in this family, Blackstone thought. They assumed, for example, that the kidnapping was the *only* crime that had occurred, and conveniently brushed to one side the fact that two men had been murdered. And they assumed – or, at least, Virginia did – that he was the sort of man who *could* produce a tuxedo, if he were only given enough advance warning.

'I'm sure if you and Harold put the tuxedo problem in the hands of your valets, they'll be able to come up with a perfectly satisfactory solution, George,' Virginia said airily.

'Besides, if they stay to dinner, how will they ever get back to New York tonight?' George asked, fighting an increasingly desperate rearguard action.

'They don't *have to* get back to New York tonight, you silly boy,' the seemingly irrepressible Virginia said. 'They can spend the night here.'

'Here?' George repeated bleakly.

'Here,' Virginia confirmed. 'Just think how convenient that would be. If they stayed in Ocean Heights, they could be up bright and early, and have questioned all the servants before the rest of us had even risen.' She turned from her brother-in-law to Blackstone. 'I can't believe you'd be cruel enough to deny us the pleasure of your company, so I'm absolutely confident that when I ask you dine with us – as a special favour to me – you'll have no choice but to say "yes". You *will* say "yes", won't you, Inspector?'

There were several advantages to agreeing to the proposal, Blackstone thought. The first was that he hadn't eaten since breakfast time, and was ravenously hungry. The second was that it made sense to stay at Ocean Heights rather than travel back to the city – and if they *were* staying, they might as well eat. Add to that the fact that spending more time with the family might throw up information useful to the case, and there were good solid grounds for staying.

But the *real* reason that he felt not the slightest hesitation in accepting the offer, he acknowledged to himself, was the look of horror on George Holt's face as he contemplated the possibility. It would do George good not to get his own way for once – and his obvious discomfort would only add an extra relish to whatever they were served.

'We'd be delighted to stay to dinner,' he told Mrs Holt.

'Oh, good!' Virginia said, clapping her hands together like a small child. 'We'll have such *fun*!'

You might, Blackstone thought, but I doubt if, once it's over, the other members of your family will retain any fond memories of the evening.

ELEVEN

I t was at the end of the meal that the two uniformed footmen, previously unseen, appeared in the doorway of the dining room.

'Ah, your escorts have arrived!' Virginia Holt said to Meade and Blackstone. 'And if you're wondering why there's two of them, it's because George doesn't want you wandering about the ancestral home – which isn't really ancestral at all, and bears very little resemblance to a home – without at least two pairs of eyes following every move you make.'

'Really, Virginia, sometimes you go too far,' George said sullenly.

'You mean, I *usually* go too far,' his sister-in-law replied. 'It was only a joke,' she assured the detectives. 'The reason you need a footman each is that, as chance would have it, your rooms are in different parts of the house.'

But there was no *chance* about it, Blackstone thought, as he followed the mute flunkey down a maze of corridors.

Alex Meade was one of the *Connecticut* Meades. He wore a tuxedo as if he had been born to it, and suitable accommodation would have been provided for him close to the family's bedrooms.

He, on the other hand, was one of the East End of London Blackstones, a far less distinguished line. When *he* had donned his borrowed tuxedo, it had *looked* as if it were borrowed, and when it came to the matter of selecting *his* sleeping accommodation, anything would do.

The footman stopped at a door halfway along the corridor.

'This is it,' he said, in a voice he might have used when showing the rat-catcher where to catch the rats. 'Anything else you want?'

'A little subservience – however insincere – might be nice,' Blackstone said, mainly for his own amusement.

'A little *what*?' the footman asked.

'Subservience,' Blackstone repeated. 'If you're interested, you can borrow a dictionary and look it up.'

He opened the door and said, 'Goodnight,' over his shoulder. The footman, making no reply, turned and retreated down the corridor.

The room which Blackstone entered contained a single bed, a wardrobe which had seen better days, and a side table on which had been placed a bowl and a jug of water.

It had probably been specifically selected by George to make him aware of his place in the pecking order, he decided – but only someone as stupid as George would even have thought such a demonstration necessary. Besides, as far as Blackstone was concerned, the room was more than acceptable – in fact, as basic as it was, it was a great improvement on both his lodgings in London and his crummy hotel room in New York City.

As he closed the door behind him, he noticed that though there was a keyhole, there was no key. It didn't matter. He had never had anything that was worth stealing, anyway.

He walked over to the open window and lit a cigarette. From outside came the sound of the ocean crashing against the shoreline – a peaceful sound, despite the power and violence which was producing it.

In terms of his investigation, the dinner had been something of a disappointment, he thought.

With the donning of their evening wear, the Holt family also seemed to have slipped into an altogether more civilized way of behaving. George had been polite to his guests – even gracious, as far as he was able. Harold had told some amusing anecdotes about his time at Harvard University. Virginia – apart from her final comments – had refrained from saying anything outlandish. And even Elizabeth had managed to seem a little more relaxed. Altogether, it could have been called a thoroughly convivial gathering – if you liked that sort of thing.

It was only when Blackstone brought up the subject of Big Bill that the atmosphere had suddenly become as chill as the lemon sorbet they were all eating at the time.

'*There's one way, at least, in which your father is better off than most kidnap victims,*' *he'd said.*

'*Oh yes?*' *George had replied, in a tone which indicated that he had no particular desire to find out what that one way might be.*

'*Indeed,*' *Blackstone said, ignoring the lack of interest.* '*Most victims, you see, are not used to being locked up in confined spaces – and of all the frightening things they have to deal with, that's what often terrifies them the most. But your father won't have that problem, will he? After all, he has lived in a very confined space for seven years.*'

'*Yes, he has,*' *George agreed – and said no more.*

None of them really cared about Big Bill, Blackstone thought, taking a drag on his cigarette. They certainly wanted the head of the family back safely with them – and were prepared to pay a substantial ransom to *get* him back – but that was more to do with the price of stocks and shares than with any bonds of affection.

But then, who was to say that William Holt *deserved* his family's love and concern?

The picture that had emerged of him so far was of a man prepared to trample any business rival – or even any business *partner* – into the ground, if it brought him a profit. And perhaps he had adopted a similar cavalier attitude with his own kith and kin.

Blackstone stubbed out his cigarette, undressed, and climbed into bed.

It had been a long day, he thought – and given that he had less than seventy-two hours to prove that he was as good as Alex Meade *thought* he was, more long days were about to follow.

It was around two in the morning when the bedroom door clicked softly open, and Blackstone's survival instincts – developed during his time in India – dragged him from exhausted sleep to complete alertness in less than a second.

The door clicked closed again, and the intruder was now inside the room.

If he'd been back in New York City, he would have had his gun under his pillow. But this wasn't New York – and even in a house where there had already been two murders, he had seen no need to take his weapon to bed with him.

Fool!

Blackstone lay perfectly still, and began to breathe like a man who was still asleep.

The intruder took first one cautious step closer to the bed, and then a second one, and from the sound his feet made on the floor, it was obvious that he was barefoot.

Blackstone's eyes had begun to adjust to the darkness, and now he could see a vague shape which was halfway across the room and still moving cautiously.

Whatever was about to happen, it would all be over in the next ten seconds, he told himself.

How would his assailant choose to attack him? Not with a gun. In a sleeping house, guns were far too noisy.

Nine!

The intruder would expect his victim to be asleep, and only able to put up token resistance, so maybe he might try to strangle or smother him.

Eight!

Or perhaps his weapon of choice was a hammer – in which case, the head on the pillow would be what he was aiming for.

Seven!

It *might* be a hammer, but a knife was more likely. He would lift his arm back, then swing the knife in a wide forceful arc towards the supine body.

Six!

The only advantage he himself had in this fight was the element of surprise, Blackstone told himself – and if he moved now, even that would be gone.

Five!

He needed to time it perfectly, to wait until the knife was coming down, and then twist out of the way.

Four!

However hard the assassin tried, he wouldn't be able to stop himself mid-swing. The knife would cut through the empty air where the body should have been, and bury its blade in the mattress.

Three!

The assassin would pull back his arm for a second attack, but by then – if things went right – the counter-attack would be underway, and he would have his own pain to deal with.

Two!

That's what will happen if you get it *right*, Blackstone's brain told him. If you get it *wrong*, you'll never see another sunrise.

One.

The dark shape had almost reached the bed now, and had still not raised its arm.

Blackstone could hear it breathing, and had the smell of it in his nostrils.

There would *be* no attack, he realized – or, at least, no attack meant to do him harm.

'Mrs Holt?' he asked.

The woman jumped slightly, but when she said, 'Call me Virginia,' her voice was steady enough.

'What are you doing here?' he asked.

She laughed. 'You're not much of a detective, are you, Sam? Didn't you notice, when you first came into this room, that there was no key in the door?'

'Yes, I noticed,' he admitted.

'And didn't you realize *why* there was no key?'

'No, I didn't.'

'Then you can't have been watching the way I looked at you over dinner. I would have thought that, after that, any man with even *half* a brain would have been expecting me.'

'What makes me so privileged?' Blackstone wondered. 'Why didn't you choose Alex Meade instead?'

Virginia laughed again. 'Alex is a boy,' she said. 'A very beautiful one – but still a boy.'

'And I'm a middle-aged man,' Blackstone pointed out.

'Yes, you are,' Virginia agreed. 'A middle-aged man who's taken a battering from life. But that's your appeal, you see – because however much you're battered, you'll still fight back. And I like that.'

'I think you should go,' Blackstone told her.

'Do you?' she asked.

He had only a single sheet covering him, and her hand was under it in a second, grasping him between the legs.

'Well, there's at least *one* part of you that doesn't want me to go,' she said huskily.

He said nothing.

He *did* nothing – even when she began to move her hand up and down his shaft.

'What's the matter with you, Sam?' she demanded. 'Are you dead or something?'

'Perhaps,' he replied. 'If I am, that would certainly explain the stiffness, wouldn't it?'

He could not see her face in the darkness, but he sensed that a battle between amusement and anger was being fought out on it.

'I'm not used to getting this sort of reception,' she told him.

'And I'm not used to people taking what they want from me without asking me first,' he said.

She released her grip on him and pulled her hand clear of the bed.

'Is that it?' she asked, and now it was clear that anger had won. 'Other men can't believe their own luck when I go to them, but *you* want me to *beg* you to screw me?'

'No, I don't want you to beg at all,' Blackstone said. 'What I want you to do is leave.'

'Bastard!' Virginia hissed.

She turned, and headed towards the door. She would have liked to have flounced out of the room – slamming the door behind her – but she was obviously afraid that if she did that, she would wake up the whole house.

He groped in the dark for his cigarettes, lit one up, and wondered why he had turned Virginia Holt's offer down.

It was certainly not because he found her unattractive. There wasn't a man on the planet who would have found her that.

Perhaps, then, it was because she was a married woman – though he had slept with married women before.

So maybe it was because she was involved in the case he was investigating.

'No, it's not that, either,' he groaned aloud. 'It's because of Ellie.'

Yes, it was because of Ellie.

Even though he hadn't seen her for months!

Even though, when they *were* seeing each other, they had never actually been lovers!

'Do you really think that *she's* being celibate herself?' he asked himself. 'Do you think that *she's* paying abstemious homage to an affair that was never really an affair at all?'

He was a fool, he decided – a *bloody* fool!

But there was nothing he could do about that, and, stubbing out his cigarette, he fell into an uneasy sleep.

TWELVE

The slowly rising sun coloured the ocean with a gentle red tint rather like a slight flush on pale skin – or perhaps like blood diluted by water.

Blackstone, his back to the house, looked out over that ocean and wished he was on the other side of it, among people who he knew – people he understood.

'Well, it is a surprise to find you out here,' said a voice from somewhere to his left. 'On this island of late nights, I thought I was the only one who rose early enough to watch the sun come up.'

Blackstone turned to face Harold.

'I couldn't sleep,' he said – and found himself wondering, the moment the words were out of his mouth, what interpretation the other man would choose to put on them.

Did Harold know that his wife had left him in the middle of the night, in search of another man's arms?

And if he did know, was he pretending not to?

Had he learned, over time, that the best way to deal with his wife's infidelities was to ignore them?

'You're planning to question the servants this morning, aren't you, Inspector?' asked Harold, as if in an attempt to move away from a subject that had never really even been raised.

'Yes, I am planning to question them,' Blackstone agreed.

'And where were you intending to do that?'

'We've been given one of the upstairs rooms as our office. I thought we could use that.'

Harold frowned. 'Do you know, I'm not sure that that's such a good idea,' he said.

'No?'

'It doesn't bother me *where* you talk to them, but George won't like it. He's very much a man for believing that everyone should know their place – and stay in it. He wouldn't be happy at the thought of some of the servants tramping through parts of the house in which they're not usually allowed.'

'I see,' Blackstone said, non-committally.

'Would it bother you awfully if you had to use one of the rooms in the servants' area, instead?' Harold asked.

'No, I don't think so,' Blackstone replied. 'Not as long as we have some privacy.'

'That should be easy enough to arrange,' Harold said, sounding relieved. 'In fact, I'll go and see to it now.' He turned to go, then checked himself. 'I sometimes sleep rather badly myself,' he added.

'Do you?'

'Oh yes. In fact, sometimes it's so bad that, in order not to disturb my wife during the night, I sleep in my dressing room.'

It was pathetic, Blackstone thought.

He wanted to say, 'Nothing *happened*! She may have put the horns on you with half the men on Coney Island, but nothing happened *with me*!'

But all he *actually* said was, 'That's very considerate of you, and I'm sure Mrs Holt appreciates it.'

Harold shrugged awkwardly. 'Yes, well, I . . . I suppose I'd better go and see about getting a room you can use.'

'That would be very kind of you,' Blackstone agreed.

The sign on the door said 'Assistant Housekeeper', and when Blackstone and Meade had first entered the room at eight o'clock, it had seemed – with its desk and three chairs – to be the perfect place in which to question the staff.

It began to feel less perfect by nine o'clock, when it started to get hot, and by nine thirty the heat was so sweltering that it reminded Blackstone of his days serving in India.

'Did Harold do this on purpose?' Alex Meade asked peevishly, wiping the sweat from his brow with the back of his hand. 'Is putting us in this oven his idea of a good joke?'

'No, I'm sure it isn't,' Blackstone replied.

It would simply never have occurred to someone like Harold Holt that a room between the bakery and laundry was bound to become unpleasant once both those places had started working at full pelt. He had been shielded from such things from birth, and whilst he might accept – on an intellectual level – that other people's lives were less comfortable than his own, he had no real concept of what that discomfort might feel like.

'I wouldn't mind the heat if I felt that we were getting some-where,' Meade said.

But they weren't, Blackstone agreed.

They had questioned almost the entire staff, and not one person had provided them with even a scrap of information which might just possibly be of some help in their investigation.

Mr Fanshawe had kept himself to himself, the cook had said. If he'd had any friends away from the house, then she certainly knew nothing about them.

There hadn't been any strangers loitering in or near the grounds of Ocean Heights in the previous few days – or even the previous few months – the head gardener had said firmly. If there had been, he'd certainly have heard about it, because this wasn't the city, where people went unnoticed, it was a village – and everybody knew everybody else's business.

'There's only one of the staff who we still haven't seen,' Meade said, looking despondently down at his list. 'Still,' he added, brightening, 'she might be just the breakthrough we're looking for – because she's Judith Hawthorne, the girl who cleans Big Bill's bunker.'

Blackstone chuckled. 'Big Bill's Bunker!' he repeated. 'I like that!'

'Then how about Holt's Hideaway?' Meade suggested eagerly. 'Or William's Warren? Then again, there's always Billie's Bolt-hole and . . .' He paused, and a look of concern crossed his face. 'Do you think I'm getting hysterical, Sam?' he asked, worriedly.

Blackstone shook his head. 'You're just exhausted.'

'But it's not even noon yet.'

'Doesn't matter what time it is, or how long you've been at it,' Blackstone said. 'Getting nowhere in an investigation can wear you out quicker than anything else I know. But, as you said, we could be on the verge of a big breakthrough.'

'Yes, we could,' Meade agreed, without much conviction.

The signs were not hopeful, Blackstone told himself, as he watched Judith slouch into the room.

'Please take a chair, Miss Hawthorne,' Alex Meade said.

The girl looked around her.

'Which one?' she asked.

'Why not take the only one that's free?' Meade suggested, with an encouraging smile.

The girl nodded lethargically, and sat down.

There were some servants whose intelligence naturally shone through, even when they were doing their best to hide it, Blackstone thought.

But Judith Hawthorne was not one of them. Her blank eyes showed no possible interest in the world around her. She had a way of moving, and even sitting, which suggested that she found most – if not all – of the things she had to do too much of an effort, and that, left to herself, she would do nothing at all. She did not even seem to be

affected by the fact that handsome young Alex Meade had smiled at
her, though most ugly girls – and she was undoubtedly ugly – would
have been over the moon about it.

'You know that you could be of great help to us, don't you, Judith?'
Meade asked.

'Could I?' the girl replied, indifferently.

'You most certainly could,' Meade told her. 'Since you've spent
more time with Mr Holt than practically anyone else in the house,
you might be the one who can provide the vital piece of information which will help us to find him.'

'Oh,' Judith said, though she did not seem particularly excited
about the prospect.

'How long have you been responsible for cleaning Mr Holt's
rooms?' Blackstone asked.

'Since Mr George hired me,' the girl said, in a flat tone.

'And that would be . . .?'

'I don't know.'

'Take a guess,' Meade urged her. 'Remember how old you were
then, and take it away from how old you are now.

'It would have been about three years ago,' Judith said, in a tone
which suggested she was reluctant to part with so many words in
one breath.

'Are you the only one of the servants, apart from Mr Fanshawe,
who goes in there?'

'Yes.'

'So keeping the place presentable is all down to you? That's quite
a lot of responsibility for a girl of your age, isn't it? You must be
quite proud of what you've achieved.'

The girl shook her head, but so sparingly that, had the two detectives not been watching her closely, they would probably have missed
it.

'Not really,' she said.

Meade and Blackstone exchanged exasperated glances.

'I expect Mr Holt really appreciated your company, Judith,' Meade
ploughed on determinedly. 'It must have been nice for him, living
down there, all alone, to have someone to talk to.'

'We didn't talk.'

'Not at all?'

'No.'

'You must surely have exchanged a few pleasantries. "How are
you today, Mr Holt?", "Is there anything special you'd like me to do
for you?" You know the sort of thing.'

Judith shrugged – and even that seemed to take her a great deal of effort.

'It wasn't allowed,' she said.

'What wasn't?'

'Talking to him.'

'He *told* you that you weren't to talk to him?'

'No.'

'Then how do you know it wasn't allowed?'

'Mr Fanshawe told me – before I ever started working down there.'

'So Mr Holt never gave you any instructions?' Blackstone asked. 'He didn't say . . .' he searched around for inspiration, and found it in the laundry cart which was being trundled past the door. 'He didn't say, for example, "I want these shirts laundered, Judith. Could you please see to it"?'

'No. I never brought his clothes to the laundry. I only brought the sheets that I'd stripped off the bed.'

'So what happened to his dirty clothes? Someone must have taken them away for laundering, mustn't they?'

'I suppose so.'

'And who do you think that someone might have been?'

'I saw Mr Fanshawe with a bag of his laundry once or twice,' Judith admitted reluctantly.

'Ah, now we're getting somewhere,' Meade said. 'But what I still don't see is why Mr Fanshawe should have taken the dirty clothes to the laundry, when you could quite easily have done it when you were bringing the sheets.'

'He didn't,' Judith said.

'Didn't what?'

'Didn't bring the clothes to the laundry.'

'Are you sure about that?'

'You can ask Mrs Mills, the washerwoman, if you don't believe me.'

'So where did he take the dirty clothes?'

'Don't know.'

'Thank you, Judith, you've been very helpful,' Meade said, with an apparent sincerity which Blackstone could not help but admire.

After the heat of the assistant housekeeper's office, it was a real pleasure to be outside, with a gentle sea breeze blowing through their hair.

'You know you told me I should always try to get inside the heads of all the people involved in an investigation?' Meade asked, as the two detectives stood looking out at the ocean.

'Yes?'

'Well, I'm having real trouble getting inside Big Bill Holt's head.'

'In any particular way?'

'In all sorts of ways. But mostly, I don't understand why, when he could have had any of the female staff in this household as his personal maid, he was prepared to tolerate Judith.'

'What's wrong with her?'

'Don't you *know*?'

'Perhaps, but tell me anyway.'

'Well, for a start, I don't get the impression she's very good at her job,' Meade said.

'I think we can take that as read,' Blackstone agreed.

'But more importantly, you have to consider Holt's situation. If I was locked away in an underground vault, and my maid was one of only four people – apart from the occasional prostitute – who ever came to see me, I'd have chosen someone I could talk to.'

'Judith said she wasn't allowed to talk.'

'Yes, I believe her, because she's really too stupid to lie. But *why* was she told not to talk?'

'I don't know.'

'And then there's the fact that Holt has an eye for the ladies. We've seen a number of quite pretty maids while we've been here, haven't we?'

'We have.'

'So why didn't Holt ask for one of them, instead of a buck-toothed, sallow-complexioned drudge like Judith?'

'I don't know,' Blackstone said, for a second time.

'It's almost as if he was deliberately punishing himself – but from what we've learned about him so far, he doesn't seem like the *kind of man* to ever even think of doing that.'

'No, he doesn't,' Blackstone agreed. 'He seems more like the kind of man who'll grab what he wants simply *because* he wants it, and, as far as he's concerned, everyone else can go hang.'

'So none of it makes sense!'

'I'll tell you something else that doesn't make sense,' Blackstone said. 'The laundry question.'

'The fact that wherever Big Bill's laundry was done, it wasn't done in the house?'

'Exactly. But *why* wasn't it done in the house? I thought at first

it could be because he was afraid his enemies might take the opportunity to slip some kind of poison into his clothes.'

'But you don't think that any longer?'

'No, I don't. If he was worried about being poisoned, the thing
he'd be *most* careful about would be his food. But all the food he
ate was cooked right here in the house – and that didn't seem to
bother him at all.'

'Fanshawe would have known why he was happy with Judith as
his maid,' Meade said moodily. 'Fanshawe would have known why
he wouldn't have his clothes washed in the Ocean Heights laundry.'

Indeed he would, Blackstone thought, but we can't *ask* him now,
can we – because I had him in my hand and then I let him slip
through my fingers!

'So what do we do now?' Meade asked despondently. 'Go back
to the city?'

Blackstone nodded. In terms of making progress in the investigation, there were half a dozen solid reasons for abandoning Ocean
Heights in favour of New York City. It was a decision any seasoned
investigator would have taken – and the fact that, in taking it, he
would be putting a good few miles between himself and Virginia
Holt, was no more than a happy coincidence.

THIRTEEN

He was standing just inside the woods, a short distance from the spot where Fanshawe had last been seen alive.

He had been there for half an hour, observing the house through his binoculars. He had seen the chambermaids open the upstairs windows and vigorously shake rugs and bedding out of them, and the gardeners change the plants in the flower beds. He had watched Mrs Virginia Holt set out on her morning ride, and half-wondered if she'd perhaps been involved in an entirely different kind of riding the night before.

But none of that had really interested him – none of that was why he was there.

At eleven thirty, there was the clip-clopping sound of a horse's hooves as a carriage approached. When he turned to look at it, he saw it was the official police carriage from his own precinct – which could only mean that Blackstone and Meade were leaving for the city.

He should have been expecting it, Flynn thought – should have known that Blackstone was a smart enough policeman to realize he would never get to the bottom of the mystery by sitting around on his ass in Ocean Heights.

Yes, he *should have* expected it – but seeing it actually happen still came as a blow.

The two detectives emerged from the house, side by side. As they walked towards the carriage, they seemed hardly aware of their surroundings. In fact, Flynn thought, they appeared to be engaged in an animated – possibly even heated – discussion.

Flynn glanced at his watch – even though he fully understood that the time he had left could not be measured in a given number of hours, but would instead be determined by what the policeman from Scotland Yard decided to do next.

He watched the carriage pull away, and accepted that the clock had already started ticking.

'You'll have to change your plans, Michael,' he said softly to himself. 'You've no choice in the matter.'

Mary Turner had been on her knees in prayer for over an hour when she saw the police carriage pass by the front window of her cottage.

'They're leaving, oh Lord,' she moaned. 'They're leaving, and now there will be no justice for my Joseph.'

She realized, with horror, that what she had just said might well be interpreted by the Almighty as a complaint.

'I know, oh Lord, that my Joseph will get his reward in heaven, and that those who took his life will burn forever in hellfire,' she said quickly, 'but is it so wrong for me to wish for justice in this world, as well as the next?'

She waited for an answer, but though she was practised in praying, she did not know how to listen.

It had always been Joseph who'd listened – who'd got the answer directly from God and had passed it on to her. And now Joseph could tell her no longer, because he was dead.

She rose stiffly to her feet, and walked over to the table, where her Bible was resting.

She was as poor a reader as she was a listener, but she knew there were countless examples in the Good Book of the wicked being punished for their sins on earth.

Perhaps it was not part of the Lord's plan for Joseph's murderers to be punished in the here and now, she thought. Perhaps, by striving for that herself, she was going against His wishes. But if she was, He would forgive her in time, because that was what an all-merciful God did.

She paced the room, and slowly the life came back to her aching knees.

She had no idea what to do next, she thought, almost in despair.

There had been times when – weak woman that she was – she had silently questioned the wisdom of the rule that the womenfolk of the Soldiers of God should be kept well away from the affairs of the corrupt world in which they lived.

Not any more!

She'd needed that protection, because she was useless – because she couldn't think of a single way in which she could help avenge her husband's death.

Unless . . .

Unless his unexplained trips to New York really *had had* something to do with his murder.

'*He was not killed because of* who *he was, he was killed because of* where *he was*,' she had said to Blackstone.

And part of her – most of her – still believed that.

But there was also a small – insistent – voice nagging away at the back of her mind, which said if there was even the *slightest* chance he could have died for another reason, it was her duty to find out what that reason was.

She came to a halt at the table, almost as if it had been pre-ordained that she should do so.

It was at this table that Joseph had spent hour upon hour studying the Holy Writ. But it was at the same table that he had written his reports to the Vicar General, and nightly recorded his efforts to carry out God's work in his journal.

She had never seen the journal – it was another of the things she was to be shielded from.

But she knew where he kept it!

It was in the locked drawer under the table top.

She found herself wondering – for the first time in her married life – *why* Joseph had kept the drawer locked.

Was it that he hadn't trusted her?

No, that couldn't be it!

He had trusted her, but he hadn't trusted the *Devil*, who might find a way to tempt her at any time.

And was it the Devil who was tempting her at that moment, now that she no longer had her husband's protection?

If it was, she didn't care. She wanted to see her husband's journals – more than she could ever remember wanting *anything*.

The drawer was locked, as it always was, and no amount of tugging would force it to open.

But she was not to be deterred. Not now.

Using her husband's hammer and chisel, she set to attacking the drawer. She was not very adept – this, again, was man's work – but she was determined, and kept at it even after she cut herself.

At the end of five minutes, the drawer and a chunk of the table top were all but destroyed – but she had the journal in her bloody hand, and had never felt so empowered in her life.

The animated conversation between Blackstone and Meade – which Flynn had so accurately noted from his hiding place in the woods – continued as the police carriage drew ever closer to the Coney Island streetcar terminal.

'Holt's kidnapping just has to have been a professional job, Sam,' Meade argued, for perhaps the fifth or sixth time.

'I'm not saying it wasn't *carried out* by professionals,' Blackstone countered, 'only that it wasn't *commissioned* by them.'

'So the guys who Holt had ruined finally decided to have their revenge on him?' Meade asked sceptically.

'It's a possibility.'

'Why would they wait seven years?'

'I don't know,' Blackstone admitted. 'Perhaps, after they had the bookkeeper killed, they lost their nerve.'

'That's a weak argument even if Rudge *was* murdered,' Meade said. 'And if he wasn't . . .' he added with a shrug.

Blackstone felt a sense of pride that his protégé had enough confidence to argue his case so strongly – and also a sense of grievance that this still-wet-behind-the-ears pipsqueak was daring to question his judgement.

'If it *was* them – and if they *do* hate him so much – why didn't they just have him killed?' Meade demanded.

'If they'd had him killed, they'd never get the ransom money, which they probably see as a small return for what they lost,' Blackstone said. 'Besides, they may not want him dead. They may just want to see him humiliated. They may want to show that they can buy and sell him – just as he bought and sold them!'

'And if a couple of guards get killed along the way, that's no concern of theirs?' Meade asked.

'If the businessmen *are* behind it, I don't think they ever intended the guards to die,' Blackstone said.

'They must have known that if you employ thugs—'

'They knew *nothing*! That's the point! They come from the cosy civilized world of New York society – they have no idea of just how violent some men from outside that world can be.'

'I still don't see it,' Alex Meade said stubbornly.

'So let's look at *your* theory,' Blackstone said, trying not to sound irritated. 'A gang of criminals, somewhere on – say – the Lower East Side, decide to kidnap a rich man and hold him for ransom. Right?'

'Right,' Meade agreed cautiously.

'They sit around and discuss their possible targets. They know that they only have to go along Fifth Avenue, late at night, to see any number of millionaires returning from a party, guarded only by their coachmen. But they reject that idea. And what do they choose to do instead? They choose to go way beyond their normal stamping ground and snatch a man from a bunker which is guarded by two armed Pinkertons!'

'For God's sake, Sam, they knew the Pinkertons would be no problem, because they were working with Fanshawe. And that's also precisely why they selected Holt rather than any other millionaire – because it was *Fanshawe's* plan!'

Blackstone shook his head. 'However are we going to conduct

this investigation when we can't even agree on a starting point?' he asked.

'Maybe we could conduct *two* investigations,' Meade said. 'You follow up any leads you can find on the disgruntled businessmen, and I'll go and listen to the rumblings in the underworld.'

It sounded like a suggestion, Blackstone thought, but it wasn't – it was a challenge!

Apart from a ball of fluffy cotton-wool hair perched precariously over each of his ears, the Dean of the Cornell University Medical School was totally bald. He had a largish – almost Roman – nose, on which rested a pair of half-moon glasses, and he seemed to Ellie Carr to look *more* like a dean than any dean had a right to.

'It really is most kind of you to give up some of your valuable time to instruct our students,' the Dean said.

'It's my pleasure,' Ellie replied.

And so it was. The Americans were treating her like a princess, and while she told herself that a serious scientist like her didn't need that kind of adulation, she was rather starting to enjoy it.

'It has been proposed that we schedule you to perform an autopsy which some of our brighter students would be allowed to monitor,' the Dean said. 'Would you have any objection to that?'

'None at all,' Ellie replied.

The Dean coughed awkwardly. 'I must admit that I was opposed to it at first, and it was only with some reluctance that I allowed my colleagues to talk me round to the idea.'

'Oh?' Ellie said. 'And why were you opposed to it, if I may ask?'

'I was afraid you might find our young men a little hard to handle.'

'Because I'm a woman?'

'Partly. And partly because you're English.'

'Well, there's nothing I can do about either of those things,' Ellie said airily.

'Quite,' the Dean agreed. 'But I thought it was only fair to warn you that, in the past, some of our colleagues from England have found our American ways a little brash for their taste.'

'Yer don't know what brash is till yer've been fru the East End of a Sat'dy night,' Ellie said.

'I beg your pardon?'

'I'm sure I'll be able to handle it.'

'The problem is exacerbated, you see, by the type of young men we have here,' the Dean pressed on. 'Naturally, they all come from very good families.'

'Naturally,' Ellie agreed drily.

'And no doubt, in time, they'll all make excellent physicians. But their background does tend to give them rather more self-confidence in their own abilities than one might consider desirable in someone who is here mainly to learn.'

'In other words, they're arrogant little bleeders.'

'I beg your pardon!' the Dean said, for a second time.

'I said, "That doesn't matter, as long as they're good readers."'

'I'm not sure I quite follow you, but no matter,' the Dean said. He consulted the sheet of paper which lay on the desk in front of him. 'The particular cadaver we have in mind for you is a suicide victim,' he continued. 'You have no objection to that, do you?'

'No objection at all, but if you have a corpse that's had an argument with an express train – and lost – then you'd really be giving me something to work with,' Ellie said.

'I'm not sure we can—' the Dean began.

'Only joking,' Ellie told him. 'A suicide will do me fine. After all, we don't want to give your nice young men nightmares. How did this suicide victim die, by the way?'

'He hanged himself.'

'Poor soul,' Ellie said. 'Still, at least he's given me an interesting prop to work with.'

They shook hands, and the Dean showed her to the door of his office.

It was only when she was in the corridor that he placed a hand on her shoulder and smiled.

'By the way, you were right, Dr Carr,' he said.

'Right?' Ellie repeated. 'Right about what?'

'They are arrogant little bleeders,' the Dean said.

Eileen O'Grady was in her late forties, and was regarded by the Irish community of Coney Island as a fine figure of woman – which was another way saying that she had childbearing hips and the strong muscular legs of a natural potato picker.

She had run her boarding house for eight years.

'There was no choice in the matter,' she would tell her cronies. 'What else could I do after that fecker O'Grady had run away with a circus midget?'

Her friends would nod, sympathetically, although they knew that the woman 'that fecker O'Grady' had run off with had been an athletic trapeze artist rather than a midget, and that, as much as Eileen might bemoan running the boarding house, she really rather enjoyed it.

Her favourite lodger was undoubtedly Inspector Flynn, who had been with her for over two years. He was quiet and somewhat withdrawn, but after twenty years of living with her loud-mouthed fecking husband, she considered that something of a bonus.

Occasionally, when they were both in the mood, she would take Flynn to her bed. She did not flatter herself that she was his ideal woman, nor did she particularly want to be *his* woman at all, but it was pleasant and comforting, and when it was all over and they went downstairs again, they found it easy enough to return to their normal landlady–tenant relationship.

It therefore came as something of a shock to her, that late morning, to find Flynn not only in his room but packing his few possessions into his suitcase.

'You're surely not thinking of moving out on me, are you, Mr Flynn?' she asked.

'My rent's paid up until the end of the month, Mrs O'Grady,' Flynn replied, avoiding the question.

'As if the thought of money had even entered my mind, Mr Flynn!' Mrs O'Grady's hands automatically moved to her hips in a gesture of displeasure.

'The fact is, Mrs O'Grady, that the police force owes me a great deal of leave, and I've finally decided to take some of it,' Flynn said.

'And where will you go?'

'To the city.'

'New York?'

'Is there any *other* city, on this side of the water, worth talking about?' Flynn asked.

'Sure, and if you're going no further than that, couldn't you keep your room here and travel in every day?'

Flynn sighed. 'I'm doing it for you,' he admitted.

'For me, is it?' Mrs O'Grady asked, far from mollified. 'And would you mind explaining exactly how you think I'd be better off without you?'

'I'm involved in something that could turn nasty, Eileen,' Flynn said. 'Very nasty indeed! And I don't want you caught in the middle of it.'

'You called me "Eileen",' Mrs O'Grady said.

'Yes, I . . .'

'You've never called me Eileen before, not even when we were . . . when we were . . .'

'Did you hear what I just told you?' Flynn persisted. 'I said things could get very nasty.'

'You called me Eileen because this is goodbye,' Mrs O'Grady
mused. 'You're never coming back from that leave of yours, are you,
Michael?'

Flynn closed his suitcase. 'I don't know,' he said. 'It all depends
on what happens in the next few days.'

'But would you like to come back if you could?' Mrs O'Grady
asked.

'Very much,' Flynn replied.

'Then I suppose that'll have to do me,' Mrs O'Grady said.

Flynn picked up his suitcase and walked over to the door. He did
not pause to kiss her, nor had she expected him to.

'I should never have told you that I was going to New York City,'
he said from the head of the stairs. 'If anybody asks you, tell them
you've no idea *where* I've gone.'

FOURTEEN

The brownstone houses on the leafy midtown New York street had probably started out life as single-family dwellings, but now – as the presence of so many bell-pushes showed – they had almost all been divided into apartments. Not that the change in circumstances made the area at all undesirable, Blackstone decided. Even on an afternoon which lacked the gentle sunshine this one had been blessed with, it must still have felt a pleasant place to live – the sort of place, in fact, that would just suit the moderately prosperous middle class.

Arthur Rudge, Big Bill Holt's head bookkeeper, had been moderately prosperous, and he had lived – and died – in the upstairs apartment which Blackstone, standing in the street, was currently gazing up at.

The report from the Fire Department said that the blaze had started in Rudge's bedroom, and spread to other rooms in the apartment, but that, due to the vigilance of one of Rudge's neighbours – a Mrs Fairbrother – assistance had been called quickly enough to prevent the house from suffering any serious structural damage.

'Vigilance,' Blackstone repeated softly to himself.

The word could have a number of meanings. It could indicate that the person who possessed it felt a strong sense of responsibility for his or her community, or that he or she had a natural gift for being aware of what was going on around them. But – more often than not – it suggested that the person in question was a nosy parker, and Blackstone was hoping that was just the case here.

The front door opened, and a woman appeared on the threshold.

'Can I help you?' she asked, but what she really meant was, 'What the hell are you doing out there in the street?'

She was displaying, Blackstone quickly decided, all the classic signs of a nosy parker, from the suspicious gleam in her eyes and the disapproving droop of her mouth, to an air of grievance she carried on her shoulders like a heavy sack of coal. She was one of those people who, almost from the moment they emerged from the womb, saw the world as both hostile and grossly unfair.

'I said, can I help you?' the woman repeated, tightening up the aggression in her voice a notch further.

Blackstone found himself wishing that Meade was by his side – because Alex could charm even this vinegary old bat, and have her eating out of his hand in five minutes. But Meade was *not* there. Meade was off somewhere else, trying to prove that he was smarter than his mentor.

'Are you Mrs Fairbrother?' Blackstone asked, though there was no doubt in his mind that that was exactly who she was.

'Yes?' the woman replied – cagey, reluctant.

Blackstone produced his temporary shield. 'I'm from the police department, madam.'

'*Police* department!' Mrs Fairbrother repeated, with contempt.

Blackstone sensed that she was on the point of slamming the door in his face.

'I'm making some enquiries, and I wondered if you could help me,' he said hastily.

'Why should I help *you*?' Mrs Fairbrother demanded. '*You've* never helped *me*. When I think of the number of times I complained to the police about Arthur Rudge – and that's just one example of the problems I've had – it makes my blood boil. And what did you do about all my complaints? Not a thing!'

'But your complaints about Rudge are precisely why I'm here now,' Blackstone said, thinking on his feet.

'What do you mean?'

'The department recognizes – belatedly, admittedly – that it has treated you very shabbily in that particular matter, and is prepared to issue a full apology.'

'A full apology?' Mrs Fairbrother said, taken aback.

In for a penny, in for a pound, Blackstone thought.

'And that apology would, of course, be printed – in full – in the newspaper,' he said.

'What newspaper?' Mrs Fairbrother asked, not quite as unyielding as she had been previously, but still unyielding enough.

'Whatever newspaper you care to choose,' Blackstone told her. 'The *New York Times*?'

'I read the *New York World*,' the woman said sulkily.

'The *New York World* it is. Our only aim is to make you happy.'

'It's a little late for that,' Mrs Fairbrother said.

It had *always* been a little late for that, Blackstone thought.

'Of course, before we can prepare the apology, we need to make sure we've got all the details right this time – which is why I'm here,' he said.

'I suppose you'd better come inside, then,' Mrs Fairbrother told him, with a lack of grace which was almost breathtaking.

*   *   *

Mrs Fairbrother's sitting room was, as might have been expected, orderly and soulless. There were, it was true, various knick-knacks – arranged with military precision – on the shelves, but Blackstone got the clear impression that they were there more because people were *supposed* to have knick-knacks than because they gave the woman any pleasure.

'You'll probably want to sit down,' Mrs Fairbrother said, with the same reluctance she had shown when inviting him in.

Blackstone sat, noting, as he did so, that one chair had been strategically positioned by the window, and that next to it was a pair of opera glasses.

'I'm not one to speak ill of the dead,' Mrs Fairbrother began, without preamble, 'but this was a very respectable neighbourhood before Arthur Rudge moved in.'

'And he brought the tone down?'

'He most certainly did.'

'How?'

'With his parties,' Mrs Fairbrother said. 'Not that I have anything against parties as such,' she added hastily. 'I often invite a few respectable ladies round for coffee mornings. But *his* parties were a positive disgrace.'

'In what way?'

'In all sorts of ways.'

She liked all this attention, and she would drag it out for as long as possible, Blackstone thought.

He suppressed a sigh and said, 'Would you care to give me an example, Mrs Fairbrother?'

'Well, there were his guests, for a start,' the woman said. 'There are only two sorts of parties a gentleman should hold – ones to which *only* gentlemen are invited, and ones which are attended mainly by married couples, with suitable escorts provided for unattached ladies. But Mr Rudge had no consideration for the proprieties. Oh no! At his parties, there were *only* women – sometimes half a dozen of them, sometimes even more.' Mrs Fairbrother paused. 'You'll have noticed I said "women", not "ladies"?'

'I have.'

'That's because that's exactly what they were. Harlots! Painted Jezebels! And once they were up there in his apartment, there were such goings on! They had a gramophone – and sometimes they'd be dancing until two or three o'clock in the morning.'

It was hard to reconcile Rudge's job as head bookkeeper with the sort of antics Mrs Fairbrother was describing, Blackstone thought.

'You don't believe me, do you?' the woman demanded, reading his expression. 'The local precinct didn't, either. And that's why I got proof.'

'Proof?'

'I bought a Kodak camera. You will have seen the advertisement – "You press the button, we do the rest".'

'Ah yes,' Blackstone lied.

'Now that the price has fallen to a dollar, every Tom, Dick and Harry has one, but when I bought mine, seven years ago, there were less than a thousand in the whole of the United States. Twenty-five dollars it cost me, and though I am not a rich woman, it was worth every cent – because it proved that I was right and those snickering officers down at the precinct were wrong.'

'You bought the camera so you could photograph the parties!' Blackstone said.

'Not the parties themselves – I was not invited, and even if I had been, I would not have attended. I bought it in order to photograph the "guests" as they arrived.'

Mrs Fairbrother walked over to the sideboard, opened a drawer, and took out a number of photographs.

'Look at these,' she ordered Blackstone.

The photograph on the top of the pile was of a short man and a much taller woman, standing in the street outside the house. The man had a nearly bald head and a waxed moustache – and looked very angry. The woman was wearing a dress which missed being stylish by just enough to make it gaudy, and though the photograph was not clear enough to say with any certainty that she was wearing a great deal of powder on her face, Blackstone *suspected* that Mrs Fairbrother's description of a "painted Jezebel" was not too far off the mark.

'It was the first photograph I took,' Mrs Fairbrother said. 'Rudge was furious. He tried to snatch the camera away from me, but I was too quick for him. After that, I had to be much more careful.'

And the fact that she was being more careful showed in the photographs which followed, Blackstone saw. The pictures were less distinct – and probably shot through Mrs Fairbrother's window – but they did, at least, support her contention that a stream of women had passed through Rudge's apartment.

So maybe despite his looks and physique, Rudge had been a real ram who had serviced half the women – rather than the *ladies* – of Manhattan.

But that didn't matter a damn, because if Rudge *had* been killed it was not because of his virility, but due to his connection with Big Bill Holt.

'Did you notice anything unusual in the days before Mr Rudge died?' he asked.

'What do mean – unusual?' Mrs Fairbrother countered.

'Well, for example, that someone seemed to be watching his apartment from the street.'

'No, if anybody had been doing that, I'd have seen them.'

I'll bet you would have, Blackstone thought.

'Then did he have any visitors, other than the women who normally visited him?' he said, changing track.

'Rudge *never* had visitors other than his harlots,' Mrs Fairbrother replied. She paused for a moment. 'Although . . .'

'Yes?'

'There were the two furniture delivery men, on the very day he died.'

'Go on,' Blackstone encouraged.

'They arrived in the late afternoon, with an armoire. I was surprised he'd ordered such a thing, because I'd seen his furniture when he moved in, and though it wasn't to my taste, it was good quality.'

'And that furniture had included an armoire?'

'Two of them – and they'd both looked new.'

'So the furniture men arrived with the armoire,' Blackstone said. 'And I suppose what happened next was that they rang the doorbell and Mr Rudge let them in.'

'No,' Mrs Fairbrother said. 'Rudge wasn't at home.'

'Are you sure of that?'

'Positive. I saw him arrive half an hour later.'

'Then how did they get into the building?'

'They had a key. Rudge probably left it at the shop for them. But it must have been a poor copy, because it wouldn't open the door at first.'

Perhaps that was true. But it was much more likely that instead of using a badly cut key provided by Rudge, the delivery man had been attempting to open the door using his own set of skeleton keys.

'What did they look like, these two men?'

'I couldn't really say,' Mrs Fairbrother admitted

Of course she couldn't.

'So they took the armoire upstairs and then left,' Blackstone said, though he would have been greatly surprised if Mrs Fairbrother had replied, 'Yes, that's exactly what happened.'

'No, they didn't leave,' the woman said. 'They were still in the apartment when Rudge arrived home from work.'

'So when *did* they eventually go?'

'About twenty minutes after that. And the funny thing was that they were carrying the same armoire out as they carried in.'

It wasn't funny at all, if the theory which was starting to form in Blackstone's mind was correct.

When the two men had carried the armoire upstairs, this theory argued, it would have contained all the ingredients necessary to start a convincing fire.

So why bring it down with them again?

For two very good reasons.

The first was that men carrying things were far less noticeable than men who weren't. Mrs Fairbrother was living proof of that, because, as nosy as she was, it was the armoire, not the men, that she'd been paying attention to.

The second reason was that there was a possibility that the armoire could be traced back to the men. An amateur pair of arsonists would have left the armoire in the apartment, believing the fire would destroy it. And these two men probably thought that too – but they were professionals, and they didn't take any chances that they didn't have to.

'How long after the men left did the fire start?' he asked.

'Don't know,' Mrs Fairbrother said.

Blackstone suppressed another sigh.

'All right, do you know how much time there was between them going and you noticing that Rudge's apartment was on fire?'

'About forty minutes.'

Yes, Blackstone thought, if they'd set a slow fuse to give them time to get well clear of the area, that was just about right.

FIFTEEN

In the daytime, the area around the Coenties Slip was about as busy as any place in New York. Steamers from Spain, Puerto Rico, Havana and Galveston constantly docked at the wooden piers which jutted out into the East River. Sailors, newly on dry land, stopped passing girls, and asked where they could find a good time – while secretly nourishing the hope that they might have already found it. Shops of all kinds buzzed with business. Cart drivers swore at their own horses – and at other cart drivers and *their* horses. And street vendors offered goods at bargain prices – often before the true owners even realized they were missing.

At night, it was different. At night, the only sounds were of drunks arguing in Jeanette Park and the East River gently lapping against the shoreline.

Blackstone and Meade stood beside a decaying canal boat, scanning the distance – and continuing to wage the battle they had been fighting all day.

'So Rudge bought an armoire on the day he died,' Meade said. 'He also probably bought half a dozen eggs and some silk underwear for one of his numerous lady friends.'

'He didn't *buy* the armoire,' Blackstone said, through gritted teeth. 'It was delivered – and then it was taken away again.'

'So it was the wrong size or the wrong colour,' Meade countered.

'And less than an hour after it was taken away, the fire started!'

'Assuming this Mrs Fairbrother is right about the timing.'

'She was right,' Blackstone said firmly.

Meade sighed. 'What you mean is, you *want* her to be right,' he said. 'I'll send some patrolmen around the big furniture stores tomorrow. The stores are famous for record keeping, and I wouldn't be the least surprised – and neither should you be – if those records show that things happened just like I think they did.'

It wasn't easy listening to his theories being disparaged in this way, Blackstone thought – especially when the disparagement was coming from a man who had spent the whole of the afternoon and part of the evening attempting – and failing – to come up with the name of an organized criminal gang that could possibly be behind the Holt kidnapping.

'I think this snitch we're waiting for could be our big break-through,' Meade said.

Yes, Blackstone thought, snitches could be invaluable – but he himself would never trust one he'd never worked with before, as Alex was about to do now.

'Of course, I'd have been happier if he'd been one of my regular snitches,' said Meade, reading Blackstone's mind, 'but none of my regular snitches were in the right place at the right time – and this guy was.'

'Or *claims* he was in the right place at the right time,' Blackstone cautioned.

'Yeah, "claims",' Meade said dismissively, as if that was good enough.

A man appeared in the near distance. He was short and narrow-shouldered, and he was moving cautiously – like a rabbit which really *wants* to reach the cabbage patch, but will still abandon that plan at even the vaguest whiff of danger.

As he drew level with them, he said, 'You Alex?'

'That's right,' Meade replied. 'Who are you?'

'Call me Ted,' the man said, making no attempt to even pretend that was his real name. 'Louie told me ya'd hit me with a five spot.'

'And he was right,' Meade agreed, holding out the money.

'Ted' grabbed the bill, and slipped it into the pocket of his ragged jacket. 'So what do ya wanna know?'

'I want to know about the two men that you say you saw in O'Connor's Saloon last night.'

'I saw 'em, all right,' Ted said, with a shudder. 'They ain't the kind of guys you forget.'

They are known as Mad Bob Tate and Jake (the Snake) Thompson. They are both big bastards, and when they walk in, a sudden hush falls over the saloon.

But this silence does not last for long.

Soon all the customers are babbling like men demented – because none of them wants to be the one who Bob or Jake singles out to ask what is wrong.

They are hard men, these two. They are vicious men. But they are also stupid and irrational men – and that is what makes them particularly dangerous.

As they approach the counter, the barkeeper can see that they have already had far too much to drink, but he is going to be the last one to tell them they can't have any more.

'Whisky!' Jake says.

As the barkeeper pours out two shots with trembling hands, he remembers the last time these two men visited the saloon – remembers how one of the customers, who didn't know them (and was too drunk to read the obvious signs), had crashed into Jake and made him spill his drink over Bob.

Other men in that situation would have laughed the incident off, or possibly demanded a fresh drink. There were a few – a very few – who would have punched the drunk in the face.

Bob and Jake had done none of these things. They had knocked him to the floor, and then, while Bob held him down, Jake had taken out his knife and blinded the man in the left eye.

The barkeeper places the two shots of whisky on the counter. He does not expect Bob and Jake to pay for their drinks – they never pay – but, this time, Jake takes out a thick roll of bills, peels off a ten, and slaps it down on the bar.

'Keep 'em comin',' he says.

Then he places the rest of the money on the counter, picks up his drink, and knocks it back in a single swallow.

Half an hour passes. Jake and Bob have several more drinks.

Jake keeps glancing down at the roll of bills, as if he wishes that someone would ask him about it.

But nobody does.

Nobody dares!

Finally, it is Jake himself who brings up the subject.

'You wanna know where I got all this dough from, barkeeper?' he asks.

The barkeeper swallows. 'I . . . uh . . . sure, if you want to tell me, Mr Thompson,' he replies.

'We bin over to Coney Island,' Jake says. 'Lot o' money rollin' around on Coney Island – just waitin' to be plucked.'

The barkeeper wonders if he is expected to say something else, and decides that he probably is.

'That so, Mr Thompson? Thank you for telling me. Maybe I'll get over there sometime myself.'

It is the wrong thing to say, and he knows it the moment the words are out of his mouth.

Jake gives him a stare which could freeze blood.

'Just what are you sayin'?' he demands. 'That you could make this kinda money?

'Hell no, Mr Thompson,' the barkeeper says, almost soiling himself. 'There's no way I could make the kinda money you make. I just meant that maybe I could pick up a little.'

'You got no chance,' Jake says, as if he hasn't really been listening.
'You gotta be a real *man to earn this kinda money. You gotta be*
willin' to kill *for this kinda money.'*

'Is that it?' Meade asked, sounding partly impatient – but mostly
betrayed. 'You drag us out here, in the middle of the night, you take
five bucks off me, and all you can tell me is that you heard some
guy in a bar say he'd been over to Coney Island and that you've got
to kill to earn big money.'

'Shut up, Alex,' said Blackstone, who was reluctantly coming round
to the view that they might actually be on to something. He turned
to the snitch. 'There's more, isn't there?'

'Yeah,' the snitch agreed. 'There's more.'

Jake, fired up by alcohol, isn't finished yet. Just in case anyone on
the saloon hasn't seen the roll of bills, he picks it up and waves it
around in the air.

'Yep, to get this money we had to kill three guys,' he says.

'You're sure that's what he said?' Blackstone asked. 'That they'd had
to kill *three* men?'

'I'm sure – 'cos while he was speakin', he held up three fingers.'

Three men!

The two security guards!

And William Holt!

But if they *had* killed Holt, Blackstone thought, they couldn't have
done it until after the ransom call.

'Anybody could *claim* to have killed three men,' Meade said, his
earlier disappointment still evident. 'It doesn't prove a thing. Did he
say how they killed them?'

'Oh yeah,' the snitch replied. 'He said, all right.'

Jake is the centre of attention, and is revelling in it.

'Slit the throats of two o' the bastards!' he says, and as he speaks,
he draws two of the fingers on his free hand across his own throat.
'Stood behind 'em, an' slit their throats right open. Shoulda heard
the noise they made – kinda like a drinkin' fountain, just before the
water comes up.' He turns to his partner for confirmation. 'Ain't that
right, Bob?'

'Damn straight!' Mad Bob agrees.

'Do you wanna tell 'em what we did with the third guy, Bob?'
Jake asks. 'Or do ya want me to do it?'

'I'll tell 'em.' Bob says. 'It was real funny with the third guy, cos—'

The door of the saloon swings open, and the uniformed patrolman whose beat this is walks in.

He has not come to arrest these two self-confessed murderers, or even to check on whether or not the barkeeper is maintaining an orderly house. He has no interest at all in what is going on in the saloon – he is there merely to pick up the weekly bribe, from which he will take his own cut before passing the rest of it on up through the command structure.

Everybody – including Bob and Jake – knows this, but even so, the two men are not quite drunk enough to carry on their boasting as if he were not there.

The patrolman picks up his envelope and leaves, but like actors whose most dramatic speech has been cut off in the middle, Bob and Jake no longer seem to have any appetite for finishing their performance. They drain their drinks and leave themselves, and once they are out of the door the rest of the customers breathe a sigh of relief that this time nobody was hurt.

'So they never said how they killed the third man?' Meade asked.

'No, they just said it was kinda funny,' the snitch replied.

'They didn't even give you an idea of *when* they killed him?'

'Like I said, after the cop had gone, they kinda clammed up.'

Could they have killed Holt, Blackstone wondered.

And if they had, had they done it on their own initiative, or because they'd been told to?

Killing him might make sense from the kidnappers' point of view – but not before the ransom was paid, because surely George would insist on speaking to his father again before handing over half a million dollars.

'I got somethin' else for you,' the snitch said. 'But it's gonna cost you an extra five.'

'You've already been paid to tell us all you know,' Meade said, with a hint of anger creeping into his voice.

'No, I ain't,' replied the snitch, nervous, but determined to hold his ground. 'I was paid to tell you about Bob an' Jake – an' I done that. But the other thing I got happened later, when they'd gone.'

Meade handed over a second five dollar bill. 'This had better be good,' he said menacingly.

'It's maybe half an hour before this other man comes into the saloon,' the snitch said. 'I notice him straight away – even before I see his face – because he ain't dressed like a regular guy.'

'And how does a "regular guy" dress?' Meade asked.

'Like your buddy there. This guy was dressed more like you.'

'I get the picture,' Meade said.

'When I get a look at his face, I know I've seen him before, but I can't put a name to him,' the snitch continued. 'Anyway, he walks into the saloon, and he don't look like he's done it by accident. I mean, it ain't his kind o' place, but he don't seem uncomfortable, if ya know what I mean.'

'I know what you mean,' Meade confirmed.

'So then he starts asking questions.'

'What kind of questions?'

'Stuff like, "Have there been any guys in here tonight with money to burn?" That kinda thing.'

'And what did you tell him?'

'I didn't tell him nothin',' the snitch said, sounding offended. 'I can't be seen talkin' to cops – I got my reputation to consider.'

'He was a policeman?' Meade asked.

'Yeah, he was. Didn't I say that?'

'Not that I recall.'

'OK, so I ain't sayin' nothin' 'cos of my rep, but there's this low-life called Freddie Burns who ain't got my . . . what's the word?'

'Scruples?' Blackstone suggested, with a half-smile on his face.

'Yeah that's it,' the snitch agreed. 'He ain't got my *scruples*. So Freddie takes him into the corner, an' they're talkin' for a while. Then the cop gives Freddie twenty dollars for tellin' him just what I told you.'

'He gave him *twenty dollars*!' Meade asked, disbelievingly. 'Do you think I came here straight from Ellis Island?'

'All right, maybe he give him five, the same as you give me,' the snitch admitted. 'The thing is, as the guy was headin' for the door, I managed to put a name to the face.'

'And are you going to tell us what it is – or would you like us to guess?' Meade asked, with growing irritation.

'I knew him from the old days, see. He wasn't like the other cops. He never took no bribes, an' he never did nobody any favours.'

'The name!' Meade said.

'Seems to be that if you want the name so bad, it must be worth another five,' the snitch said.

'And it seems to me that if you don't give me the name in the next ten seconds, I'll be obliged to take back the ten bucks I've already given you, cuff you, and take you down to the nearest station house – where I'm sure they'll find a way to make you talk,' Alex Meade said.

'My old mom told me never to trust a cop – an' she was right,' the snitch whined.

'Tick tock!' Meade said.

'People used to call him the Frozen Mick, on account of he never showed his feelings,' the snitch said, in a sulky mumble.

'And what was his *real* name?'

'It was Flynn,' the snitch admitted. 'Sergeant Flynn.'

SIXTEEN

I t was mid-morning, and as he walked down Fourth Avenue with Meade at his side, Blackstone was playing the numbers game in his head.

Big Bill Holt's kidnapping had occurred early on Monday morning – say, fifty-three or fifty-four hours previously.

The kidnappers had demanded that the ransom be paid on Friday – which meant, roughly speaking, that they would expect it in their hands somewhere between forty-eight and fifty-two hours from that moment.

Fifty-four and fifty-two, repeated grimly.

He didn't have to be Isaac Newton to work out that more time had already gone than was now remaining. Nor did it take a great brain to realize that if as little progress was made in the fifty-two hours as had been made in the fifty-four, the Holt brothers would probably lose half a million dollars and their father would probably lose his life.

'We're there,' Meade said.

Blackstone looked up.

The Wall Street Gentlemen's Club was not actually located on Wall Street itself, but it was close enough for all but the most bloated capitalist to reach on foot from their brokerage houses. Its portal was guarded by an impressively uniformed doorman, who looked at Blackstone's suit with disdain, and was probably on the point of telling him to push off when he noticed that the semi-tramp was accompanied by a younger – much more smartly dressed – man.

'Mr Meade, sir,' he gushed, like an over-pressurized fountain. 'What a pleasure it is to see you.'

'Good to see you, too, Alfred,' Meade replied. 'Is there anyone inside who I might know?'

'I should imagine there'll be at least a dozen gentlemen who would count it an honour to be thought of as your friend,' the doorman said ingratiatingly. 'And even if – by some unhappy chance – there aren't, there'll be at least a score more who hold your father in the highest esteem.'

You saw a different world when you went places with Alex Meade, Blackstone thought.

But that had nothing to do with the fact that he was an *American* policemen, rather than an *English* one – cops everywhere were regarded as little more than servants by everyone but the lower orders.

No, it was because his family had money, and – in a country still too young to have developed an entrenched inflexible aristocracy – they also had what passed for *class*.

He wondered if he would still have been a policeman if his father had been *Lord* Blackstone, instead of a private soldier who had been killed in battle even before he was born.

Yes, he decided, he would have. He could have been born into the royal family and still ended up a copper – because that was always what he was *meant* to be.

'Is there any chance you could bring one of the members who might know me to the door?' he heard Meade ask.

'Now why should you want me to do that, sir?' Alfred wondered.

'Well, this is a very exclusive club, and since I'm not a member, I'll need someone to sign me in,' Meade said, guilelessly.

The doorman laughed. 'Oh, I think we can waive the rules on this occasion, sir,' he said.

A different world, Blackstone reiterated to himself. A *very* different world indeed.

There had been occasions when, in connection with one of the cases he'd been investigating, Blackstone had been granted access to the gentlemen's clubs in London. What he remembered – standing there while the man he was questioning sat – was large rooms filled with worn, overstuffed leather armchairs which the merely prosperous would have thrown out long ago, but the very rich clung on to as if they were heirlooms.

The Smoking Room of the Wall Street Club could have been in one of these London clubs. In fact, he suspected it had been *copied* from those clubs.

But from what I've seen, the Yanks won't be copying us for much longer, he thought. Give it a few years, and *we'll* be copying *them*.

Meade scanned the room with his eyes.

'Looking for anyone in particular?' Blackstone asked, reaching for his cigarettes.

'Yeah,' Meade replied. 'Someone who likes to gossip but also has a brain – and men with both those attributes are thinner on the ground than you might think.'

A club servant, dressed in the full penguin suit, appeared at

Blackstone's side with such discretion that it was almost as if he had materialized there.

'I'm terribly sorry, sir, but while cigars are more than acceptable within the precincts of this establishment, the smoking of cigarettes is not permitted' he said – laying much the same emphasis on the word "cigarettes" as some people would have laid on "leprosy". He held out an ash tray in his immaculately white-gloved hand. 'If you would care to stub out the offending article in this receptacle, sir?'

Blackstone stubbed out the offending article as requested, and the club servant instantly faded away into the background.

'You can't take me anywhere, can you?' Blackstone asked Meade with a grin. 'It's like the old saying goes – "You can put a peasant in the best shabby second-hand suit that money can buy, but he'll still be a peasant".'

A couple of days earlier, Meade would have come back with a sharp reply, but he was no longer as comfortable with Blackstone as he had been, and now all he said was, 'I think I've found the man we want.'

He led Blackstone across the room to a group of armchairs arranged around a coffee table, where a solid white-haired man was sitting alone.

'Mr Maxwell!' Meade said. 'What a pleasure! Would you mind if we joined you?'

The man looked up through heavily hooded eyes.

'I don't mind at all, Alexander,' he said, 'but I do wish that you'd drop the act.'

'The act?' Meade repeated innocently.

'The delight you just displayed! The sheer joy you appear to feel at finding me here! This meeting is no happy coincidence, Alexander. You're here specifically because you want to talk to me – or someone very *like* me. Isn't that true?'

'Perhaps,' Meade conceded.

'The bonhomie is totally unnecessary, Alexander,' Maxwell continued. 'If you want something from me – and we both know you do – you only have to ask.'

Meade grinned sheepishly. 'This is my colleague, Inspector Blackstone, from New Scotland Yard,' he said.

'Ah, so that's who he is!' Maxwell said. 'Your fame justly precedes you, Inspector.'

'I see you've heard about how he tracked down Inspector O'Brien's killer,' Meade said.

'I've heard, but that's not what I was referring to,' Maxwell said airily, brushing away, with a gesture of his podgy hand, the idea that a major murder investigation could be of much interest.

'Then what . . .?' Meade asked, puzzled.

'There's any number of policemen who could track down a killer,' Maxwell said, 'but, as far as I know, Inspector Blackstone's the only cop who's ever made Captain Bull O'Shaugnessy jump through hoops – a feat previously considered nigh on impossible without the payment of a very large bribe.'

It was true that he *had* made O'Shaugnessy 'jump through hoops' – or, at least, hit him hard in the wallet by pressuring him to temporarily close down a brothel – Blackstone thought.

But O'Shaugnessy had got ample revenge by 'losing' the prisoner who Blackstone had been sent over to America to collect – and pretty much condemned him to staying in the new world until that prisoner was recaptured.

'Why don't you both sit down and tell me exactly what it is you want?' Maxwell suggested.

They sat, and though they did so with some care, the old leather chairs creaked in protest.

'I'm investigating the Holt kidnapping,' Meade said.

Maxwell nodded. 'There's been a ransom demand, I take it,' he said.

'There has.'

'And what did the kidnappers say in their note?' Maxwell chuckled. 'That if those two sons of Big Bill's *don't* pay the ransom, they'll send him back home to them?'

'I take it you're not a great admirer of Holt's,' Meade said.

'Nobody I've ever talked to is an admirer of Big Bill's,' Maxwell said simply. 'To know William Holt is to loathe him.'

'Is that right?'

'Indeed it is. I've been acquainted with all the wheelers and dealers in my time. Mellon, Gould, Morgan, I knew the whole bunch. They were, without doubt, some of most vicious, arrogant, unscrupulous men ever to walk on the face of the earth, but none of them could hold a candle to Big Bill in the son-of-a-bitch stakes. He ruined dozens of good men, but I think it's his sons I feel *most* sorry for.'

'He was hard on them?' Meade asked.

'Damned hard. He wanted them to be just like him, you see – men of iron, who didn't mind the pain they inflicted on themselves as long as everyone else was suffering more.' He took a puff on his cigar. 'Let me tell you one story I heard. When George was nine, Big Bill decided it was time for him to learn to ride. But he didn't get him a pony – that would have been too easy – he bought him a full-sized horse, and a bad-tempered one at that, by all accounts. Well, George fell off, and lay on ground, crying. Big Bill told him to get back on the horse, but he said it hurt too much. So Bill started kicking him – and kept on kicking until he eventually struggled back to his feet and mounted the horse again. When the doctor examined George later, he discovered he had two serious injuries. One was a broken leg, from falling off the damned horse – and the other was two broken ribs from the kicking his father had given him.'

So was it any wonder that the main reason the brothers wanted their father back alive was to protect the value of their shares? Blackstone thought.

And who could blame them for eating a hearty meal on the very day that monster of a father had been kidnapped?

If he'd been in their shoes, he'd have cracked open a dozen bottles of the best French Champagne.

'The only way George survived was by working as hard as he could to become the man his father wanted him to be,' Maxwell continued, 'and in many ways he's succeeded, though, of course, the old man isn't satisfied with the result, because he'd *never* be satisfied. Harold, on the other hand, was smarter than his brother, though I'm not sure whether what he did turned out to be *so* smart in the end.'

'What *did* he do?' Meade asked.

'He pretended to be someone who he knew that his father would despise – someone Big Bill wouldn't bully because he *wasn't* worth bullying. The problem with that, of course, is that if you act a part long enough, you eventually *become* the part. You've met Harold, I take it?'

'We have,' Meade agreed.

'Not much of a man, is he? But then, in quite another way, neither is George. If you could weld them together, you might just end up with a complete person, but even then, I wouldn't put any money on it.' Maxwell took another puff of his cigar. 'Wall Street's quite right to be jittery about this kidnapping. If Big Bill *does* end up dead, the company's finished. Maybe it won't happen next week, maybe not even next year, but, in the long run, it *is* doomed – because neither of those boys are anywhere near big enough to step into Big Bill's shoes.'

According to Fanshawe, they already *had* stepped into his shoes, and all Big Bill did now was sign the paperwork, Blackstone reminded himself.

But then the butler had lied about other things, so why should he have been telling the truth about that?

'Thank you for filling in some of the background on his sons, Mr Maxwell,' Alex Meade said politely. 'I'm sure it will be very helpful to our investigation – but what we'd really like to hear about is some of the men that Holt ruined.'

A sudden chill filled the air around them.

'You'd like to hear about some of the men that Holt ruined?' Maxwell repeated.

'That's right,' Meade said. 'Just for background.'

'Bullshit!' Maxwell said. His hooded eyes closed for a second, and when he opened them again, he said, 'The men he ruined are now either old, or broken in spirit, or both. Can you really see them carrying out a kidnapping?'

'No,' Blackstone said, 'but we could see them hiring someone else to do the work for them.'

Not quite true, he admitted to himself. *He* could see it. Alex, on the other hand, was still refusing to entertain it as a possibility. Yet despite that, Meade had agreed to go through this whole charade, and, for that, Blackstone was grateful.

'You can see them hiring someone else, can you?' Maxwell asked. 'Well, I sure can't. If Big Bill had ruined me, I'd have had no idea where to look for the men I would need to get my revenge.'

No, Blackstone thought, you probably wouldn't. But being the kind of man you so obviously are, you'd make it your business to *find out.*

'I understand that you might find it hard to give us information on men who have probably been your friends and colleagues for years—' Meade began.

'You're right, I would find it hard,' Maxwell interrupted – and now there was a hint of anger in his voice. 'Damned hard – especially when you consider that what I'd really be doing is helping to save the skin of a snake like Bill Holt. Well, let me tell you, Alex,' Maxwell jabbed a podgy finger in Meade's direction to punctuate his words, 'if Holt does turn up somewhere with a bullet in his head, I'm not about to lose a minute's sleep over that.'

'I don't suppose many people will,' Meade said reasonably.

Alex had done all that could be expected of him for a cause he didn't believe in, Blackstone decided. If the young detective stood up and walked away now, the older detective couldn't really blame him.

But Meade *didn't* stand up and walk away. Instead, he leant forward, so that he was now closer to Maxwell.

'Believe me, I do sympathize with your predicament,' he said. 'But the problem is that Holt's not the only victim of the kidnapping. Two guards – two *good* men – had to have their throats slashed. And do you think it's right that their widows and children may never know who took their husbands and fathers away?'

Nicely done, Alex, Blackstone thought. Not strictly the truth – given that the Turners had no children, and Cody had been a bachelor – but nicely done anyway.

Maxwell was probably the kind of man who gambled a hundred thousand dollars without a moment's thought, but what Meade had said had hit home, and now he seemed uncertain of *what* to say.

'I'll give you one name – and it's a good one,' he said finally. 'One name – and that's it.'

'I'm listening,' Meade told him.

'Edward Knox.'

'Oh, come on, Mr Maxwell!' Meade said exasperatedly. 'Please don't treat me like a fool!'

'How is that treating you like a fool? Holt ruined Knox, and Knox, out of all that bastard's victims, was the one man with enough balls to try and do something about it. Doesn't it seem likely that if anyone was going to get together a plot against Big Bill, it would be Knox?'

Meade sighed. 'Except that Knox is in jail,' he said, 'and it must be almost impossible to organize something like that from a prison cell.'

'Who told you he was in jail?' Maxwell asked, surprised.

'Nobody did. I just assumed that since he was guilty of attempted murder, he'd have been sent away for at least twenty years.'

'Knox never went to jail.'

'He was *arrested*, wasn't he?'

'Of course he was arrested. After he'd failed in his murder attempt, George Holt knocked him out cold and then called the police. But he was never *tried* for the crime.'

'Why, in God's name?' Meade asked.

'I've no idea,' Maxwell admitted. 'But if you want to find out, maybe the prosecutor's office will tell you.' His good humour was returning, and he chuckled again. 'And if you get no answer there, you can always ask the captain of the precinct that Knox was taken to when he was arrested.'

'Do you know which captain it was?' Meade asked.

'Sure do,' Maxwell said. 'It was Inspector Blackstone's old friend, Bull O'Shaugnessy.'

SEVENTEEN

The black mood, which Alex Meade had been drifting in and out of for the past two days, descended on him again as he and Blackstone sat at the back of the streetcar which was slowly making its way up Fourth Avenue.

'If the NYPD was a *real* police force, we'd have Mad Bob and Jake the Snake in the holding cells by now,' he said morosely. 'Hell, if it was a *real* police force, we'd have taken them both off the streets a long time ago.'

'Have you got any leads on them at all?' Blackstone asked.

'Not a goddam one. Sure, when I ask them, the patrolmen say they're keeping their eyes peeled, but—' He suddenly stopped talking, and tapped the shoulder of the man sitting in front of them. 'Hey, you!' he said.

The man turned around.

'Yes?' he said.

He was in his early twenties, but somehow had managed to maintain a look of boyish enthusiasm which made even the fresh-faced Alex Meade look grave and staid. He was probably a college student, who threw himself into his work with a joyousness which quite exhausted his professors, Blackstone guessed.

'Are you listening to our conversation?' Meade asked aggressively.

'Of course not!' the young man protested in a voice of deepest innocence, then he spoiled it all by adding, 'Are you guys *really* detectives?'

'You better believe it,' Meade said, producing his shield. 'You want to move further up the car, before I arrest you?'

'Arrest me? What for?'

'I'll think of something,' Meade promised.

The young man rose heavily to his feet.

'And they say this is a free country,' he complained.

'*Who* says?' Meade demanded. 'You tell me who they are, and I'll have them behind bars before you can say "Bill of Rights".'

'Feeling better now, Alex?' Blackstone asked, as he watched the young man move further up the car.

'Yeah,' Meade said, automatically. Then he changed his mind, and continued, 'No, I'm not. See Sam, what just happened *shouldn't* have happened. We're city officials, engaged on important city business, and we should have our own transportation.'

Meade's mood had very little to do with his current complaint, Blackstone thought, but if he had to blow off steam at something – and he clearly did – then transportation was a relatively harmless target.

'So what you're saying you want is your own *personal* carriage?' he prodded.

'No,' Meade replied. 'I don't want my own personal carriage – I want my own personal *automobile*. Every police officer should have one – and it won't be long before we all do.'

He had seen one – or possibly two – automobiles in Manhattan that day, Blackstone thought, and there were days when he saw none at all – so the idea of every cop in the city driving around in one definitely qualified as one of Alex's more fanciful ideas.

'You think I'm wrong, don't you?' Meade challenged, still looking for a fight.

'Maybe, in time, every police officer who has a *private income* – like you do yourself – will have one,' said Blackstone, in a placatory tone, 'but I certainly can't see them being anything like as widely used as you seem to—'

'The price will come down,' said Meade firmly.

'They're handmade, by professional carriage makers,' Blackstone pointed out. 'It takes weeks, if not months, to—'

'I met a guy called Olds, at one of my father's dinner parties,' Meade interrupted. 'He's building a factory in Detroit, Michigan, which will use something he's invented called a "mass production technique". He reckons he should be able to turn out five thousand automobiles *every single year* – and I believe him.'

'Five thousand a year!' Blackstone repeated, incredulously. 'Well, if you say so.'

'I do say so!' Meade said, forcefully. Then he grinned, looked a little sheepish, and said, 'Shall we get back to the case?'

'If you're ready,' Blackstone agreed. 'You were saying that you'd got no leads on Tate and Thompson.'

'I've got no leads on Inspector Flynn, either. He's taken some leave he was owed, and has completely disappeared.'

'Maybe he's gone on holiday,' Blackstone said.

But he didn't really believe that himself, because any man who'd been on the trail of Tate and Thompson no more than twelve or fourteen hours after the kidnapping wasn't going to get any rest until the whole thing was over.

'Do you know what's got me puzzled?' Meade asked.

'You're wondering why Captain O'Shaugnessy is willing to see us?' Blackstone guessed.

'Damn straight,' Meade agreed. 'The man hates your guts.'

'It's because he hates my guts that he's agreed to the meeting. He wants to see me squirm.'

'And will he?'

'I'm not planning on it. In fact, I'm rather hoping that it will be the other way around.'

Precinct Captain Michael O'Shaugnessy sat in his office chair, his feet on the desk and his hands locked behind his bull-like neck. A cigar drooped from the corner of his mouth, and he had a smug expression on his face which Blackstone would very much have liked to rearrange with a ball-peen hammer.

Even in a police department which was justly famous for being rotten from top to bottom, O'Shaugnessy stood out as a shining beacon of deviousness and corruption. He had personally broken more heads than a boatload of invading Vikings, and he had amassed a larger fortune – through bribery and graft – than all but the most successful of the city's politicians.

'Well, well, well,' he said, 'what have we here? The Limey cop and his little buddy Detective Sergeant Meade. Remember when that prisoner of yours escaped, Inspector Blackstone?'

'I remember,' Blackstone said.

He was not likely to forget. In fact, every day he spent in New York City was a reminder of it.

'Yeah, that was some prison break,' O'Shaugnessy said, really enjoying himself. 'Steel bars as thick as your arm, four men on guard – an' he still managed to get out.'

'I thought your story at the time was that he escaped en route to your cells,' Blackstone said.

'Maybe it was,' O'Shaugnessy agreed. 'Maybe it was. It's kinda hard for me to keep track of *all* my lies an' deceits.' He took a puff on his cigar, and blew the smoke contemptuously in Blackstone and Meade's direction. 'So just what can I do for you guys?'

'We'd like some information,' Blackstone said.

'Now, ain't that nice?' O'Shaugnessy said lazily. 'And what do I get in return?'

'The satisfaction of upholding the oath you've *sworn* to uphold, and of doing the job you're *paid* to do?' Meade suggested.

'I was talkin' to the organ grinder, not his monkey,' O'Shaugnessy pointed out. 'Well, Inspector Blackstone?'

'You don't get anything,' Blackstone said.

'Then I got nothin' to say,' O'Shaugnessy replied.

Blackstone turned to Meade. 'That's five dollars you owe me' he said.

'Have you boys been betting against each other?' Shaugnessy asked.

'That's right,' Blackstone agreed.

'So you bet five dollars that I wouldn't help you, and Meade bet five dollars that I would.' O'Shaugnessy turned to Alex. 'You really are one *dumb* asshole, ain't you, Sergeant Meade?'

'That wasn't the bet,' Blackstone told him.

'No?'

'No. It wasn't about whether you *would* help us or not – it was about whether you'd be too *scared* to help us.'

'Scared?' O'Shaugnessy repeated. 'Scared of what?'

'That for all your boasting about how smart you are – and how *safe* you are – you're still worried that, if you say too much, a Limey and a humble detective sergeant from your own department might find some way to bring you down.'

'Boy, you sure do live in some kinda dream world, don't you?' O'Shaugnessy asked, with a smirk.

'In his position, that's what *I'd* say,' Blackstone told Meade. 'I'd smile just like he is now, and I'd produce just the same line of bull-shit – even if I was crapping my pants at the time.'

'You got it all wrong, you Limey bastard,' O'Shaugnessy said, angry now. 'I could tell you *everythin'* that goes on in this precinct. I could tell you exactly who pays the bribes an' exactly how much they pay. Hell, I could even give you the numbers of my secret bank accounts – and even with all that, you still wouldn't be able to bring me down, because this is New York City, an' I'm only doin' the same as every other captain.'

'Prove it,' Blackstone challenged.

'Prove what?'

'That you're not scared.'

'How? Do you actually *want* to know the numbers of them secret bank accounts of mine?'

'No, I want to know about a man called Knox, who, seven years ago, tried to kill William Holt. Do you remember that?'

'Sure do. Not likely to forget it, 'cos Holt was a big wheel in the city at the time.'

'Yes, he was,' Blackstone agreed. 'And the fact that he was impor-tant makes it all the more surprising that his would-be assassin never went to prison. Would you mind explaining how that came about?'

'The case was all set to go to court – an' then the evidence went missing.'

'What evidence?'

'Well, for openers, the gun that Knox shot Holt with. One minute we had it safely locked up in the evidence room down in the basement, and the next minute it was gone.'

'And, of course, you launched an inquiry to find out just what had happened to it?'

'There didn't seem much point in doing that.'

'No?'

'No. See, the way I had it figured out, the sergeant in charge of the case had removed the evidence himself.'

'And why would he have done that?'

O'Shaugnessy chuckled. 'You *know* why he'd have done it – because Knox had *bribed* him to do it.'

'And you didn't expect any trouble from the powerful Holt family over the fact that the evidence had disappeared?'

'Hell, no! They knew the way things work in this city, just like everybody else did. If they wanted the case to go to court, all they had to do was pay the sergeant a bigger bribe than Knox had – which they could well afford to do – and the evidence would turn up again.'

'Wouldn't Knox have kicked up a stink if that had happened?'

'What could he have said – that the sergeant hadn't lived up to his part of the bargain? If he'd done that, he'd have been admitting to bribery, and that would have added five or six years to his sentence.'

'Ah, now I get the point!' Blackstone said.

'You do?'

'You'd get a cut of the bribe that *Knox* paid the sergeant, whatever happened. But if you recovered the evidence yourself, that's *all* you'd get. On the other hand, if you just sat there and waited, you'd get a cut of the *second* bribe – the one which the Holts would have to offer – and that bribe would be much larger than the one from Knox.'

'Now you're catching on,' O'Shaugnessy said.

'But the Holts never did pay a bribe?'

'That's right, and that was a real surprise to me, because Big Bill was known to be one of the most vengeful men in whole of New York City.'

'But at least you got part of the Knox bribe.'

O'Shaugnessy frowned. 'Not even that. See, the sergeant said there'd *been* no bribe, and that the evidence had just gone missing.'

'And did you believe him?'

'Sorta yes, and sorta no. When I spoke to him, he looked me straight in the eye and told me there'd been no bribe. And I did believe *that*.'

'So where does the "sorta no" come into it?'

'I also asked him if he'd removed the evidence, and when he said he hadn't, he had to look away.'

'So why do you think he did it?'

'Who the hell knows? And if there's no money to be made out of it – which there wasn't – who the hell cares?'

'It must have come as a shock to you to realize you had even a *halfway* decent and honest officer working for you,' Blackstone said.

'Damn straight,' O'Shaugnessy agreed.

'And is he *still* working for you?'

'Do I *look* like a rube to you?' O'Shaugnessy demanded. 'Do you really think I'd tolerate that kinda guy in my precinct? Course he ain't still working for me! I got him promoted to inspector, then had him transferred the hell away from Manhattan. The last I heard, he was working way out in the sticks.'

Blackstone's mind was racing.

The sergeant in question had lost the evidence against Knox, but he had not done it for money – because O'Shaugnessy was completely convinced no bribe had been paid.

So what *had been* his motive?

Was it perhaps less to do with Knox himself than with the man he had tried to kill?

And there was more – the sergeant had been promoted to inspector, and was now working way out in the sticks.

But just what did O'Shaugnessy *mean* by 'the sticks'?

'Are you talking about Coney Island?' he asked.

'What?'

'Is this man you had promoted to inspector based on Coney Island now?'

'Yeah,' O'Shaugnessy said. 'How did you know that? Wait a minute! I ain't made the connection before, but Big Bill Holt lives on Coney Island, don't he?'

'Yes, he does,' Blackstone agreed. 'The other thing you never told us is the policeman's name. It wouldn't be *Flynn*, by any chance, would it?'

'Goddam right it's Flynn,' O'Shaugnessy said.

'I told you we shouldn't trust Flynn,' Alex Meade said, once they had left that cesspool of corruption which was O'Shaugnessy's office behind them. 'I told you right from the very start.'

It could all be traced back to Flynn, Blackstone thought. Alex's dark moods, his aggression, his refusal to consider any viewpoint but his own, could all be traced back to that first meeting with Inspector Flynn.

Yet despite everything that had happened, Blackstone could not bring himself to share his partner's feeling about the man. There was a singleness of purpose and deadly earnestness about the inspector which reminded him a little of himself, and though he had no idea what the singleness of purpose was directed *towards*, or what had occurred to *forge* that deadly earnestness, he couldn't help feeling a sneaking admiration for him.

'He certainly did a good snow job on O'Shaugnessy,' Meade said. 'Bull really *doesn't* believe he took a bribe to lose Knox's gun.'

Neither do I, Blackstone thought.

'And what the hell was he doing sending a cable to Scotland Yard about Fanshawe, even *before* the kidnapping?' Meade demanded.

'I don't know,' Blackstone admitted. 'Nor can I explain why he seems to have made it his personal mission to track down the kidnappers of a man who he appears to despise.'

'*If* that's what he's doing,' Meade said, enigmatically.

'And just what do you mean by that?' Blackstone wondered.

'Maybe what he's actually doing is covering his own tracks – because he's the brains behind the kidnapping,' Meade said.

'Oh, come on, Alex,' Blackstone protested.

'Think about it!' Meade urged. 'He deliberately got himself posted to Coney Island, where Holt has his home.'

'We don't know that for a fact.'

'He did a background check on Fanshawe to see if he was a suitable man to use in the kidnapping.'

'Then why would he tell *me* he'd done it?' Blackstone asked.

But Meade was not to be deterred.

'Who had more reason to get to know the Pinkerton men than the local inspector?' he continued. 'And who was in a better position to recruit some New York thugs for the job than a man who'd worked among them?'

'It's not Flynn,' Blackstone said firmly.

'I don't know where the bastard is,' Meade said, ignoring him. 'But wherever he is, he's not on vacation.'

EIGHTEEN

I t was too dark in the warehouse for him to *see* the rat, but he heard it scuttle past him clearly enough, and, seconds later, when the scuttling had stopped, his ears picked up the sound of its defiant squeak.

He laughed, both at the absurdity of the rat's situation and at the absurdity of his own.

'You're just like me,' he told the furry rodent in a soft voice. 'When you're scared, you run like hell – and it's only when you feel safe again that you take the time to show you were never scared at all.'

But he wouldn't run this time, he promised himself. This time, he would draw his inspiration from Edward Knox, a pathetic little man who – because he overcame his fear and stood his ground – transformed himself into a real hero.

The timbers of the decaying warehouse creaked complainingly. The squeaking rat – or it may have been some other rodent – indulged in another mad dash. Other than that, there was silence.

How long had he been standing there, he wondered.

Half an hour?

More than that?

Waiting, waiting, waiting – though he still did not know whether the men he was waiting *for* would actually come – or whether he would be able to handle them if they did.

He was a bloody fool, he told himself – though that was not exactly news to him.

But what else was he to do? For seven long years, he had been chasing a phantom, and then – when he had finally found a way to pen it up – it had managed to slip away again.

But it would not be allowed to escape.

It *could not* be allowed to escape.

Because if it did, that would mean he would have wasted the best years of his life on *nothing*.

He heard the warehouse door creak open, and felt his heart starting to beat a little faster.

'I shouldn't have gone into this thing without someone to back me up,' he thought.

But in the whole of New York – perhaps in the whole wide world – there was no one else he could trust.

The men had stopped in the doorway, and he could see their silhouettes clearly, against the light of the full moon behind them.

'Are yer there?' one of them called out.

'I'm here,' he said.

'I can't see ya. Why are yer in the dark?'

Because that tips the odds slightly more in my favour, he thought. Because there are two of them and one of me – and I need all the help against the odds that I can get.

'Why are yer in the dark?' the other man asked for a second time.

'Because I don't want you to see my face,' he said aloud. 'You can understand that, can't you?'

'We like to know who we're workin' for,' the man said.

'Why? Does it really matter to you who I am, or why I want somebody killed – as long as you get the *money*?'

'Still don't like the dark,' the man complained.

'There's a hurricane lamp about twelve feet ahead of you. I'll light your way there with my flashlight.'

'With yer *what*?'

'With my flashlight. It's a new thing – just come out.'

And used almost exclusively by the New York City Police Department, he added silently to himself.

He took the cardboard tube out of his pocket, switched it on, and aimed the beam of light at their feet.

'Come on!' he urged.

Still, they hesitated.

'What's the matter? Are you frightened?' he taunted. 'It's professional killers that I need to hire. I've no use at all for candy-assed little boys who are afraid of the dark.'

They stepped forward, closing the door behind them, and advanced cautiously. They followed the beam of the flashlight to the lamp, then one of them struck a match and lit the wick.

He studied them in the glow of the lantern. They were thugs – mindless thugs. They deserved to be put down like rabid dogs for what they had done, but – again like rabid dogs – it would be pointless to try and make them feel any responsibility for their actions.

'We still can't see yer,' one of them complained.

'That's the idea, my boy,' he replied. 'Which one are you – Mad Bob or Jake?'

'Don't call me that!'

'So you must be Bob, which makes your friend Jake.'

'Who do yer want us to kill?' asked the one he had now identified as Jake.

'Nobody,' he said.

'But we was told—'

'I'm much more interested in who you've *already* killed. And before you make any sudden moves, I should warn you that I've got my revolver pointing at you, and I could shoot you both before you'd gone more than a couple of feet.'

'Who the hell are yer?' Bob demanded.

'Didn't I mention that before?' he asked. 'I'm Detective Inspector Michael Flynn. But don't worry, boys, it's not you that I'm after. You're of about as much interest to me as the knives you used, and if you help me to find out what I want to know, I just might let you go.'

'I don't know what yer talkin' about,' Bob said.

'Now, you see, that's not *at all* helpful,' Flynn said, 'and if you carry on like that, I might just shoot you, as an incentive to make Jake more cooperative.'

'Yer wouldn't do that,' Bob said. 'Not if yer a cop.'

'I *am* a cop,' Flynn said. 'But I'm also a man with a mission – and that trumps being a police officer every time.'

'Yer bluffin',' Bob said.

'I can soon prove I'm not - by pulling the trigger - but I'm sure we all wish to avoid that,' Flynn countered. 'Now where was I? Oh yes! Two nights ago, you went to a house on Concy Island and slit the throats of two Pinkerton men called Cody and Turner.'

'Yer crazy!' Bob said.

Flynn squeezed the trigger. There was a sudden flash of light, followed by a loud explosion which echoed round the empty warehouse, and then Bob crumpled and hit the floor.

Flynn watched him writhing in agony for two or three seconds before he said, 'For God's sake, Bob, it's only your leg – I could have aimed at something *much* more painful. And you can't say I didn't warn you.' He turned his attention to Jake. 'I've got that right, haven't I?' he asked. 'You did kill the guards.'

'Yeah,' Jake admitted shakily. 'We killed 'em.'

'Good boy,' Flynn said approvingly. 'Now what I'm really interested in – as I said earlier – is who *paid you* to kill them. Actually, that's not true,' he corrected himself. 'I already *know* who it was who paid you. What I need you to tell me is where he is now.'

'He's . . . he's on Coney Island,' Jake said.

'Don't lie to me,' Flynn said angrily. 'He wouldn't have *dared* stay there – not after what he's done.'

'I swear to yer—'

'If I shoot you, it won't just be a leg wound, like I gave Bob,' Flynn threatened. 'This time, I'll be aiming for your nuts.'

'Please . . .!'

'Tell me where the bastard is!'

The door to the warehouse suddenly crashed open, and standing there – silhouetted just as Bob and Jake had been earlier – were three men.

'This is police business – keep away!' Flynn shouted.

But even as he was saying the words, there was a part of his brain which knew he was wasting his time.

The three men in the doorway opened fire almost simultaneously, their guns spitting flames into the darkness which was all that separated them from the oasis of light in which Bob and Jake were standing.

Three more shots followed in rapid succession.

And another three.

As the bullets slammed into him, Jake performed a grotesque dance of death in the flickering light of the lantern.

Flynn raised his own weapon to return the fire. But before he could get off even a single shot, a giant sledge hammer struck him in the chest, and he was suddenly flying backwards.

He must have blacked out – he had no idea for how long – but when he regained consciousness, there were four things he was immediately aware of.

The first – the most pressing – was the pain in his chest.

The second was the groans coming from either Bob or Jake – he didn't know which.

The third was the acrid smell of cordite, which filled the air and was almost choking him.

And the fourth was the sound of footsteps, as the men who had been standing in the doorway drew ever closer.

'Mad Bob's still alive,' he heard one of the men say.

Yes, that was logical, Flynn's fevered mind thought irrelevantly. A man who was already lying on the ground had a much smaller chance of being hit by a fatal bullet than one who was presenting himself as an upright target.

'Did yer hear what I said?' the assassin asked one of his companions. 'Bob ain't dead.'

'Well, yer can soon change that, can't yer?'

The part of Flynn's brain which was still working like a policeman's noted that, from their accents, they were probably from the Lower East Side, the natural training ground for this type of killing.

The closest man bent down – Flynn could just see him from the corner of his eye – placed his revolver against Bob's head, and pulled the trigger. Bob's legs kicked out convulsively – once – and then he was still.

Where's your gun? the policeman's brain screamed. You had it in your hand when you were shot – so it can't be far away now.

No, it couldn't be, could it, the rest of the brain agreed.

The pain, when he moved his arm, was almost unbearable, but by an effort of will he forced the arm to keep moving while the hand on the end of it groped on the dirt floor for his weapon.

Nothing to the right.

He would command the arm to undertake the epic journey to the left, he told himself, gritting his teeth.

Nothing to the left, either.

So that was it, then. The end of his mission – the end of his life!

'What about the other guy?' the man who'd finished off Bob asked.

'He ain't part of the deal.'

'So do I put a bullet in him as well?'

'Hell, I don't know – do what yer want.'

The first man looked down at Flynn. 'Yer not part of the contract, so I guess this is yer lucky day, feller,' he said.

The three men turned and headed towards the door.

Left alone, Flynn wondered just how long it would take him to die.

NINETEEN

The bright morning sunlight streamed in through the windows, bathing the busy nurses, who were rushing up and down, in an almost angelic glow.

'I'm not entirely happy about you talking to my patient, because he's still very weak,' the young doctor said, as he led Blackstone down the corridor.

'But he *wants* to talk to me, doesn't he?' Blackstone countered.

'Yes, indeed,' the doctor agreed. 'He was most insistent on it. But if it seems to be too much of a strain on him—'

'I'll leave immediately,' Blackstone promised.

They had passed a row of bustling public wards, and now entered an area of the hospital which seemed much more serene.

When they came to a halt in front of a door which looked as if it would be more at home in a medium-priced hotel than in a hospital, Blackstone said, with some surprise, 'He's in a *private* room, is he?'

'That is correct,' the doctor confirmed.

How the hell could Flynn afford a private room on *his* pay? Blackstone wondered.

He couldn't, unless, of course, he wasn't as straight as he pretended to be – unless he was just as corrupt as most of the other officers working for the NYPD.

'He's not paying for the room himself,' said the doctor, as if reading the other man's mind.

'No?'

'No. While he was still in surgery, a messenger arrived with a plain envelope stuffed with cash and a note which said that Inspector Flynn was to be given the best care that money could buy. I suspect the anonymous donor was a concerned member of the public.'

Suspect what you like, Blackstone thought. I think I know *exactly* who the money came from.

The doctor opened the door, said, 'Well, I've got a lot to do, so I'll leave you to it,' and was gone.

Flynn lay in the bed, looking very pale, and was swathed from neck to stomach in bandages.

'Well, well, if it isn't the famous English detective,' he said weakly, by way of greeting.

'You're lucky to be alive, you know,' Blackstone said. 'It was a patrolman who'd heard the shooting who found you, and that was pure chance, because he shouldn't even have been in the area. The official line is that he was pursuing a suspect, but Alex Meade's theory is that he'd gone there to take advantage of the complementary service that the local whores feel obliged to provide for policemen.'

'Piss on Meade's theory,' Flynn said, without rancour.

'They took two bullets out of you, both of which came within half an inch of killing you,' Blackstone continued. 'So, all in all, it really *does* look like it was your lucky day.'

'The bastard who shot me said the same thing – and you're both wrong,' Flynn told him, wincing as he spoke. 'If it *had* been my lucky day, I'd have been somewhere else when Bob and Jake got hit.'

'The entire New York Police Department was told to look out for Tate and Thompson – so how is it that you're the one who found them?'

'The cops in this city only do their job properly when there's something in it for them,' Flynn said. 'Besides, the fact that the police were looking for them gave them a reason to hide – but I was offering them money, and that gave them a reason to come out.'

'Do you want to start at the beginning?' Blackstone suggested.

'Start *what* at the beginning?'

'The story of how you became involved in all this.'

Flynn thought about it for a moment, then said, 'Sure.'

'I'm listening.'

'My father came over to this country with nothing. He wanted to make a completely new start in the new world. He even changed his name from *Flynn* to *Fines*, because he thought that sounded better in business. Then, for the next twenty-five years, he worked like a dog, and at the end of that, he'd managed to get some capital behind him. Not a great deal, you understand, but enough.'

'And he invested it with William Holt?' Blackstone guessed.

'Indeed he did. And the day he learned he'd lost everything, he went out into the backyard and hanged himself. He didn't kill my mother, too, but he might as well have done, because she adored him, and six months later she was dead from grief herself.'

'You were already a cop by then.'

'Yes, I was – a sergeant.'

'And you'd changed your name back to Flynn?'

'The biggest mistake my father ever made was to trust William

Holt,' Flynn said. 'But the second biggest was to turn his back on his heritage. I'm *proud* to be Irish,' he added, defiantly.

'And why wouldn't you be?' Blackstone asked. 'I'm guessing that the day your father died, you made a promise to yourself.'

'I did. I swore I'd get back at Holt for what he'd done to my father. I swore I'd build up a file on him that would send him to prison for the rest of his natural days. It became my sole purpose in life.'

'You deliberately lost the evidence against Edward Knox, didn't you?'

'Knox had tried to do something I didn't have the balls for myself – which was to kill Holt. It seemed to me that the least *I* could do for *him* was to make sure he didn't go to jail.'

'And when Captain O'Shaugnessy wanted you posted away from Manhattan, you made sure you were sent to Coney Island – so you could continue your investigation?'

'No,' Flynn said. 'I got myself posted to Coney Island because I'm a dumb Mick – full of the romance of Ireland – who sometimes thinks he's living in the middle of a Gothic novel.'

'You've lost me,' Blackstone confessed.

'I wasn't making the case against Holt on *Coney Island* – I couldn't get near enough to him to do that. All the evidence I've built up has been collected in the city. But I *liked* living close to him, you see. I *liked* walking past that big house of his, and feeling the evil and greed emanating from the place.' Flynn grinned. 'I *told* you I was a dumb Mick.'

'How much evidence have you collected?'

'More than enough to build up a watertight case against Holt. Fraud, bribery, theft, embezzlement, conspiracy to pervert the course of justice – it's all there in my dossier.'

'And where is it now?'

'I gave it to the District Attorney. He was over the moon about it. He's been polishing it up for the past month, and next week he was due to subpoena Holt to appear before the Grand Jury.'

'Did Holt know that?'

Flynn snorted contemptuously. 'The DA's office leaks like a sieve, so of course he knew.' He paused. 'I can tell by the look on your face that you still don't understand.'

'Understand what?'

'That that subpoena is what this kidnapping was all about!'

'You've lost me again.'

'Holt knew that once he'd been arrested – once the cell door had closed behind him – they'd never let him out again. He had to disappear before that happened – and *that's* why he faked his own kidnapping.'

Jesus! Blackstone thought, how could the man be so right about so many things and yet put them all together and draw the totally wrong conclusion?

'You've been through a hell of a time, and you're tired,' he said.

'You don't believe me!' Flynn said, incredulously.

'The best thing for you is to get some rest.'

'You have to see that's what he's done,' Flynn said, frantic. 'You have to understand that he's out there somewhere – laughing at us.'

'Flynn got too close to it,' Blackstone said to Meade, as they shared a jug of beer in the nearest saloon to the hospital. 'And when you get too close to a thing, you can see all the little details, but not the big picture.'

'So you don't think there's any chance at all that he might be right, Sam?' Meade asked.

'None,' Blackstone said firmly.

'I don't think you should brush his ideas aside just like that,' Meade said hotly. 'When a man nearly dies trying to prove a theory, that theory should be shown some respect.'

'It was only yesterday that you were convinced it was Flynn himself who was behind the kidnapping,' Blackstone pointed out.

Meade looked down at the table. 'Yeah, well, I was wrong,' he mumbled. His raised his head again, and looked Blackstone squarely in the eyes. 'There was a part of me that always knew Flynn was a good cop,' he said. 'There was a part of me which always suspected he was a better cop than *I* am.'

'You kept that part of you well hidden,' Blackstone said.

'And not just from you,' Meade conceded. 'From myself, as well.' He paused again. 'Do you know what it's like to have an influential father, Sam?'

'You know I don't.'

'You tell yourself that you've got the job on your own merit, and that when you get promoted *that* will be on merit too, and not just because you've paid a bribe. And then you meet somebody like Flynn – who so obviously really *has* risen on merit – and you begin to ask yourself if you'd even be a *sergeant* if you didn't have Daddy behind you.'

And that's when it becomes important to you that *your* theories on the case are the right ones, Blackstone thought. *That's* when it becomes vital that you solve the case *unaided* – because it's the only way you think you can convince yourself you're up to the job.

'You're the one who paid for Flynn's private room at the hospital, aren't you?' he asked.

Meade nodded. 'Yeah, I am.'

'Because you felt guilty?'

'Maybe.'

'Then you have to be careful not to let that guilt get in the way of your doing good police work,' Blackstone said sternly.

'Is that what I'm doing?'

'I think so – otherwise you'd see I was right about Flynn's theory.'

'*Prove* to me that you're right!' Meade demanded.

'All right, I will,' Blackstone agreed. 'Put yourself in Big Bill's shoes, Alex. You learn from a contact in the District Attorney's office that you're about to be subpoenaed – and that an arrest is likely to follow. What do you do?'

'Grab all the money I can lay my hands on and make a run for it.'

'Exactly! What you *don't* do is draw more attention to yourself than you have to, by, for example, staging your own kidnapping.'

'Holt could have thought that the kidnapping would throw us off the scent for a few days,' Meade pointed out.

'He didn't *need* to throw us off the scent,' Blackstone argued. 'Flynn said it would have been at least another week before the subpoena was served.'

'So?'

'So what was the most sensible course of action for Big Bill to follow? Was it to take the money and run, knowing that, because he hasn't been seen for years, no one was going to miss him until the subpoena *was* served? Or was it to do something that involved the death of two Pinkerton agents, which would mean that if he was eventually caught, he'd not only be charged with fraud, but prosecuted for murder as well?'

Meade sighed heavily. 'You're right, Sam. Inspector Flynn's theory makes no sense at all.'

'Big Bill probably *was* planning to make a run for it,' Blackstone said, 'but the kidnappers struck before he'd had time to get it properly organized.'

'So where, *exactly*, does that leave us?' Meade asked despondently.

'In a deep, dark hole,' Blackstone said. 'Our best chance of solving this case was to get our hands on Mad Bob and Jake. Once we had them behind bars, we could have sweated them for the name of whoever hired them. But the kidnappers realized that they were the weak link in the chain, too – and that's why they had them gunned down.'

'Maybe if we could catch the killers . . .' Meade began.

But there was no chance of that – and they both knew it.

The men who had murdered Bob and Jake had been professionals, and had carried out their work with the same cold-blooded detachment as butchers in an abattoir. It was unlikely they'd known – or cared – why the two men had to die, and just as unlikely that they knew who wanted them dead. Even if the police managed to arrest them – and that would be a big 'if' even in London, where the coppers actually saw it as their *job* to solve crime – it was unlikely to lead the investigation anywhere.

Meade sighed again. 'What's our next move?' he asked.

What indeed, Blackstone wondered.

'We could go to the Cornell University Medical School, and pick up Fanshawe's autopsy report,' he suggested.

'Why would we bother?' Meade asked. 'We know *how* he died.'

'And we think we know *why* he killed himself,' Blackstone said. 'But what if we're wrong? What if, for example, he was totally innocent of the kidnapping, but had some incurable disease?'

'Then why wait until the place was swarming with police before topping himself?'

'Maybe because he found the additional strain of the investigation just too much to take?' Blackstone drew a deep breath. 'Listen, Alex, I'm not saying it's probable that he had a disease. The most *likely* explanation is that he *was* involved in the kidnapping, and hanged himself because he thought he was about to be arrested. But we can't say that *definitively* until we've eliminated all the other possibilities. And the autopsy report will help us to eliminate at least a few of them.'

'You're clutching at straws, Sam,' Meade said.

'You're right,' Blackstone agreed. 'And I'm sure you have at least a dozen *much* better ideas about what do next – so why don't you tell me what they are?'

Meade thought about it for a moment. 'Why don't we go and pick up Fanshawe's autopsy report?' he suggested.

TWENTY

The clerk sitting at the main desk of the Cornell University Medical School was a pretty girl in her mid-twenties. She had intelligent, expressive eyes and once they laid sight on Alex Meade, they said quite clearly that she was smitten.

'Is there anything I can do for you?' she asked, in a voice which suggested that the services she offered might well extend far beyond those available in the hospital complex.

'We've come for the autopsy report on Robert Fanshawe,' Meade said, his own voice perhaps slightly higher than it normally was.

The clerk checked her records. 'I don't have it,' she admitted. She examined a second list. 'Oh, that's the reason – it's being performed right now in Lecture Theatre Three.'

'It's being done in a *lecture theatre*?' Blackstone exploded.

'Sure, this is a teaching hospital,' the clerk said, looking at Meade again. 'There'll be students there to watch.'

'The hospital *has* been informed Robert Fanshawe was involved in a murder inquiry, hasn't it?' Blackstone asked.

The clerk glanced briefly down at her notes again. 'It says here that it was a suicide.'

He was being unreasonably bad-tempered, Blackstone realized. Fanshawe *had* taken his own life, so did it really matter that he was being cut up in front of an audience, when the autopsy was likely to give them *nothing*?

Even so, he could not help hearing a mocking voice in the back of his mind – a voice, furthermore, which sounded uncannily like Inspector Flynn's – say, 'Now why give the body to our simple Coney Island doctor, when you can have a big shot in New York slice through him for the instruction and delectation of all his runny-nosed trainee sawbones?'

'You can go and see the process yourselves, if you want to,' the clerk said helpfully.

'We can?' Meade asked.

'Sure, there's a gallery above the lecture hall. It's only supposed to be for doctors, but sometimes *our* doctors bring guests with them.' She winked. 'And those guests, I have to say, look as if they're loaded.'

'Drunk?' Meade asked.

'Rich,' the clerk replied. 'But sometimes drunk *as well*,' she added. 'I suppose people can do what they like with their money, but even if I had a fortune, I still wouldn't pay to watch anything as gruesome as an autopsy.'

Standing in the gallery, Blackstone and Meade looked down at the lecture theatre. There was only one person there at that moment, and he was lying on an operating table at the centre of the theatre, covered with a white sheet, bathed in a brilliant white light – and quite dead.

'This is kinda weird,' Meade admitted.

'Is this your first autopsy?' Blackstone asked.

'Hell, no, but at all the others I hadn't met the guy until *after* he'd died. This is somebody I actually talked to – and who talked back – and, like I said, it feels kinda weird.'

A lab technician entered the theatre, pushing a trolley on which knives, saws and tweezers were neatly laid out. He parked the trolley beside the operating table, stepped back to see if it was properly aligned, and then left.

The students arrived next. There were a dozen of them, all wearing surgical gowns, masks and caps. Whilst trying not to appear to do so, they jostled for position around the operating table, though none of them crossed the line which – though invisible – was clearly understood by them to exist.

Now all we're waiting for is the star of the show – the great doctor, Blackstone thought.

The doctor arrived right on cue. He was a small man – at least a head shorter than any of his students – yet even from the gallery, he seemed to have a presence about him which almost made it appear as if was towering over them.

He reached the table, and walked around to the top of it, from where he could see all his students.

'Well, gentlemen, here we all are, so let's get to work shall we?' said a voice from behind the doctor's mask that Blackstone knew all too well.

'Good God! It's Ellie!' he gasped.

'Ellie?' Meade repeated, mystified.

'Ellie Carr!'

'You mean *your* Ellie?'

'Exactly,' Blackstone agreed, although he was not at all sure that she was – or ever would be – *his* Ellie.

Not after what had happened between them in London.

*   *   *

It is ten o'clock in the evening. He is sitting in a pub, with Charlotte Devaraux, a beautiful and talented actress. They have been talking for some time when she makes her proposal.

'You do understand that I'm not offering you a lifetime of love, don't you?' she says.

'Yes, I do understand.'

'I'm not even offering you companionship – at least, not beyond one single night. But if companionship for that single night would suit you, then it's there for the taking.'

It should be every man's dream, but instead of agreeing to it immediately, he says, 'If you'll excuse me, there's a phone call I have to make.'

He rings the lab, where he knows Ellie will still be hard at work.

'Listen, Sam,' she says the moment he has identified himself – and before *he has had time to say why he called, 'I think I may have found the source of that poison of yours, but it's far too early for me to be able to give you any definite results, so don't even bother to ask.'*

'I wasn't going to ask. Forget work.'

'I beg your pardon?' Ellie retorts, as if he's suddenly started speaking in a foreign language.

'Forget work,' he repeats, with just a hint of a plea in his voice. 'Give it a rest for tonight. It's still a couple of hours until the pubs close. I could meet you outside the hospital and we could go and have a drink somewhere.'

'The kind of work that I'm involved in at the moment can't just be dropped whenever I feel the inclination,' she answers, talking slowly, as if to an idiot.

'What does that mean?' he demands. 'That you can't *stop? Or that you* won't *stop?'*

'A little of both, I suppose,' she says honestly – because she is *always honest, except when it is only herself she is fooling. 'I think I may be breaking new ground here, and it's very difficult to tear yourself away from something like that.'*

'Is it?' he says, the plaintive tone more evident now – at least to him! 'Even if I asked you to? Even if I say that I'm feeling low, and would really *appreciate your company tonight?'*

'For heaven's sake, Sam, stop being so difficult. If you want company, why don't you give Sergeant Patterson a ring?'

'It wouldn't be the same.'

'No, since he's a man and I'm a woman, it would obviously be somewhat different,' Ellie says, with maddening scientific logic. 'But

Patterson can keep you amused tonight, and, once the investigation's over, I'll find a way to make it up to you.'

'You really don't *understand, do you?'*

'Understand what? I understand that you want the results from my tests. You do *still want them, don't you?'*

'Yes, but . . .'

'So I'm doing my level best to get them for you as soon as possible. And I promise you this, Sam – in the morning you'll be glad that at least one of us has shown some self-discipline.'

He gives up.

'Who knows how I'll feel in the morning,' he says. 'Goodnight, Ellie.'

When he gets back to the bar, he is hoping that the actress – offended by his cavalier behaviour – will have gone. But she is still there, and they spend a night of wild passion together.

Who has betrayed who, he wonders, even in the throes of that passion?

Has Ellie betrayed him by putting her work above his desperate need for her?

Has he betrayed Ellie by refusing to wait for what – they both knew – was bound to happen between them sooner or later?

Or since nothing has happened yet, is all talk of betrayal meaningless?

He doesn't know.

But later, looking back on it, he knows that since that night, things have never been the same between them.

'So, now that we're all here, what shall we do first?' Ellie asked the students.

One of them raised his hand tentatively in the air.

'Yes?' Ellie said.

'The first thing that we should do, ma'am, is make a chest incision,' he suggested.

Ellie reached on to the trolley, took hold of a scalpel, and held it up under the brilliant white light for all the students to see.

'Does everyone agree that should be our first step?' she asked.

The students nodded enthusiastically.

Ellie returned the scalpel to the trolley.

'Say you were going to cut up some cloth to make curtains,' Ellie began. She paused. 'Sorry, that analogy wouldn't work for you, would it? I forgot for a moment that even though this university has an admissions policy which – in theory – puts men and women on an equal footing, there are, in fact, no women present.' She looked around, as if to confirm the truth of her statement. 'All right, then, let's try something else. Say you were going to build yourself a chest of drawers – would you start cutting the wood before you'd taken your measurements and studied the grain?'

Even from the gallery, it was possible to sense the students' feeling of bemusement, and when someone chuckled, Blackstone was slightly surprised to discover that that someone was him.

'None of you has *ever* built a chest of drawers, have you?' Ellie enquired.

The students shook their heads.

'Of course not,' Ellie said heavily. 'Coming from the background you *have* come from, you've never felt the need to. In fact, even though you may end up as surgeons, the chances are that you've probably never really done *anything* with your hands – not even make an omelette.'

The students looked down at the ground and shuffled their feet.

'But don't despair, gentlemen,' Ellie continued, in a much lighter tone. 'Everyone has to start somewhere. Even I – though you might find this hard to believe – was not *born* a doctor. And between now and the time that you mount the podium to be awarded your shiny new certificate under the eyes of your proud parents, you will have ample opportunity to learn.' She paused for a second. 'So, to return to my initial question, what's the first thing we should do?'

'We should study the cadaver in its current state,' said one of the students, who'd latched on to her line of thinking.

'We should study its current state,' Ellie agreed. 'This cadaver is as new to me as it is to you – I promise you, I haven't even taken a peek at it – and we'll *all* be looking at it with fresh eyes. The one thing I *can* tell you is that it was found hanging from a tree – so let's see if we can work out how the man died.'

Several of the students laughed, but when they saw the look in their instructor's eyes, the laughter quickly died away.

Ellie Carr stripped back the sheet.

'Take your time,' she said.

Almost immediately, the student who thought that he'd already got the measure of her said, 'Asphyxiation.'

Ellie covered the cadaver with the sheet again.

'What's your name?' she demanded.

'Jackson,' the student said, with less certainty now. 'Andrew Jackson. I was named after the president.'

'Which would seem to suggest that your parents had high hopes for you – at least when you were younger,' Ellie Carr mused. 'So you think he died of asphyxiation, do you, Mr Jackson?'

'Yes, ma'am, I do.'

'And you don't think the gunshot wound to his stomach had anything to do with his death?'

'The . . . the gunshot wound,' Jackson stammered. 'I didn't see any gunshot wound.'

'Didn't see a gunshot wound!' Ellie scoffed. 'And you call yourself a medical student!'

She stripped off the sheet again.

'There *is* no gunshot wound!' Jackson protested.

'No, there isn't,' Ellie Carr agreed. 'But when I said there was, you couldn't tell me there wasn't – because *you* hadn't looked.'

'Is she always as formidable as this?' Meade asked Blackstone.

'This is nothing,' Blackstone told him, and realized he was sounding quite proud of Ellie. 'She's very much the new girl here, and probably hasn't quite found her feet yet. So she's taking things carefully – holding back a little.'

'Jesus, in that case, I'd hate to meet her when she has a full head of steam,' Meade said.

'No, you wouldn't,' Blackstone countered. 'You'd find her fascinating.'

And *I* find her fascinating, he thought. I find her *much more* than that.

But he was still not sure how to come to terms with the fact that she was actually in New York.

Ellie glanced down at the corpse's face and neck.

'*Was* it asphyxiation, Mr Jackson?' she asked.

'I . . . I don't know, ma'am.'

'Then take a closer look – and this time, please don't rush it.'

The student bent over the body, and examined it for a full two minutes.

'I'd like to look at the eyes if I may, ma'am,' he said.

'Be my guest,' Ellie replied.

Jackson pulled back the eyelids, and peered at the dead eyes.

'He died from occlusion of the blood vessels, leading to cerebral oedema followed by cerebral ischaemia,' he pronounced.

'And what leads you to that particular conclusion?'

'There's evidence of petechiae – little bloodmarks – on the face. And also in the eyes.'

'There you are, Mr Jackson, you see just how good you *can* be when you let your mind – rather than your mouth – do your thinking for you?' Ellie asked.

For a moment, Jackson was unsure whether to take it as an insult or a compliment.

'It's a compliment,' Ellie said, reading his mind.

'Thank you, ma'am.'

'Now I've been nice to you – and you're pleased with yourself – and it's time to move on,' Ellie said. 'What caused the occlusions that you've so correctly noted?'

'The rope,' Jackson said.

'You're doing it again,' Ellie warned. 'Never *assume* anything, Mr Jackson. Study the neck carefully.'

'Am I wrong, ma'am?'

'I don't know,' Ellie said, deliberately looking away from the cadaver. '*You* tell *me*.'

Jackson leant over the body again. 'The bruising is in the form of a continuous band, which is certainly consistent with the ligature marks common in most hangings,' he said carefully.

'Good,' Ellie said, continuing to stare into space.

'But . . .' Jackson said tentatively.

'But what?'

'When you look closely, you can see that the pattern isn't as regular as it might be. There are some slight protuberances in it. And there's some bruising which is not part of the pattern at all.'

Ellie swung round, abandoning all show of indifference.

'Show me!' she said.

Jackson pointed out the bruising.

'Check on his hyoid bone,' Ellie ordered.

Jackson placed two of his fingers on the cadaver's neck, just below the chin.

'Not like that!' Ellie snapped. 'You're not stroking a kitten, for Christ's sake – you're checking for damage.'

Applying more pressure, Jackson ran his fingers up and down the bone.

'I think it's broken,' he said.

Ellie did not *quite* push him out of the way, but she came pretty close to it, and, once she was in position, she ran her own fingers over the bone in the same way as Jackson had done – though with a great deal more assurance and expertise.

'I think you're right,' she said. 'I think it *is* broken. And what does that tell us, Mr Jackson?'

'It tells us that . . . that he didn't die from being hanged.'

'Try again,' Ellie said severely.

'It tells us that, although the hanging may have been what actually *killed* him, there'd been some manual strangulation *before* he was strung up.'

'And since it would have been impossible for him to strangle himself – and unlikely that he'd have been in any position to hang himself once he *had* been strangled by someone else – I think we can rule out suicide,' Ellie said. 'What we have here, gentlemen, is a murder victim.'

'*Are you sure that's what he said?*' Blackstone had demanded of the snitch, after the man had told him about Jake's boast in the saloon. '*That they had to kill* three *men?*'

'*I'm sure* – '*cos while he was speakin', he held up three fingers,*' the snitch had replied.

'I think we've just found out who Jake and Bob's third victim was,' Blackstone said to Meade.

'Yeah – ain't that a bitch,' Meade replied.

TWENTY-ONE

The first meal that Blackstone and Meade had ever eaten together had been at Delmonico's on Beaver Street. Alex had claimed at the time – and on matters New York, Alex was invariably right – that not only was it the oldest restaurant in the city, but that some of the marble pillars which supported the entrance had been especially shipped out from the ruins of the ancient Roman city of Pompeii.

It had been Alex who'd paid for the meal on that occasion – which was just as well, since Blackstone's salary would have been all but eaten up by the cover charge – and it was Alex who insisted on treating Blackstone and Ellie to another Delmonico's meal after the autopsy.

'I thought you were magnificent this afternoon, Dr Carr, and you should regard this meal as nothing more than a modest repayment for your having allowed me to watch you work,' he said smoothly, as they sipped their welcome cocktail.

'Gawd, love-a-duck, if that's why yer doin' it, then I'm 'ere under false pretences, 'cos I din't know nuffink bart yer being in the gallery,' Ellie replied, in her broadest cockney.

Meade looked mystified. 'I beg your pardon?' he said.

'She goes off like that sometimes,' Blackstone told him. 'Just ignore her.'

'No, really, I couldn't,' Alex Meade protested. 'If I've offended you in any way, Dr Carr . . .'

'You haven't offended me at all,' Ellie interrupted. 'But honestly, Alex – "Regard this meal as nothing more than a modest repayment for allowing me to watch you work"? You sounded like you'd just stepped out of the pages of a badly written novel – and I just couldn't resist taking the mickey.'

Meade smiled sheepishly. 'Actually, I sounded more as if I'd just stepped out of a New York high society gathering,' he said. 'I suppose I was trying to impress you.'

'You've no need to try,' Ellie responded. 'If you're good enough for Sam Blackstone – as you clearly are – then you're good enough for me.'

She fell into a sudden silence, the expression on her face saying she thought she'd said too much – that she'd inadvertently revealed more of herself than she might have wished to.

'I've been puzzling over Fanshawe's murder, and something about it doesn't quite add up,' Meade said, coming to the rescue with a change of subject.

'You're thinking of the timing,' Blackstone said.

'I am,' Meade agreed. 'If the kidnappers had always intended for him to die, then why didn't they tell Mad Bob and Snake to do it during the actual kidnapping itself? That would surely have been easier – and safer – than having them spirit Holt away and then come back – when the police had already arrived – to finish Fanshawe off.'

'And why did they try to make it look like suicide?' Blackstone added. 'They already had the blood of the two Pinkerton men on their hands – why not just slit his throat, too?'

Ellie laughed.

'What's so funny?' Meade asked.

'I assist half a dozen inspectors from the Yard nowadays,' Ellie said, 'and almost all the cases I've worked on have been so simple that an intelligent dormouse could have cracked them. A man murders his wife, one business partner kills another, and they leave behind them a trail of forensic evidence wide enough to drive a coach and four along. But somehow, when Sam's involved, it's never simple. He's like . . . he's like the iron filings of detective work, constantly being pulled towards the magnet of complexity.' She grinned. 'It's quite clever, that – I must remember it, so I can use it again. And next time, of course, it will be much more polished, so everyone will think I'm brilliant.'

'A lot of people *already* think you're brilliant – almost as many as think you can be real pain in the arse,' Blackstone said drily.

Ellie laughed again. 'You see, Alex,' she said. '*That's* how you should talk to a woman.' She stood up. 'And now, if you'll excuse me, I must follow a biological imperative.'

'What?' Meade asked.

'She needs to go the can,' Blackstone said, practising his American.

The two men watched Ellie cross the restaurant.

Then Meade said, 'Have you told her that you love her? Have you actually put it into words?'

'No,' Blackstone admitted. 'I haven't.'

'Well, I really think you should,' Meade advised.

The more she read of her husband's journal, the more Mary Turner grew to appreciate the wisdom of the Soldiers of God in shielding their womenfolk from the evils of the world.

It was clear to her now that things were much worse than she had ever imagined. Satan stalked the earth like a proud monarch, his pathway made up of the souls that the foolish and weak had thrown at his feet. Women relinquished their virtue as if it were of no consequence. Men rolled the dice with abandon, never realizing that they were gambling not for the money on the table but with their chances of life everlasting. And even the children, so it seemed from what Joseph had written, had lost their innocence before they had even had time to become fully aware that they possessed it.

She had started the journal at the beginning, and her progress had been slow. Even in the early stages, she had often found the need to break off and pray for strength, and now she had only to read a few lines before finding herself on her knees again.

She had reached the point at which Joseph had been assigned the night shift – the point at which he had abandoned his other work on Coney Island in order to save just one man.

'*We were told by Mr Fanshawe that he would be bringing a visitor to Mr Holt tomorrow night,*' she read. '*Cody, who has been working the night shift for over a year, sniggered, and when I asked him why, he would only say that I should wait and see for myself.*'

What horrors lay in store for her on the pages which followed, Mary wondered. And would the Lord grant her the strength to deal with them?

'*The visitor was wearing a long dress and a broad hat with a veil. There are women on Coney Island (respectable women) who dress in just such a manner, but this was not one of them. This was an abomination.*'

Mary read on, hardly able to believe the words – hardly able to accept that, even in a world awash with corruption, such wickedness could exist.

'*I have been to New York City and found the Devil's Lair,*' Joseph had written on the next page. '*It is a modern Sodom called the Blue Light Club, and it is on Canal Street in the Lower East Side. I stood outside, and watched as men – almost burning up with lust – entered the place. I wanted to enter it myself, and destroy it, as Christ destroyed the money changers' stalls in the Temple. But that is not the mission that the Lord has given me. He has entrusted the soul of William Holt to my hands, and soon – when the time is right – I will confront Mr Holt and tell him that there must be no more visitors from this Blue Light, and that if he will put his faith in the Lord our God he might still be saved.*'

Tears ran down Mary's cheeks, and now – only now – did she acknowledge that there had been times when she had doubted her husband.

And what a fool she had been!

How unworthy of him!

She must tell Inspector Blackstone what she had discovered, she thought, because – though she did not understand these things herself – it might perhaps help him with his investigation.

But even if it did *not* help the investigation, telling him would still serve God's purpose, because he would surely be as outraged as her husband had been about the Blue Light Club, and take immediate steps to close it. And Joseph, who had wanted to destroy the place himself, would look down from heaven, and smile.

Meade had watched in amazement as Ellie – skinny little Ellie – had demolished the largest steak that *he* had ever seen served at Delmonico's.

Now she pushed her plate away, rubbed her stomach, and said, 'So what's for pudding?'

'I recommend that you try the Chocolate Brownie,' Meade said. He stood up. 'The maître d' has been told to charge everything to my account, so now, if you'll excuse me . . .'

'You're leaving?' Blackstone asked.

'I have another appointment,' Meade replied, unconvincingly. 'It has been a delight to meet you, Dr Carr.'

'The name's Ellie,' Ellie said. 'If you call me Dr Carr again, I swear I'll save that Chocolate Brownie, so that the next time I meet you I can stuff it right up your Khyber.'

'Up my *what*?' Meade asked.

Blackstone smiled. 'Trust me, Alex, you really don't want to know.'

They shook hands, and Meade left.

'Did he really have another appointment?' Ellie asked.

'I suspect not,' Blackstone replied. 'I rather think he was just being tactful.'

'Leaving us alone, so we could talk?'

'Exactly.'

'So what shall we talk *about*?'

What indeed, Blackstone wondered. There was so much he wanted to say – and so much he thought he shouldn't.

'Why did you come to America?' he asked.

'Well, there's certainly no beating about the bush with you these days, is there?' Ellie countered.

'You didn't answer the question,' Blackstone pointed out.

'No,' Ellie agreed. 'I didn't, did I? What do you *want* me to say, Sam? That I came to America because of you?'

'That would be nice – but only if it's true.'

'I'd have been a fool *not to* jump at the chance of coming here,' Ellie said cautiously. 'I'm helping to create a new science.'

'I know.'

'I'm a woman with so many ideas – so many theories. And the Americans are *open* to them, in a way that most people I have to deal with in England are not.'

'I understand that.'

'And yet, when I was offered the opportunity, the first thing I thought about was you.'

'But you still didn't try to contact me, once you'd landed.'

Ellie shrugged awkwardly. 'What can I say? I got wrapped up in my work. That's the problem, Sam. We *both* get wrapped up in our work.'

'We could try not to,' Blackstone suggested. 'We could make a real effort to spend more time with each other and see where that leads.'

A patrolman appeared in the doorway, looked around, and then made a beeline for their table.

'Are you Inspector Blackstone?' he asked, tentatively.

'Yes.'

'I thought they were joking when they said I should look for a man dressed like a bum,' the patrolman mused. Then a look of horror came to his face. 'I'm sorry, sir. I didn't mean . . .'

'That's all right,' Blackstone assured him. 'What's that in your hand? A message for me?'

'Yes, sir. They said at the station that it was urgent.'

Blackstone slit open the envelope, and scanned the note inside.

'I'm sorry, but I have to go,' he said to Ellie.

'What's happened?'

'The kidnappers have contacted the Holts again. They want the ransom paid tomorrow morning, and I really need to talk it through with Alex.' He stood up. 'I really am sorry.'

Ellie smiled sadly up at him. 'No problem, Sam, you can't *help* getting wrapped up in your work,' she said.

TWENTY-TWO

Alex Meade's office in the Mulberry Street police headquarters did not feel like a big room even under normal circumstances, but that morning it seemed particularly crowded.

There were six people in the room, and though they gave each other the occasional glance, most of their attention was focused on the central character in the drama, which was sliding on Meade's desk.

So *that* was what half a million dollars looked like, Blackstone thought, as he watched the two police clerks note down the serial numbers of randomly selected bills. *That* was what had inspired five deaths so far – and might yet lead to even more bloodshed.

'Why is this taking so damn *long*?' demanded George Holt.

'Calm down, George,' said his brother, soothingly. 'It's a lot of money to process, and we're still well ahead of schedule.'

'Well ahead of schedule!' George Holt snorted. 'What the hell does that mean, for God's sake?'

'It means that even if there's heavy traffic, we should still be at the saloon in plenty of time.'

'And why did the bastards choose a saloon?' George asked. 'What kind of damn stupid place is that to hand over the money?'

'It doesn't matter *why* they chose it,' Harold said reasonably. 'They're the ones who are calling the shots, so all we can do is to obey their instructions.' He turned to Meade. 'And anyway, the money won't actually be handed over in the saloon, will it, Sergeant?'

'No,' Meade agreed. 'The saloon's just the starting point.'

'We're ready for the satchel now,' one of the clerks said.

Meade handed it to him.

The satchel looked expensive – and so it had been. But the most important thing about it was its colour, because whereas most satchels were dark brown, this one was made of a pale leather which was almost yellow.

The clerks began, slowly and methodically, to fill the satchel. Gradually the pile of bills on the desk decreased, until there were none left at all.

There was a fortune in that satchel now, Blackstone thought, and yet it still barely bulged.

Funny thing, money, he told himself.

10.45 a.m.

The Silver Spur Saloon was at the intersection of 8th Street and Broadway, and was doing great mid-morning business when the six patrolmen entered it.

The arrival of the policemen unsettled a few of the customers, but most just shrugged their shoulders as if to say, 'Hell, the cops gotta drink, just like everybody else.'

But the cops were not intending to drink. Instead, they fanned out, and then the one nearest to the bar counter produced his whistle and blew on it loudly.

'Everybody out!' he shouted.

'Hey, what is this, officer?' the barkeeper asked. 'It ain't like I'm not up to date with my *payments*.'

'You got my sympathy,' the patrolman told him – though he did not *sound* very sympathetic. 'Yeah, my heart really bleeds for yer – but yer gotta go anyway, 'cos this order comes from the top.'

'So next week, when you come round for your bribe, I can give you a bit less, on account o' this, can I?' the barman asked hopefully.

The patrolman smiled bleakly.

'Dream on,' he said.

Customers who'd almost finished their drinks before the police arrived had already allowed themselves to be shepherded out on to the sidewalk, while the ones who'd just ordered new ones attempted to drain their glasses even as the patrolmen hustled them towards the door.

'This ain't right,' the barkeeper complained, as he reached for his jacket from the peg behind the bar.

'So file a complaint,' the patrolman said, unhelpfully.

10.50 a.m.

When the two carriages pulled up at the Silver Spur, some of the displaced and disgruntled customers were still milling around outside. A few of these customers – the more observant ones – noted that sitting next to the driver of the lead carriage was a large policeman holding a large shotgun, but most were too busy complaining to each other that things had come to a pretty pass in New York City when you couldn't even buy a *dishonest* cop.

Blackstone and Meade emerged from the second coach, and only when they had taken up their positions next to the door of the first coach did that door open and Harold and George climb out.

Harold was holding the almost-yellow satchel tightly in his hand, and as he made his way to the door of the saloon, the two policemen and his brother formed a tight cordon around him.

'What ya got in the bag? A million dollars?' one of the customers on the sidewalk called after them.

'Not quite,' Blackstone said, as he ushered Harold into the saloon.

The four men entered the now empty Silver Spur.

George Holt looked around him. 'Why here?' he asked, for perhaps the fifth or sixth time.

'I don't know,' Blackstone replied, wishing the bloody man would just shut up.

'We might as well make ourselves comfortable while we wait,' Meade said, sitting down at a table near the door and gesturing to the others that they should join him.

The three men sat, and Harold placed the leather satchel in the centre of the table.

'They're not just going to walk in here and *ask* for the money, are they?' George asked.

Don't you ever listen, you big oaf? Blackstone wondered silently. No, they're not going to just walk in and ask for the money – because they'd have to be as stupid as you are not to realize that the guy inspecting apples at the store across the street, and the other one leaning against the wall and reading his newspaper, are detectives!

'As Alex has already explained, this is just the starting point for the exchange,' he said, in as reasoned and measured a tone as he could muster. 'You've noticed the phone over by the counter, haven't you?'

'Well, no, I haven't actually,' George admitted.

Of course he hadn't!

'The fact that it has a phone is probably the main reason the kidnappers chose this place,' Blackstone explained. 'And, when they're ready, they'll ring and give us fresh instructions.'

'We've issued descriptions of the satchel to every officer involved in the operation,' Meade said. 'Once you've handed it over, Harold, the guy who's taken it from you will be a marked man.'

And it was the fact that he *would* be a marked man which was bothering Blackstone. The kidnappers should have specified that the money be carried in a *nondescript* bag, but they had said nothing at all on the subject – and he wished he knew why.

10.55 a.m.

They had been sitting there in uneasy silence for almost three minutes, when George, who had been looking troubled for some time, said, 'Why don't you let me deliver the ransom, little brother?'

He spoke casually, as if, since it didn't really matter which of them did it, it might as well be him – but there was no disguising the pleading tone which underlined the words.

'Well?' he asked, when Harold made no reply. 'What do you think? They won't care who makes them rich, will they?'

'They asked for *me*,' Harold said, looking pale and nervous – but also very determined. 'You know they did. They turned you down, and they asked for me.'

'But you could get hurt,' George whined.

'So could you.'

'I'm much stronger than you are.' George appealed to Blackstone. 'You tell him that it's better if I do it.'

'Harold's right,' Blackstone said. 'Only he will do. And why *should* they hurt him? He's nothing more than a delivery boy.'

'They'll hurt him because they hate the Holts,' George said.

'How do you know?'

'I can feel it – and if Harold won't let me deliver the ransom, then I want to call the whole thing off.'

'And let Father die?' Harold asked.

George put his hand on his brother's shoulder.

'The chances are that they'll kill Father whatever we do,' he said gently.

'We'll have the satchel in our sights for nearly the whole time,' Meade assured, 'so if it's losing the money that's worrying you—'

'The money!' George said, in a voice that was almost a scream. 'Is that what you think I'm worried about – *the damned money*?'

'It would be only natural for you to be concerned . . .' Meade began, but it was clear that he realized he'd made a big mistake.

George took hold of the satchel, and slid it across the table, so it was almost in Meade's lap.

'Here's the money!' he said. '*You* take it! Give it to charity! Or keep it for yourself! I don't care! Because it doesn't *matter*! All I'm worried about is my little brother!'

Meade looked mortified. 'I'm sorry,' he said, in a subdued voice. 'I should never even have suggested that it was your main concern.'

'Damn straight you shouldn't, you bastard!' George agreed.

'Stop it!' Blackstone ordered. 'This is the time when we all need to be working together, not tearing each other apart!'

'He's right,' Harold told his brother. 'It's pointless to argue, George, because whatever you or anyone else says, *I am* the one who's going to deliver the money.'

11.02 a.m.

Even though they should have been expecting it, the metallic shriek of the phone on the bar made all four men jump.

George recovered first, and was almost on his feet when Alex Meade put a restraining hand on his shoulder, then went over to the bar himself.

Meade unhooked the earpiece and said, 'Yes?'

'Harold Holt?' asked a thick, heavily disguised voice at the other end of the line.

'Yes.'

'No, it ain't,' the voice snarled. 'Get me Holt right now – or the whole deal's off, and his father's dead.'

Meade gestured to Harold to join him, and handed him the earpiece.

'Yes?' Harold said, with a slight tremble in his voice. 'Yes, this *is* Harold James Holt . . . You want me to do *what*? . . . I'm not sure I can get there in . . . All right, I'll try . . . No, I won't tell them, but you must promise not to . . .'

He hung up the phone, and looked at the others.

'I have to go,' he said, walking across to the table and picking up the satchel.

'Go where?' George demanded.

'I can't tell you.'

George stood up, and grabbed the satchel from his brother's hands. 'If you don't tell me, I'm not going to let you go.'

'Please, George—'

'Tell me!'

'Make him give me the satchel,' Harold begged Blackstone.

'Your brother's right – we need to know where you're going,' Blackstone said firmly.

'They . . . they want me to go to S.J. Moore's. They say I'll get
fresh instructions there.'

'What the hell is S.J. Moore's?' Blackstone demanded.

'It's a big dry goods store, further down Broadway,' Meade
explained.

'He's only given me five minutes to get there, so, for God's sake,
give me the satchel, George!' Harold said.

George, finally, looked to Blackstone for guidance.

'How will you be given these new instructions?' Blackstone asked
Harold.

'I don't know!' Harold replied, on the verge of hysteria. 'They
didn't say! *Please* give me the satchel!'

Blackstone nodded, and George gave his brother the bag. The
moment he had it in his hands again, Harold turned and headed for
the door.

'You know the plan,' Blackstone said to Meade. 'Stick to it as
closely as you can.'

11.04 a.m.

When the Brush Electric Light Company had begun installing arc
lights on Broadway in late 1880, New Yorkers, watching the process
as they strolled by, had not been unduly impressed.

Sure, arc lights were a dandy idea, and the more the better, they
thought. But the lights had already lost some of the novelty value
they'd had only a couple of years earlier.

What these citizens were being kept in the dark about (so to speak)
was how much more ambitious this project was than any that had
gone before it, and what effect the arc lights – mounted on twenty-
foot-tall ornamental cast iron posts, and located on every block –
would have once they were switched on.

Then, on the 20th of December, they could see for themselves.
The work was completed, the lamps were switched on, and the whole
boulevard was bathed in a brilliant white light. It was a magical
moment. Broadway, they realized, would never be *just* Broadway
again – from now on, it was the *Great White Way*.

But the Great White Way only existed at night, and the Broadway
that Blackstone was rapidly walking down – on the trail of Harold
Holt – could have been any other wide New York City thoroughfare,
bustling with streetcars and carriages, shoppers and workmen.

Blackstone looked over his shoulder, and saw that both the detective who had been buying apples and the one who'd been reading a newspaper were close behind him.

The kidnappers' plan couldn't be as simple as it seemed at that moment, he told himself.

They must know that Broadway – and the streets which crossed it – were saturated with cops, and that the moment the switch had taken place, those same cops would close the whole area down.

So it *couldn't* be just a switch. There *had to* be some refinement to the plan. And he hadn't an idea in hell what that refinement might be.

11.07 a m

Harold Holt had reached 10th Street, where Broadway dog-legged, and Blackstone got his first real look at S.J. Moore's Dry Goods Store.

'Jesus!' he said.

He'd expected it to be big, but not the monster which was confronting him now.

Moore's frontage ran for a whole block, and the top of the building towered seven floors above the street. A non-stop line of people was entering through one of its large front doors, and a second line was leaving through another.

There were no uniformed cops in sight, but there were dozens of them close by, and if Alex Meade did his job properly – and he would – Moore's would be completely surrounded in another three minutes.

But that wouldn't do any good, would it – not if Harold Holt and the kidnappers were somewhere else entirely in three minutes' time?

Harold came to a stop in front of the store, and glanced around, as if wondering what to do next.

A ragged boy of seven or eight sidled up to him, and pulled at the edge of his jacket. When Holt looked down, the boy handed him a piece of paper and then rapidly merged into the crowd.

Blackstone signalled to the apple-buying detective to follow the boy, but even as he was doing so, he knew it would be a waste of time, because the urchin had already vanished.

Harold joined the line of people entering the building.

There had to be more instructions waiting for him inside, Blackstone thought, because it simply wasn't possible that the kidnappers would take the bait when they *must* know that the trap was already closing around them.

And yet, despite what his brain was telling him, his instinct was screaming that this was it, and that in a couple of minutes, it would all be over.

With a growing sense of foreboding, he followed Harold into the store.

TWENTY-THREE

E scalators were still a recent enough invention to be regarded
as a dangerous novelty by many shoppers. When they had been
installed in Harrods' store in London, some customers had
been so unnerved by the experience of using them that the management had had to ensure that staff were always on hand with smelling
salts and glasses of cognac. And even in S.J. Moore's – in modern,
go ahead New York City – the men and women mounting the esca
lator did not seem to be entirely at ease.

Getting on the escalator did not appear to worry Harold Holt,
Blackstone observed.

It didn't worry *him*, either, but what *was* causing him concern was
the fact that the note Holt had been handed must have instructed him
to go *upstairs*.

Going upstairs didn't make any sense at all. What the kidnappers
needed, once they had the money in their hands, was a clear escape
route. The last thing they *should have* wanted was to be three or four
floors in the air, well away from the exit.

No need to panic, they're just sending Harold up there to get more
instructions, Blackstone's brain told him.

Two minutes from now, the money will be gone, his instinct
predicted confidently.

There were perhaps fifteen steps between the two of them when
Blackstone mounted the escalator, but by the time Holt had reached
the top – Haberdashery, Silks, Bonnets and Cloaks – the policeman
had narrowed the gap to five steps.

And that was just about right, Blackstone thought, because he was
close enough to keep Holt in view when he reached the top, yet not
so close that it was obvious he was following the man.

Holt got off the escalator, and immediately mounted the one travelling up to the next floor.

Just how bloody high were they going?

Say his instinct – rather than his brain – was right, Blackstone
argued. Say the kidnappers were planning to take the money from
Harold in this store. How, then, did they plan to get away? By making
some kind of daring high wire escape from one of the windows?

At the second floor, Holt got the escalator to the third. On the third he mounted the escalator to the fourth – the fur coat department.

There were no more sales floors beyond the fourth. This would be where the journey ended.

Since there was no longer any need to stay so close, Blackstone allowed himself to drop back a little, and by the time he mounted this final escalator himself, Holt had almost reached the top.

This *was* where the exchange would take place – he was convinced of that now.

But it still didn't make sense!

He was two-thirds of the way up the escalator when the screaming began.

'Fire!'

'It's on fire! Oh, sweet Jesus, the whole place is *on fire!*'

'We're all going to die!'

The people on the fourth floor rushed madly towards the down escalator, elbowing each other aside in their effort to escape. The first few made it without incident, and rushed down the steps to the safety of the floor below. Then – inevitably – one man lost his footing. He fell, and the woman behind him fell *over him*, and soon bodies were bouncing down the escalator like snowballs down an icy slope.

Only seconds had passed since the first alarm had been raised, but already pandemonium ruled.

The falling people tried to stop themselves by jamming their hands and legs against the sides of the escalator. Sometimes they succeeded. But now they presented an obstruction both to the further falling bodies – which slammed into them – and to the more nimble of foot – who tried to kick them out of the way.

The noise swelled with the panic. There was screaming and cursing and sobbing and praying.

'Please let me through – I have three little children waiting for me at home.'

'Help me save my baby! For the love of God, won't somebody help me save my baby?'

The customers who had been on the fourth floor were not the *only* ones trying to escape. Those who had been on the up escalator when the fire started had turned around, and were attempting to fight against the movement of the escalator and return to the safety of the floor below. And to make matters even worse, the down escalator was now so jammed with bodies that some of the fourth-floor customers had turned to the up escalator as their means of salvation.

Blackstone struggled against the tide, trying to force his way up to the fourth floor – but it was an impossible task. The sheer collective weight of the people coming down slammed into him, knocking him off his feet – and he became no more than a part of the tumbling mass of humanity which gravity was rapidly propelling back to the floor below.

When he landed, it was on the bodies of those who had fallen before him, and even before he had time to raise his arms in order to protect himself, more of the human avalanche was piling on top of him.

'Keep calm!' Blackstone told the man he had landed on – and the man who had landed on *him*, and the people who were sandwiching him in from both sides. 'Keep calm! You'll do less damage that way.'

But he might as well as saved what little breath he had left, because within the mound – within this Chinese puzzle of flesh and bone – there was already movement. Trunks squirmed and twisted, legs kicked, and hands clawed, as people tried to pull themselves clear.

Gradually, the situation eased. Gradually, some of the fallen freed themselves from this horrendous mêlée, and some were assisted by shop assistants and other customers.

Once he was clear of the mound himself, Blackstone conducted a rapid assessment of damages.

His head ached. His cheek – after an unwelcome encounter with someone else's boot – was throbbing furiously, and a knee smashing into the small of his back had not helped matters either.

But there was nothing seriously wrong.

Nothing to prevent him from seeing – right through to the bitter bloody end – what had turned out to be a disastrous operation.

He looked up at the escalator. A few remaining refugees from the fourth floor were still trickling down it – but Harold Holt was not one of them.

Of course he wasn't one of them, Blackstone told himself. Harold was still upstairs – being robbed of his money and possibly his life!

The air on the fourth floor was thick with smoke, but through it Blackstone could still see several assistants who were standing in one corner, holding fire extinguishers in their hands.

He turned, and scanned the rest of the floor. He already knew what he was expecting to find, he thought despondently – he just had no idea, for the moment, where he would find it.

The counters, behind which the assistants normally stood, were too much in the open to have been used. The mannequin displays –

set up eye-catchingly in the middle of the room – offered nothing like the amount of cover that would have been needed. But the several racks of bargain fur coats – bunched together at the far corner of the floor, almost as if the management were ashamed to be even selling them – would have proved ideal.

Hoping that he was wrong – and *knowing* that he was right – Blackstone dashed across the floor to the racks. As he drew level with them, he heard the sound of a man groaning, and recognized the voice as Harold Holt's.

Holt was lying on the floor, between two racks of coats. There was blood on his face and his hands, but he did not have the appearance of a man who had been *seriously* injured.

He looked up, and recognized Blackstone.

'Where were you?' he asked.

I was downstairs, Blackstone thought angrily. I was bloody well downstairs – letting the kidnappers run rings round me.

He let his gaze move from Holt to the distinctive leather satchel which lay a couple of feet from him. It was open and – of course – it was empty.

The patrolmen who'd originally converged on Moore's to catch a kidnapper were now fully employed in holding back the ever-swelling crowd. The fire brigade had arrived, though there was little for it to do, and a dozen horse-drawn ambulances stood at the Broadway entrance of the store, while two dozen stretcher-bearers ferried the worst of the injured from the building to the waiting vehicles.

It was a mess, Blackstone thought, looking out of the window at what was happening in the street. It was a *huge* bloody mess!

He turned to the pale-looking man with the bandaged head, who was sitting on the chair next to him.

'What can you remember, Harold?' he asked.

'You shouldn't be questioning him now – not in his condition,' George Holt protested.

'It's . . . it's all right,' Harold said weakly. 'What I got was little more than a scratch. I was lucky, in comparison to most people.'

'Even so—' George began.

'I *want* to help,' Harold interrupted him.

George sighed. 'Go ahead,' he said, resignedly.

'When I got to the fourth floor, I didn't know what was supposed to happen next, so I started to walk towards the window. I think I must have been about midway between the escalator and the window when the screaming started.'

'What did you do then?' Blackstone asked.

'I panicked, along with everyone else,' Harold said. 'Isn't that shameful? I forgot all about Father and the ransom, and all I wanted to do was get out of there as quickly as possible.'

'So you turned back to the escalator?'

'I would have done – if they hadn't grabbed me.'

'How many of them were there?'

'I know for certain that there were two – but there may have been more. One of them pinned my hands behind my back, and another forced my head forward, so all I could see was the floor. Then they half-pushed me, half-dragged me towards the racks of fur coats, and once we were there, one of them must have hit me over the head – because that's when I blacked out.'

And while he was unconscious, the kidnappers transferred the ransom money from the leather satchel to whatever they'd brought with them to carry it away in, Blackstone thought.

'Can you describe the men?' he asked.

'Not really. It all happened so quickly. They were both bigger than me – though that's not saying much – and one of them had a beard, but it didn't feel like a *real* one, if you know what I mean.'

'Can I take my brother home?' George asked.

'Yes,' Blackstone said wearily. 'Why not?'

'What will happen to Father now?' Harold asked. 'Will they release him?'

'It's a possibility,' Blackstone lied.

'It's a funny thing, you know, but there have been times when I *did* wish Father dead,' Harold said quietly. 'But not now. Now I know there's a chance he might never come back again, all I feel is a great emptiness inside.'

TWENTY-FOUR

The beer was ice-cold, and as it washed away the smoke which had coated his throat, Blackstone began to feel better – but not much.

'Tell me about the fire,' he said to Alex Meade.

'It started near the stairs,' Meade replied.

'There were stairs!' Blackstone exploded. 'I never saw any bloody stairs!'

'No, you wouldn't have. All the exit doors leading to the stair wells were covered with thick curtains. In fact, it seems to have been those curtains which caught fire first.'

'There were *curtains* over the *exit doors*?' Blackstone asked incredulously. 'Why, for God's sake?'

'They were there to hide the fact that there *was* an exit door.'

'That's insane!'

'Not from the store's point of view,' Meade said. 'This is a city that worships the new and exciting. Moore's – and all the other big stores – *loves* publicity. It wanted its customers to ride the escalator, because it was an experience they'd tell their friends about – and then *the friends* would come to Moore's, to try it out for themselves. See what I'm getting at, Sam? Nobody ever bothers to tell their friends they've *walked* upstairs.'

'So the incendiary devices were probably placed between the curtains and the doors,' Blackstone said.

'That's what the evidence suggests.'

'And did the devices have timers?'

'The fire department isn't willing to say *definitely* that they did – but that's the way its thoughts are going.'

There would have been timers, Blackstone thought. And if the fire in Arthur Rudge's apartment – seven years earlier – had also been caused by incendiary devices, then there'd probably have been timers on them too, because the fire hadn't started until half an hour after the men carrying the armoire had left.

'We've been outclassed and out-thought all the way,' he said gloomily. 'When the kidnappers told Harold that he only had five minutes to get to the store, we thought that was because they didn't want to give us time to get organized. Wrong! They limited it to five minutes because they'd already set the clock – and wanted him there just as the devices went off.'

'Yes, I suppose that *was* smart,' Meade conceded, 'but just because they made *one* smart move, it doesn't mean that they're criminal masterminds who will always be able to—'

'And starting the fire by the stairs was brilliant too,' Blackstone interrupted. 'If it had started *anywhere else*, the staff would have told some of the people on the fourth floor to use those stairs as their means of escape.'

'There'd still have been a panic,' Meade pointed out.

'Yes, there would – but nowhere near as much as there was when the customers realized that the escalator was the *only* way out for them. Do you think that just *happened*? Or is it more likely that it was all part of the kidnappers' calculation?'

'They probably calculated it,' Meade admitted reluctantly.

'And then there's the leather satchel,' Blackstone continued.

'What about it?'

'It always bothered me that they didn't specify what kind of bag Harold carry the money in. And *why* didn't they specify it?'

'I don't know.'

'They'd figured out that if they left it to us, we'd buy the most conspicuous bag we could. That was exactly what they *wanted* us to do – and we fell for it!'

'We told our men to look out for a yellow satchel!' Meade exclaimed, getting the point. 'We made it *central* to identifying the kidnappers.'

'Every cop was focusing on that satchel – which meant they weren't looking so closely at *other things*.'

'You're right, we were outclassed,' Meade said miserably.

'And do you know what the real irony of the whole fiasco is?' Blackstone asked. 'I probably saw the kidnappers!'

'You probably *saw* them!'

'That's right – because I saw nearly everybody who came down the escalator. But there were at least two hundred people, and maybe half of them were men, so I've no idea which of them it could be.'

Meade went to the bar, and when he returned he was holding a tray with two beers and two whiskies on it.

'What's this?' Blackstone asked, looking down at the shot glasses. 'Is it a reward for figuring everything out just half an hour too late, or is it an attempt to cheer me up?'

'It's neither of those things,' Meade told him. 'It's more like an attempt to fortify you.'

'And why would I need fortifying?'

'Because Commissioner Comstock asked if we could see him half an hour from now – except that it wasn't really a request.'

'Is that right?' Blackstone asked, picking up the shot glass and swallowing the fiery liquid in a single gulp.

The first time Blackstone had met Commissioner Comstock, the commissioner had shaken his hand warmly and invited him to sit down – two things which would never have happened to the inspector in New Scotland Yard. It had struck him at that time that Comstock was a decent, well-meaning man who wanted to do the right thing – but would have been much more at home on a small university campus than he could ever be in a large police department.

This meeting was entirely different. Comstock did not ask Blackstone and Meade to sit down, but instead gestured that they should stand in front of his desk. Nor did he have the look of a slightly bemused academic any more. Now, the expression on his face was strained, and his eyes were those of a wild animal which had suddenly found itself trapped in a corner.

'When you solved the O'Brien case, do you know what I thought?' he asked Blackstone.

'No, sir.'

'I thought, "Here is a man who really understands police work. Here is a man who could teach us a great deal." But I was wrong, wasn't I? It wasn't brilliant detective work which led you to solve that case – it was pure dumb luck.'

'With respect, sir, I hardly think you're being fair,' Meade said.

'Shut up, Sergeant!' the commissioner shouted. 'You'll have your say when it's *your* turn to be hauled over the coals!'

'I guess I will,' Meade agreed.

Comstock turned his attention back to Blackstone. 'So when the next important case came up, I immediately thought, "Let's give it to the 'expert' from Scotland Yard." But that was a mistake, wasn't it?'

None of this is about me, Blackstone told himself. It's all about him.

Comstock knew that the only way he was going to survive this particular debacle was by getting someone else to take the fall, he thought. But the commissioner knew, too – deep inside himself – that what he was about to do to his English guest was both dishonest and dishonourable. So, like all *decent* men who also happened to be *weak*, he was attempting to cajole his victim into saying that what he was doing was *right*.

'I said it was a mistake, wasn't it?' the commissioner repeated.

'We did all we could,' Blackstone said. 'We did all that *any two policemen* in our situation could have done.'

But did we? he found himself wondering.

Perhaps another copper would have realized the significance of the leather satchel before he had.

Perhaps another copper would have realized that what he was being led into was a trap.

'Do you know how many policemen I assigned to this case?' the commissioner asked.

'Over one hundred.' Blackstone guessed.

'Over a hundred,' the commissioner agreed. 'I personally removed them from their normal duties – I let crime run rampant through this city – so you could have the manpower you needed.'

If most New York cops had seen it as part of their duties to combat crime, the commissioner might have had a point, Blackstone thought, but since they were mainly concerned with feathering their own nests, it was unlikely that taking them off the streets had made any difference at all to the crime figures.

Not that any of that mattered a jot. This was a classic mud-throwing exercise, and only *some of it* had to stick.

'Over one hundred and fifty people were injured in Moore's, some of them quite seriously,' Comstock continued. 'What have you got to say about *that*, Inspector Blackstone?'

Blackstone shrugged. 'I didn't start the fire, sir. That was the kidnappers' work.'

But *could he* have foreseen it, he wondered. *Should he* have foreseen it?

Of course not!

So why did he still feel guilty?

'The kidnappers did start the fire, it is true, but it happened on *your* watch,' Comstock pointed out.

Ah yes, that was it – it happened on his watch.

'Although the New York Police Department is temporarily paying your salary, I have no real jurisdiction over you, Inspector Blackstone,' Comstock said. 'And that being the case, I have cabled all the details of what has happened to Assistant Commissioner Todd in New Scotland Yard, and will leave it to him to decide what disciplinary action should be taken.'

'Pontius Pilate himself couldn't have said it better,' Blackstone told him.

'Would you care to repeat that, Inspector?' Comstock asked.

'Not really, sir,' Blackstone said. 'There doesn't seem to be much point, when you so obviously heard me clearly the first time.'

'I will not tolerate—' Comstock began. And then he stopped himself, because he had realized that he *would* tolerate it – realized that being angry at Blackstone made his task a lot easier.

The commissioner turned to Meade. 'Have you anything to say for yourself, Sergeant?'

'Yes, sir, I have,' Meade replied. 'Wouldn't it save us all a lot of time if, instead of going through all this rigmarole that none of us is taking seriously, you just suspended me right now?'

'Suspend you?' the commissioner repeated. 'I have no intention of *suspending you*, Sergeant – at least for the moment.'

Of course he hadn't, Blackstone thought. It wouldn't be good politics to suspend Meade then. It would be far better to wait – until they found out *exactly* what had happened to William Holt.

TWENTY-FIVE

Under normal circumstances, Blackstone would have enjoyed eating in the little restaurant on the corner of 9th Street. He would have enjoyed it because the food was good and the staff were friendly – and because the place had no pretension of its own, and expected its customers to leave any pretensions *they* might have behind them in the cloakroom. But most of all, he would have enjoyed it because he was dining there with Ellie Carr.

Yet tonight, even Ellie's presence was failing to work its magic, and the food might just as easily have been fried sawdust for all he noticed it.

'Alex and I always knew that we'd been given this investigation simply because we'd be convenient scapegoats if anything went wrong,' he said, 'but I never thought that if it *did* go wrong, they'd try to *crucify* us.'

'He hasn't actually taken you *off* the investigation yet,' Ellie pointed out.

'No, he hasn't,' Blackstone agreed. 'But in my case, he's only waiting for a cable from Assistant Commissioner Todd, who, as you know, is not a great admirer of mine.'

'And in Alex's case?'

'When William Holt's body turns up, the newspapers will go to town on it – because he was an important man, and you're not supposed to get away with killing important men. Whoever's in charge of the investigation at that point will be for the chop, whether or not they're culpable. And since Alex *is* culpable—'

'You're not being fair on him,' Ellie interrupted.

'He made mistakes,' Blackstone said firmly. 'Not as many as me, but enough. So, since he's already doomed, it makes sense to leave him in his post for a while longer.'

'There's no question that when William Holt turns up he *will* be dead, is there?' Ellie asked.

'None at all,' Blackstone replied. 'The kidnappers are already responsible for the deaths of at least four people, and if they're ever caught, they'll go to the electric chair whatever happens. So why run the risk of letting Holt live, even if there's only the vaguest possibility that he might be able to give the police a lead?'

'What if they *were* caught?' Ellie wondered. 'And what if you and Alex were the ones who caught them? Would it make a difference?'

'It might,' Blackstone said. 'But to catch them, we need a trail to follow – and the trail ends in S.J. Moore's.'

'If you've lost the end of the trail, why not go back to the beginning?' Ellie suggested.

'The beginning?'

'You're convinced that whoever kidnapped Holt also murdered Rudge, seven years ago, aren't you?'

'Yes,' Blackstone agreed, 'I am.'

'So why not take another look at Rudge's murder, and see where it leads you?'

'That trail's so cold you could skate along it,' Blackstone told her.

'Maybe not,' Ellie countered. 'The dead still have their story to tell – especially to someone like me.'

'I appreciate you trying to help me—' Blackstone began.

'And so you should,' Ellie interrupted, 'because where would the great Sam Blackstone be without the great Ellie Carr somewhere behind him?'

Blackstone grinned. 'Nowhere at all,' he admitted. He took a sip of his wine. 'Let's change the subject. How's *your* work going?'

'Fine,' Ellie said, sounding uncharacteristically evasive.

'Fine?' Blackstone repeated.

Ellie hesitated before speaking again. 'I've got some *good* news,' she said finally. 'Good news for me, I mean. But I'm not sure you'll want to hear it at the moment.'

'*Why* wouldn't I?' Blackstone asked. 'It'd be quite reassuring to hear that there are at least *some* people in the world who don't have their bollocks resting on the edge of the guillotine.'

Ellie laughed. 'What an absolutely *charming* image.'

'So what's the good news?' Blackstone persisted.

'I've been offered a lecture tour of America. It would involve lecturing at nearly every prestigious medical school in the country.'

Blackstone smiled. 'I'm proud of you.'

'And you could come with me,' Ellie said. She reached across the table and took his hand. 'We could discover America together.'

'I'm not sure that would work,' Blackstone told her, pulling away.

'Why not? You're finished as far as the New York Police Department is concerned, aren't you?

'I'm as dead as a doornail. I'm probably finished with Scotland Yard, as well.'

'So there's nothing to keep you in New York.'

'Not a thing.'

'Which means that's there's also nothing to prevent you from coming with me.'

'And what would I do on this lecture tour of yours?'

'Do?'

'I'm not the kind of man who can convince himself that he's paying his way just by carrying your bag now and again.'

'The Yanks have offered me a small fortune, so there's absolutely no need to pay your way,' Ellie said.

He had grown up an orphan, Blackstone reminded himself. Many of the boys he had known back then had become criminals and had died in their early twenties – and he could easily have become one of them. But he hadn't. Instead, he'd joined the army and fought his way through the ranks to sergeant. Then he'd started at the bottom again, and – against all odds – become a police inspector. He had achieved something in his life. Not much, maybe, but he *had* achieved it.

'I said there's absolutely no need for you to pay your own way,' Ellie repeated.

'I can't do it,' Blackstone told her sadly. 'Shall we get the bill?'

They summoned the waiter, and when the bill came, Ellie opened her purse to pay it.

'I'll get this,' Blackstone said, putting the last money he had in the whole world down on the plate.

'Are you sure?' Ellie asked.

'I'm sure.'

'We could always split it.'

'I said I'm sure.'

Ellie sighed. 'If that's what you want. But can I ask you one more thing before we leave?'

'Of course.'

'Up until now, we couldn't be together as much as we wanted to be because we both had demanding jobs. That's right, isn't it?'

'Yes, it is.'

'But now we can't be together because you probably have *no job at all*. Does that about sum it up?'

'Perfectly,' Blackstone agreed. He shook his head slowly. 'Funny old thing, life, don't you think?'

As he walked along the deserted dock, he found his mind drifting back – almost inevitably – to a night which seemed like a lifetime ago, though he was prepared to accept that it had been little more than three years.

He had been walking along the Albert Embankment, listening to the river lap against the shore, just as he now listened to the ocean lap against the pier. He had been thinking of Hannah, his first true love, who, hours earlier, had been willing to sacrifice him for the cause she had followed all her life – and only minutes later, had been dead herself.

He had come to a halt, and looked down at the river – and at the lights of the ships anchored midway between the two shores. And he had been tempted, at that moment, to walk down the nearest set of steps which led to the river, and to keep on walking.

Until he had drowned.

Until he had made himself at one with the heart of the city he loved.

It had been the intervention of Vladimir – the Tsarist agent who killed Hannah – which had saved his life.

'But who'll save my life tonight?' he wondered aloud.

His own words surprised him, because he did not think, up until that point, that he had been even contemplating killing himself.

Yet the more he thought about it, the more he was surprised that he *had* been surprised.

He was a man without a career – or soon would be. And that made him a man who was already living in the shadow of the workhouse, where a man ceased to be a man at all, and became nothing more than a creature which ate when it was told to, slept when it was told to, and probably even shat when it was told to.

It didn't have to be that way, of course.

He could carve out a new life for himself – but it would never be the life he'd had.

He could become Ellie's pet – a kept man – but though he knew she would never remind him of that, he was sure that he would not be able to forget it himself for a moment.

It occurred to him that he had been courting death his entire life, but always – at the last second – had chosen to fight back.

Well, maybe this time he wouldn't.

Maybe this time he would give in gracefully.

'I want your money!' said a voice from the darkness.

'I haven't got any money, son,' he said. 'If I had, you'd be more than welcome to it – but I haven't.'

The man stepped out of the shadows. He was in his early twenties, and had a pock-marked face and hard, cruel eyes. There was a knife in his hands.

'You're lying,' he said.

'No, I'm not,' Blackstone replied. 'I'm telling you the truth, and you know I am.'

'But I've been following you for over half an hour,' the man complained.

'Then you've been wasting your time,' Blackstone told him. 'But it's not my fault you don't know how to pick your victims properly.'

The man's lip curled in an ugly gesture of rage. 'I think I'll stick you anyway,' he decided.

'I wouldn't try that, if I was you,' Blackstone advised.

'Oh, you wouldn't, wouldn't you? An' why not?'

'Because if you do, I'll make sure you'll never be able to threaten anybody with a knife again.'

'Big words!' the man scoffed. 'Let's see if you're still so cocky when you've got a blade stickin' in your gut.'

He lunged forward, the knife aimed at Blackstone's stomach.

But Blackstone, reading the signals from the other man's body, knew it was not the right hand, holding the knife, which was the danger – that the real threat was the left hand, with which his assailant would attempt to grab him by the neck, or by the shoulder, and pull him on to the blade.

He swung around, out of the path of the knife, and grabbed his attacker's left arm with his right hand, while his left fist smashed into the other man's chin with an uppercut. The assailant's head rocked backwards, but he kept his grip on the knife until Blackstone followed through with a rabbit punch to his Adam's apple.

The man hit the ground, gasping for breath, yet hardly aware of where he was. Blackstone stamped down on his right hand with the heel of his boot, and then ground until he could feel the bones breaking.

'I did warn you what I'd do,' he said.

He turned and walked away.

You chose to fight back again, didn't you? asked a voice in his head.

Yes, I do appear to have done, Blackstone agreed.

TWENTY-SIX

The sun had been up for less than an hour when Timmy Tyler and his dog, Skipper, entered the woods that surrounded Ocean Heights. To Timmy, the woods were a magical place, where he could give free rein to all the adventures which were constantly playing in his head, without any grown-ups around to tell him he was being stupid. And since he'd had Skipper, it had been even better. The big black Labrador loved to run and chase and hide, and if he had any objections to being cast in the role of grizzly bear or wild stallion in one of Timmy's stories, then he certainly didn't show it.

That early morning, they had not been in the woods long when Skipper came to a sudden halt in a small clearing, and began to growl at the ground.

'Come on, Skip!' Timmy urged him, dashing between the trees in the direction of home.

But turning around, he saw that, though the dog should have been at his heel, it was still in the clearing.

Timmy walked back to the animal.

'Look what I've got, Skip,' he said, holding up a twig he had broken off on the way.

Timmy knew what should happen next. The stick should become the centre of the Labrador's whole world. He should focus on it with excited eyes, while tensing his muscles so that when Timmy threw it, he could be off after it like a shot.

The dog showed no interest.

'Stick!' Timmy said, in case, for some reason, the dog had failed to recognize this particular piece of wood for what it was.

He feigned throwing the stick, an action which would usually heighten the dog's excitement, but that had no effect, and when he finally released it, Skipper could not have cared less.

'What's the matter with you, Skipper, boy?' Timmy asked. 'Are you feeling ill?'

The dog barked vigorously, which his owner took to indicate that this was one of stupidest questions he had ever heard.

'Then if it's not *that*, I honestly don't know what it is,' the boy confessed helplessly.

The dog looked quizzical for a moment, then – apparently deciding keep to the point. Sometimes she spoke with the voice which imitated an evangelic preacher's. At others she would suddenly transform herself into the poor lonely widow she actually was. But sandwiched between the righteous fire of indignation and the tragic expression of loss there were words which – to an investigator – were pure gold.

When Blackstone hung up the phone, there was a smile on his face. He could never remember a case in which one piece of information had made so much difference – in which one single fact could change the whole way he looked at the investigation and provided him with the answers he had been so desperately searching for.

He thought about Inspector Flynn and his theory.

Flynn had said that the kidnapping had been faked – and he had been quite right.

Flynn had said that the *reason* it had needed to be faked was that William Holt was about to be subpoenaed to appear before a grand jury – and he had been quite right about that, too.

There was just one thing that Flynn had been wrong about. But it was a *huge* thing – a *gigantic* thing!

The office door opened, and Alex Meade entered. His shoulders were slumped and he looked utterly defeated.

'A body's been discovered in the woods near Ocean Heights,' he said miserably. 'The Coney Island police haven't identified it yet, but there's no doubt that when they do, they'll find that it's Big Bill Holt.'

'It's *not* Holt,' Blackstone said.

'How can you possibly say that?'

'Because I know who it *actually* is.'

'Have you lost your mind?' Meade wondered aloud.

'Not at all,' Blackstone said airily. 'It's never been clearer. And that's because I've just been talking to Mrs Turner, and she's told me all about the whores who visited the Ocean Heights bunker.'

'So what?' Meade asked.

'So they were the wrong *kind* of whores,' Blackstone replied.

TWENTY-SEVEN

Meade and Blackstone stood at the corner of Canal Street, and watched a slow stream of men enter the Blue Light Club.

'Jesus Christ, it's only just after eleven o'clock in the morning,' Meade said with disgust. 'How could anybody think about even *normal* sex at eleven o'clock in the morning?'

Blackstone grinned. Alex, he suspected, was still a virgin, intent on keeping himself pure in the hope that Miss Clarissa Bonneville's mother would eventually overlook the fact that he had chosen to become a policeman and allow him to marry her daughter.

'Now that you've seen the place for yourself, does what I've been telling you make sense?' he asked.

'Maybe,' Meade said reluctantly. 'Maybe more than maybe, but I'll still be happier when I've heard it straight from the whore's mouth.' He smiled self-consciously. 'No pun intended,' he apologized.

One of the patrolmen whose regular beat was Canal Street sidled up to them. 'The boys are ready,' he said.

Meade nodded. 'Good.'

'The thing is, they all want to know if we really *have to* do it,' the patrolman said.

'Have to do it?' Meade repeated.

'See, this *finocchio* club hands over its brown envelope regular as clockwork every week,' the patrolman explained, 'so the boys figure it has the same right to privacy as everybody else who pays a bribe.'

A look of deep contempt filled Meade's face for just a moment, and then, though it obviously took him some effort, was replaced by a bland, uncritical expression.

'Tell "the boys" they've no need to worry,' he said. 'We're not here to close the place down, or even arrest anybody. All we want to do is scare a couple of people into cooperating with us. You've no problem with that, have you?'

'No problem at all,' the patrolman agreed.

Meade watched him walk away. 'One day . . .' he said, in a half-growl, 'one day, when I'm the Commissioner of Police for New York, I'll clean up this whole rotten city.'

that his owner would never get the point without a practical demonstration – began to dig up the ground with his paws.

Now Timmy understood!

In his mind's eye, he saw a bunch of olden-day pirates, rowing away from their ship.

They moor in the shallows close to Ocean Heights – although, of course, there is no Ocean Heights there at that time – and wade ashore carrying a large wooden chest. The head pirate – who has a big black beard and a patch over one eye – looks around him, and points a hooked hand towards the woods. The buccaneers carry the chest into the woods, dig a hole, and put the chest into it. They intend to come back for it later – but they never do!

The dog was still digging furiously.

'Good boy!' Timmy said.

There would be all kinds of wonderful things in that chest!

Gold coins and bracelets!

Ancient pistols and bottles of rum!

Once he had uncovered the chest, he would go home and tell his parents all about it. And they would laugh at him, his father saying it was time he grew up, his mother cooing that he was still such a sweet little thing. But they wouldn't laugh when he put his hand in his pocket and laid some pieces of eight on the table, would they? No, they wouldn't be laughing then!

Skipper was still determinedly digging.

'Let me give you a hand, boy,' Timmy suggested.

The Labrador did not seem particularly enthused by the idea, but he knew his place in the hierarchy of things, and when Timmy knelt down beside him and edged him out of the way, he withdrew gracefully.

It was much easier to scoop out the hole than Timmy had thought it would be, and it did occur to him, as he worked, that any soil hiding a hundred-year-old treasure chest should have been more tightly packed.

It also occurred to him, when his fingers brushed against something solid which was definitely *not* earth, that the pirates had made a pretty sloppy job of things, and should really have buried their treasure *much* deeper.

And it was at that point that he cleared a little more of the earth away and saw a pair of dead eyes staring blankly up at him.

Blackstone lay on his bed, in his ratty hotel room, watching the El railway thunder past his window as it carried people with some purpose in their lives towards their destination.

He lit a cigarette, and reviewed his own situation. His fate was in the hands of Assistant Commissioner Todd, and until Todd decided what that fate would be, he was still officially on secondment to the NYPD. So there was nothing – in theory – to stop him going to the Mulberry Street police headquarters that morning.

Nothing in *theory*!

But in *practice*, what was the point?

'The point is that young Alex will be there,' he said softly, answering his own question.

Meade would be there – because Meade was ever the conscientious policeman – and when the news came through that Holt's body had been found, and his own career was in ashes, he would need the support of a good friend.

Hauling himself reluctantly off the bed, Blackstone accepted that he would have *to play* at being a policeman for just a while longer.

Despite her excitement at being in New York, Ellie Carr had slept like a log during the first few nights of her stay there, but the previous night – after her meal with Blackstone – had proved to be an exception to the rule.

She had tossed and turned for hours, and had woken up once in a hot sweat and once in a cold one. It was probably a fever, she thought, as she dropped off into an uneasy doze, but when she woke up and took her temperature, everything appeared to be normal.

'So it must be that I'm concerned about Sam,' she told herself, as she dressed. 'Yes, that's who's knocking me off balance – bloody Sam Blackstone!'

She was not even sure she had any *right* to be worried about him, she argued, as she made her way down to the street – and certainly proud, independent Sam wouldn't *thank* her for worrying. But there it was – this unsought worry – quite clearly at the centre of her being, so she supposed she was stuck with it.

She reached the City Morgue at half past eight and presented her credentials, and ten minutes later she already had the post-mortem file which she'd requested in her hand.

The office he shared with Meade was empty, though Meade's straw boater on the hat stand was proof that the detective sergeant was somewhere in the building.

Blackstone sat down at his desk, and waited.

The phone rang.

'We got a woman on the line called Mary Turner who wants to talk to you,' the operator said. 'You want me to put her through?'

He really didn't need someone informing him about the overwhelming goodness of Almighty God, Blackstone thought.

'No, tell her I'm out,' he said.

And, almost immediately, he felt ashamed of himself.

The woman had lost her husband, and if it brought her some comfort to talk about eternal certainties to some almost-stranger who believed in no such thing, then who was he to deny her the opportunity?

'Are you still there?' he asked the switchboard operator.

'Sure.'

'I've changed my mind. Put her through.'

The phone clicked, and then a new voice – which he recognized as belonging to Mary Turner – said, 'Inspector Blackstone? I have some very important information for you.'

'Go ahead,' he said, waiting to be told that salvation was his for the taking, if only he would abandon his sinful ways.

'Have you heard of a place called the Blue Light Club?'

'I can't say that I have.'

'It is a wicked, sinful place, and you must close it down immediately.'

Blackstone sighed. 'I really don't have the power to do that, Mrs Turner.'

'Then talk to someone who does,' the woman urged him. 'For it is an abhorrent place – a modern Sodom – and it must be destroyed.'

'How do you even know about this club?' Blackstone wondered.

'I learned of it from my dear husband's journal. It is this Blue Light Club – I can barely force myself to utter the name – which took Joseph to the city, and it was his dearest wish that it should be obliterated from the face of the earth.'

The wheels began to turn in Blackstone's head. Joseph Turner had been on duty the night one of the prostitutes had visited Holt in his bunker, he recalled. And that had had such an effect on Turner that he had abandoned his work with the whores of Coney Island, and devoted himself to this new mission.

'Tell me more,' he said.

The style and nature of a post-mortem report could often tell the experienced reader almost as much about the writer as the subject he was writing about, Ellie Carr thought, as she studied the report on Arthur Rudge.

In this case, she guessed, it had been written by an eager young doctor who had not yet had the time or experience to develop the cavalier attitude so often displayed by more hardened professionals. He had been careful. He had been thorough. And he had produced a very credible report, considering the material he had had to work with.

There was no doubt that Rudge had been very badly burned. Large sections of his hypodermis had been destroyed, sometimes down to the bone – but at least the bones themselves hadn't been turned to ash.

What exactly was she looking for? she asked herself, as she pored over the report.

Something that would help pull Sam out of the shit, she answered.

And while she had no idea what that *something* might be, she hoped she would recognize it when she saw it.

If Rudge had been murdered, as Blackstone suspected, then he must either have been knocked unconscious before the fire was started, or else tied up so that he could not escape from it. If the latter had occurred, then any evidence of it would have been burned away. But if it was the former, it would have been noted in the section of the report dealing with the skull.

The young doctor had found no signs of any damage to Rudge's cranium. The only injury he commented on at all was a slight chipping of the right scapula – but that could have happened long before Rudge met his death.

'This isn't going to help, Sam,' she sighed.

And you were an optimistic fool to ever think it would, she added silently.

It was as she was reading about the pelvis that she began to feel a slight, familiar tingle, and by the time she had reached the description of the fibula, it had become a positive itch.

If she'd listened correctly to what Sam had had to say about Rudge, then she was definitely on to something, she told herself.

But what if she'd misheard or misunderstood, which was always possible?

There was only one way to find out for sure – and that was to ring Sam.

But when she placed the call through to the Mulberry Street police headquarters, the switchboard operator told her that the inspector's line was engaged.

Except for the times when Blackstone interrupted her with a question, Mrs Turner talked solidly for another five minutes. She did not always keep to the point. Sometimes she spoke with the voice which imitated an evangelic preacher's. At others she would suddenly transform herself into the poor lonely widow she actually was. But sandwiched between the righteous fire of indignation and the tragic expression of loss there were words which – to an investigator – were pure gold.

When Blackstone hung up the phone, there was a smile on his face. He could never remember a case in which one piece of information had made so much difference – in which one single fact could change the whole way he looked at the investigation and provided him with the answers he had been so desperately searching for.

He thought about Inspector Flynn and his theory.

Flynn had said that the kidnapping had been faked – and he had been quite right.

Flynn had said that the *reason* it had needed to be faked was that William Holt was about to be subpoenaed to appear before a grand jury – and he had been quite right about that, too.

There was just one thing that Flynn had been wrong about. But it was a *huge* thing – a *gigantic* thing!

The office door opened, and Alex Meade entered. His shoulders were slumped and he looked utterly defeated.

'A body's been discovered in the woods near Ocean Heights,' he said miserably. 'The Coney Island police haven't identified it yet, but there's no doubt that when they do, they'll find that it's Big Bill Holt.'

'It's *not* Holt,' Blackstone said.

'How can you possibly say that?'

'Because I know who it *actually* is.'

'Have you lost your mind?' Meade wondered aloud.

'Not at all,' Blackstone said airily. 'It's never been clearer. And that's because I've just been talking to Mrs Turner, and she's told me all about the whores who visited the Ocean Heights bunker.'

'So what?' Meade asked.

'So they were the wrong *kind* of whores,' Blackstone replied.

TWENTY-SEVEN

Meade and Blackstone stood at the corner of Canal Street, and watched a slow stream of men enter the Blue Light Club.

'Jesus Christ, it's only just after eleven o'clock in the morning,' Meade said with disgust. 'How could anybody think about even *normal* sex at eleven o'clock in the morning?'

Blackstone grinned. Alex, he suspected, was still a virgin, intent on keeping himself pure in the hope that Miss Clarissa Bonneville's mother would eventually overlook the fact that he had chosen to become a policeman and allow him to marry her daughter.

'Now that you've seen the place for yourself, does what I've been telling you make sense?' he asked.

'Maybe,' Meade said reluctantly. 'Maybe more than maybe, but I'll still be happier when I've heard it straight from the whore's mouth.' He smiled self-consciously. 'No pun intended,' he apologized.

One of the patrolmen whose regular beat was Canal Street sidled up to them. 'The boys are ready,' he said.

Meade nodded. 'Good.'

'The thing is, they all want to know if we really *have to* do it,' the patrolman said.

'Have to do it?' Meade repeated.

'See, this *finocchio* club hands over its brown envelope regular as clockwork every week,' the patrolman explained, 'so the boys figure it has the same right to privacy as everybody else who pays a bribe.'

A look of deep contempt filled Meade's face for just a moment, and then, though it obviously took him some effort, was replaced by a bland, uncritical expression.

'Tell "the boys" they've no need to worry,' he said. 'We're not here to close the place down, or even arrest anybody. All we want to do is scare a couple of people into cooperating with us. You've no problem with that, have you?'

'No problem at all,' the patrolman agreed.

Meade watched him walk away. 'One day . . .' he said, in a half-growl, 'one day, when I'm the Commissioner of Police for New York, I'll clean up this whole rotten city.'

And he probably would, Blackstone thought.

'What does *finocchio* mean?' he asked.

'It means "fairy",' Meade said. 'It's an Italian word for what – in the Lower East Side at least – is mainly an Italian vice.'

The arrival of four uniformed policemen, blowing their whistles and waving their nightsticks, sent a wave of panic through the clients at the Blue Light Club.

'I just walked in off the street. I swear to you, officers, I had no idea what was going on in here!' babbled one portly middle-aged man, as he struggled to button up his pants.

'Look, you gotta let me go,' pleaded another man. 'I'm not a bad guy. I'm a deacon at St Mary's.'

'Everybody shut the hell up – or I'll start making arrests right here and now!' Meade bawled from the doorway.

Gradually the noise subsided.

'I'm not here to judge you,' Meade continued, 'but if that was my intention, I'd have to say that you're the biggest collection of sick bastards I've ever come across, and you should all be thoroughly ashamed of yourselves.'

'I am,' a stick-thin man in a flashy suit moaned. 'I am – and I promise I'll never do it again.'

'The customers can go,' Meade said. 'The people who work here – if that's what you want to call it – will stay.'

There was no real difficulty in telling the two groups apart. The customers – who shuffled through the door with their eyes fixed on the ground – were mostly in their thirties and forties, and wearing their business suits. The workers were much younger – in their teens and twenties – and though some of them were wearing men's clothing, they all had painted faces and heavily blackened eyebrows.

'Right,' Meade said, when all the customers had gone, 'now I'd like to talk to the boss.'

The boss was a thickset man in a blue dress, and even the heavy make-up he was wearing did not quite obscure the stubble on his square jaw. He said he'd like to be addressed as Miss Annie, if they didn't mind, and Meade bit on the bullet and said he didn't mind at all.

'You know, it's really not fair that you should disrupt my business in this way,' Miss Annie said, in a high falsetto voice which didn't quite come off. 'I should be very cross indeed, but,' looking directly into Meade's eyes, 'it's hard to be cross with such a pretty boy as you.'

Meade shrank away, and it was all Blackstone could do to stop himself from laughing out loud.

'I . . .' Meade began, with a crack in his voice which showed just how dry his throat had suddenly become.

'You do *know* you're a pretty boy, don't you?' Miss Annie interrupted.

'And *you* do know that we could haul you – and all your nancy boys – down to the jail, don't you?' Blackstone asked, deciding the time had come to rescue his partner.

Miss Annie flashed him a look of pure hatred. 'And how long do you think you could *keep* us in jail?'

'Not long,' Blackstone admitted. 'But then, consider this – you don't have to go jail *at all*. If you were to answer a few simple questions, we'd be out of here before you could say, "Bent as Dickie's hat band".'

'What kind of questions?' Miss Annie asked suspiciously.

'Let's start with an easy one,' Blackstone suggested. 'How long have you been sending out your whores to the house on Coney Island?'

'Entertainers,' Miss Annie said. 'They are *entertainers*.'

'Your entertainers, then. *How long?*'

'I'm really not sure I know what you're talking about,' Miss Annie said huffily.

'Call for a paddy wagon,' Blackstone told Meade. 'It's time to make a few arrests.'

'There's no need to be so hasty,' Miss Annie told him. 'Did you say a house on Coney Island?'

'Yes.'

'I suppose I must have been sending my entertainers there for six or seven years, now.'

'And how is it arranged?'

'A gentleman called Fanshawe – an *English* gentleman like yourself, though with more manners – visits us about once a month. Not for his own benefit, you understand, but merely acting as an agent for another gentleman.'

'I understand.'

'Mr Fanshawe knows the other gentleman's taste, and selects an appropriate entertainer to meet his needs. The entertainer travels back to Coney Island in the afternoon, and returns to the city the next morning.'

'What's the name of this other gentleman?' Blackstone asked.

'I have no idea, but my girls tell me he likes them to call him "Daddy".'

'And what does he look like?'

'How would I know that? I've never met the gentleman.'

'If your "girls" have told you what he wants them to call him, I'm sure they've also given you a description of him,' Blackstone said.

Miss Annie sighed. 'This is all most unprofessional, you know.'

'Give me a description, and that's the last you'll see of us,' Blackstone promised.

Miss Annie nodded, and did as requested.

'Now do you believe me?' Blackstone asked Meade.

'Now I don't think there's any doubt about it,' Meade said.

When Blackstone, Meade and Ellie Carr got off the streetcar at its terminal on Coney Island, the veteran Sergeant Jones was already waiting for them with the police carriage.

'How's our Inspector Flynn?' the sergeant asked, once the introductions had been performed.

'Inspector Flynn is growing stronger all the time,' Blackstone told him. 'And when I get back to city and report to him on what's happened here, I wouldn't be at all surprised if he rises up from his sick bed and does a jig.'

'I'm delighted he's improving,' Jones said, 'but I think you're wrong about the jig. It's not Mr Flynn's style.'

But maybe it would be, now that the heavy weight he'd been carrying on his shoulders for seven years was finally about to be lifted, Blackstone thought.

'Did you seal off the house?' he asked.

'We did,' Jones confirmed, sounding a little worried. 'But I can't say the family were exactly happy about it. Mr George said,' he glanced at Ellie, 'excuse my language, ma'am – he said that first he'd have my balls on a platter, and then he'd have my job.'

'That's just the sort of thing Mr George *would* say, but your job is safe enough – and so are your balls,' Blackstone assured him. 'You didn't tell him *why* you'd sealed it off, did you?'

'No, only that I'd been instructed to.'

'So nobody in Ocean Heights knows anything about the corpse that was found in the woods?'

'Not a thing.'

'And where is the corpse now?'

'It's in the local mortuary,' Jones turned to Ellie. 'Will you want him moved somewhere else, ma'am?'

'No,' Ellie replied. 'I can cut him up in the mortuary just as easily as I can cut him up anywhere else.'

'It's a strange job for a lady,' Jones said, almost to himself.

'Well, then, it's just as well that I ain't one,' Ellie countered, in her best cockney.

The man lying on the mortician's table was in his middle to late forties. He was five feet five inches tall, and had a bald head and waxed moustache which looked considerably less elegant than it must have done before it had been covered with earth.

Ellie studied him for a moment, then said, 'I'll have to cut him up, of course, but I'd be surprised if the cause of death was anything other than a single – rather professionally delivered – puncture wound to the heart.'

Jake and Bob had bragged about killing three men in the saloon – the Pinkerton men and one other. For a while, Blackstone and Meade had thought that the third victim might be Big Bill Holt, and then that it was Fanshawe the butler. But it had been neither of them – it was this man lying on the table.

'I'll need to do some tests, but I'd guess he's been dead for about four days,' Ellie said.

'You may be right,' Blackstone told her. 'In fact, I *know* you're right – although, legally speaking, he's been dead for seven years.'

TWENTY-EIGHT

Blackstone and Meade were shown into the parlour in which they'd first met the two Holt families, and, as on the previous occasion, Harold and Virginia were sitting on one sofa and George and Elizabeth on another. This time, however, there were no straight-backed chairs for the two detectives to sit on – this time, it was plain, their visit was unwelcome.

'I must complain in the strongest possible terms, Inspector Blackstone!' George said. 'We have been told by your police officials that under no circumstances are we to be allowed to leave the house. We have, in short, been treated like common criminals, and I very much resent it!'

'Shut up, George,' Harold said firmly.

'What was that, little brother?' George asked, amazed.

'It takes a brave man to forcibly detain an important family like ours, George. Do you think Inspector Blackstone would ever have contemplated such an action if he didn't believe he could more than justify it to some higher police authority?'

George frowned. 'No, I . . . err . . . suppose not,' he said doubtfully.

'So your best plan would be to shut up, and let him tell us exactly what's *made* him so brave, wouldn't it?'

'I still think it's a damned impertinence,' George said.

'I have something that I wish to say to you, Inspector,' Virginia told Blackstone.

He turned towards her. She had on a dress with a flared skirt and a finely beaded bodice which swept down to her magnificent cleavage, and she was wearing silk flowers in her hair. She looked stunning, he thought.

'Yes, ma'am?' he said.

Virginia gave him a look which would have reduced a lesser man to a smouldering crisp.

'I thought you should know that I have better things to do with my time than sit here listening to a man in a shabby suit expound his improbable theories,' Virginia said. 'And so, for that matter, does my sister-in-law,' she added, standing up. 'Come, Elizabeth.'

Elizabeth looked up at Virginia with startled eyes. *She* was wearing a day dress of finely striped cotton, and though it – like Virginia's – had a plunging neckline, what bosom she had was chastely covered by the cotton blouse she wore beneath the dress.

'Come, Elizabeth,' Virginia repeated.

The other woman studied her hands. 'I'm not sure . . .' she mumbled.

'Now!' Virginia said firmly.

And Elizabeth rose reluctantly to her feet.

'It's all right with *you* if we leave, isn't it, Inspector Blackstone?' Virginia asked.

'It's all right with me,' Blackstone agreed.

Virginia shook her head, and her magnificent curls swirled around her shoulders,

'That is a pity,' she said. 'I *was* rather hoping you'd forbid it, so I could have the pleasure of ignoring you.'

She walked out of the room with the stately glide of a galleon, while Elizabeth followed meekly in her wake.

'She has some spirit, that wife of yours, Mr Holt,' Blackstone said.

'Yes,' Harold agreed, in a suddenly subdued voice. 'Yes, she does.'

'How's your head now?' Blackstone continued, looking at the bandage swathed around the top of Harold's skull.

'Much improved,' Harold replied.

Blackstone nodded. 'Good! But then it wasn't really that serious an injury in the first place, was it? Self-inflicted ones never are.'

'Self-inflicted ones!' George sputtered. 'What the hell are you talking about? My poor brother was dragged across the fourth floor of Moore's Dry Goods Store by two large men—'

'No, he wasn't,' Blackstone interrupted. 'Those men never existed. Oh, I know you had to have someone else to make the phone calls and plant the incendiary devices, but it would have been far too risky to get your accomplices more *actively* involved in the plot – because there was always the chance they might get caught. And, after all, they weren't really necessary, were they?'

'Involved in the plot?' George repeated. '*What* plot?'

'I'd like you to think back to the moment in the Silver Spur Saloon when the kidnappers called,' Blackstone said.

'Why should I do that?' George asked.

'Because you asked me *what* plot – and I'm about to tell you.'

'Waste of time,' George said.

'But you'll do it?'

'I suppose so.'

When the phone rings, it is Alex Meade who answers it.

'*Harold Holt?*' *asks the man on the other end of the line.*
'*Yes.*'
'*No, it ain't. Get me Holt right now – or the whole deal's off, and his father's dead.*'
'How did the kidnapper know it wasn't Harold he was talking to?' Blackstone asked George.
'I should have thought it was obvious. He didn't *sound* like Harold.'
'No, that's not it at all. Alex's problem was that he didn't know the password.'
Meade gestures to Harold to join him, and hands him the earpiece.
'*Yes?*' *Harold says, with a slight tremble in his voice.* '*Yes, this is Harold James Holt.*'
'Harold *James* Holt,' Blackstone said. 'Like all good passwords, it was simple and innocuous – so simple, in fact, that I didn't recognize it for what it was at the time, though looking back, it's obvious.'
'This is insane!' George said.
'I must admit, you put on a good double act in that saloon,' Blackstone continued, ignoring him. 'You with your concern for your brother's safety, him nervous, yet determined to go through with it. But that's all it was – an act!'
'So what you're saying is that there *were* no kidnappers in Moore's?' George asked.
'Yes, that's exactly what I'm saying.'
'Then what happened to the money?'
'Interesting question,' Blackstone said. 'The disappearance of the money is crucial to the illusion you wanted to create, because it was meant to prove that the kidnappers *were* there.'
'Well, exactly!' George said. 'I mean, there wasn't an illusion, but—'
'So it's possible that, in order to make it disappear, Harold simply threw it on one of the fires that were blazing merrily away on Moore's fourth floor.'
'You're saying that he would have been willing to *burn* half a million dollars?'
'Then again, it's possible that on the journey between the police station and the saloon you switched the money for dollar-sized pieces of paper, and *that* was what Harold threw on to the fire. I don't know which of those two things actually happened, but I expect, now they know what they're looking for, the fire department should be able to tell us in a day or two.'
'So we took Father's ransom money and either burned it or hid it?' George asked.

'Now you're catching on,' Blackstone agreed. 'After all, why would you *want* to pay a ransom for a man who's been dead for seven years?'

'Dead for seven years! Father was alive *four days ago*,' George protested. 'He may *still* be alive – and you should be looking for him now, rather than wasting time by persecuting us!'

'The man in the bunker *wasn't* your father,' Blackstone said. 'And once we'd realized that, a number of things that had been puzzling us suddenly started to make sense. For instance, we wondered why you would have employed such a lifeless creature as Judith to clean your father's apartment, and, of course, it was her very lifelessness – her lack of interest in anything – that recommended her. She never questioned that the man she was cleaning for was Big Bill Holt. Bloody hell, he could have had two heads and I doubt she'd have noticed.'

'The thing you *did* have to be worried about was the laundry,' Meade said. 'Although none of the staff had ever met your father, it was just possible that one of them would have heard he was a big man, and have started to wonder why the clothes he sent to the laundry in the basement were so small. That's why none of the clothes from the bunker *ever* did go to the laundry.'

'*What happened to his dirty clothes?*' Blackstone asks Judith. '*Someone must have taken them away for laundering, mustn't they?*'

'*I saw Mr Fanshawe with a bag of his laundry, once or twice,*' the reluctant parlour maid admits.

'And Fanshawe, of course, was what we British would call "your loyal retainer", bound to you both by his sense of duty and by the fact that you probably somehow found out that he was wanted for murder in England, and thus had him completely in your power.'

'Fanshawe – a murderer! I don't believe it!' George said.

'Now that wasn't really convincing, was it?' Blackstone asked Meade.

'Not convincing at all,' Meade replied.

'If it wasn't our father in there, why did we pay the Pinkertons a small fortune to guard him?' asked George, changing tack.

'The Pinkertons were there to keep out unwanted visitors, who might discover the truth,' Blackstone said. 'Besides, it all contributed to the illusion – the place wouldn't be worth guarding if Big Bill wasn't there, but it was being guarded, so he *must* be there.'

'Let me see if I understand this,' George said. 'You're saying that our father died seven years ago, and that we've been keeping his death secret since then. Is that right?'

'Half-right,' Blackstone said. 'You had to keep his death a secret, because the business was your father, and your father was the business, and if it had become common knowledge that he was dead, the shares would have collapsed. That's when you came up with the idea of him becoming a hermit, and, I must say, you played that out to perfection.'

'How can you say that Father was cowardly to take the precautions he did?' Harold demands angrily. 'And that's what you're doing, isn't it – calling him a coward?'

George's expression softens. 'I never used that word, little brother,' he says, in a much gentler voice. 'What he did was weak, rather than cowardly.'

'You get the point?' Blackstone asked Meade. 'As long as they were discussing him in those terms, the main question we would be asking ourselves was which one of them was painting a more realistic picture of their father. And whatever side of the fence we eventually came down on, our automatic assumption would be that their father was still alive.'

'Very clever,' Meade said, with mock admiration.

'You said I was *half-right* about your preposterous theories,' George said.

'Yes, I did.'

'So in what way was I *half-wrong*?'

Blackstone walked over to the window, and looked out. Virginia and Elizabeth were walking in the garden. Virginia had her hand firmly on Elizabeth's arm, and was talking earnestly to her. Elizabeth, for her part, looked as if she might collapse at any moment.

Blackstone ran his hand across his forehead. The room was hot and sticky with guilt and denial, and what he really needed at that moment, he decided, was a breath of fresh air.

'So in what way was I *half-wrong*?' George repeated, from behind him.

Blackstone turned around.

'You were wrong to assume that I believe your father simply died,' he told George.

'But I thought you just said that he—'

'He didn't simply *die* at all. You murdered him.'

TWENTY-NINE

T he four men walked slowly through the gardens which over-
looked the ocean. They were not entirely alone. Posted at a
discreet distance were several uniformed policemen. But the
officers weren't really necessary, Blackstone thought – because
George wouldn't try anything without Harold's say-so, and Harold
was too smart for that.

'Do we have to go through this charade?' George asked.

'No, it's entirely your choice,' Blackstone told him. 'If you'd
prefer it, we can have the conversation in Coney Island police headquarters.'

'Oh, get it with it, then,' George said.

'I intend to,' Blackstone said, coming to a sudden halt. 'It was
roughly on this spot that I had my talk with Fanshawe, no more
than an hour before he died. He'd come up to the room that you'd
assigned us, to ask if we wanted anything to drink. Did you know
that?' He paused. 'But of course you knew it – because one of you
had sent him up there to be *noticed*.'

'Perhaps, rather than that, one of us sent him up there to see if
you were thirsty,' Harold said.

But he didn't say it as if he expected to be believed, because –
unlike his brother – he already knew the game was lost.

'You sent him so he could be noticed,' Blackstone said firmly,
'and so he could deliver the script which you had written for him
– a script which you hoped would establish that you stood to gain
nothing by your father's death.'

'So Big Bill's still running the business?' Blackstone asks, looking
out over the ocean.

'Not really,' Fanshawe replies. *'Mr George and Mr Harold make
most of the decisions since he signed the company over to—'*

'Since he signed the company over to them?'

*'For God's sake, don't tell anybody I told you, or I'll lose my
job.'*

'It must have been while Fanshawe and I were talking that you
realized he had made a big mistake earlier that morning,' Blackstone
said to Harold.

'Really? And what mistake might that have been?'

'Fanshawe hadn't taken a breakfast tray down to the bunker – which meant he already knew, before he even got there, what he would find. If *you* could spot that mistake, the chances were that I would too, and Fanshawe suddenly stopped being a valuable asset and became a very dangerous liability. He had to die, so George – I assume it was George – lured him into the woods, half strangled him, and then hung him from the tree.'

'So now it's not our father you're accusing us of killing, it's our butler,' George said.

'I'm accusing you of killing both of them,' Blackstone replied. 'And those two murders are just a start.' He lit up a cigarette. 'I think we'll go down to the bunker, next.'

'I . . . I don't want to go down to the bunker,' George gasped, in a half-strangled tone.

'For God's sake, George, be a man for once!' Harold said.

There was very little room for four men to stand in the small guard room, but though George and Harold seemed uncomfortable about rubbing shoulders with the others, Blackstone himself appeared to be perfectly at ease.

'I can't tell you *exactly* what happened that night, but I think I can give you a rough outline,' Blackstone said.

The guards have been told to expect two visitors – the first visitors, apart from his ladies, that Mr Holt has ever had – but when they arrive, it is a shock, because they look like such rough types that it is hard to imagine Holt ever wishing to associate with them. But Fanshawe is there, and Fanshawe says these are the people Holt wants to see, so it must be all right.

'Take them through into the boss's suite,' the butler says.

And that is strange, too, because neither of the guards has been inside the suite before.

They open the door, and step to one side to let the visitors enter first.

'You lead the way,' Fanshawe tells them.

The guards enter the suite. The boss is sitting behind his desk.

Up until this moment, they have only ever caught the occasional glance of him, when one of the Persons Permitted to Enter visited. Now, for the first time, they get a proper look at the man, and it occurs to both of them that he seems very unprepossessing for someone with so much power.

'Stand in front of my desk,' the boss says.

'Us?' one of the guards asks.

'You,' the boss replies.

The guards do as they've been ordered, and two seconds later they are gasping for breath as sharp knives slash across their throats.

The guards crumple to the ground.

'You ready?' one of the visitors asks the man behind the desk.

'I'm ready.'

'Then let's get the hell out of here.'

They meet Fanshawe on the way out. He is carrying several suits – which clearly belong to a big man – over one arm. He enters the suite, steps around the dying guards, and walks into the bedroom. He opens the wardrobe and hangs up the suits, then removes a second set of suits – made for a much smaller man – which had been hanging there. By the time he returns to the study, the guards are already dead.

'That about covers it, don't you think?' Blackstone asked.

'And just who is this man behind my father's desk supposed to have been?' George asked.

'Arthur Rudge, of course,' Blackstone said.

'But Rudge is—' George began.

But when Blackstone held up his hand for silence, he obeyed.

'Once you'd come up with your bunker idea, you had the problem of who to put in it – because there did have to be *somebody* there,' Blackstone said. 'And you had a second problem – who would actually *run* the company now your father was gone. The solution to the second problem was obvious – Arthur Rudge would do it. He was more than just the head bookkeeper – he was at least half of your father's business brain. You admitted that yourselves – or, at least Harold did.'

'If Father's enemies were brave enough to murder someone as important to the company as Rudge—' Harold says.

'He wasn't important to the company!' George interrupts. 'Hell, we've managed well enough without him, haven't we?'

'We've certainly managed,' Harold agrees cautiously. 'But it wasn't that easy at first. We made mistakes which cost us hundreds of thousands of dollars – mistakes which we'd never have made if we'd had Rudge to advise us.'

'There's that clever trick again,' Blackstone told Meade. 'Just as they talked about Big Bill as if he was alive, when in fact he was dead, they talked about Rudge as if he was dead, when the truth was that he was very much alive.'

'Rudge died in a fire in his apartment,' George said. 'Read the police report. They found his body in his bedroom.'

'They found *a* body in the bedroom,' Blackstone corrected him. 'Or rather, since the fire had been so fierce, they found the dead man's bones. And those bones, according to Dr Carr, who's recently read the report, belonged to a much bigger man than Rudge.' He paused again. 'That, of course, would explain the two men with the armoire.'

'What two men with the armoire?' George asked.

'On the day of the fire, two men arrived at Rudge's apartment while he was still at work, carrying the armoire. Twenty minutes after he'd got back, they left again, taking the armoire with them. And what was in that armoire? When they arrived, it was your dead father. When they left, it was Rudge.'

'Rudge did die in that fire in his apartment,' George said stubbornly. 'Your doctor's wrong about the bones.'

'I don't imagine he was entirely happy with the idea of living underground, but you probably gave him no choice in the matter,' Blackstone said. 'However, you had to do something to make his life bearable, and that's why you allowed him a visitor once a month – a visitor who Fanshawe brought from the Blue Light Club, and who Rudge asked to call him "Daddy".'

'Rudge's parties were a positive disgrace,' Mrs Fairbrother, the neighbour, says. 'There were only women invited – sometimes half a dozen, sometimes even more. You'll have noticed I said "women" and not "ladies"? That's because that's exactly what they were. Harlots! Painted Jezebels.'

They'd certainly been painted in the photographs that Mrs Fairbrother had shown him, Blackstone thought. And tall, too – tall enough to be men!

'It was because of Rudge's "lady" friends that the guards had to die, wasn't it?' he asked. 'I imagine your original plan was just to drug them – that would certainly have been easy enough. But then you learned – perhaps through Fanshawe – that Joseph Turner knew all about the Blue Light Club on the Lower East Side.'

'Turner had never met your father, so he didn't know that Big Bill's taste would never have run to "fairies",' Meade said. 'But there was always the danger that he'd talk to someone else about it, and that that someone would draw the correct conclusion – which was that if the man in the bunker liked fairies, then that man could never have been William Holt.'

'So Turner had to die,' Blackstone continued. 'There was simply no alternative. And by incorporating his murder into the kidnapping, you not only gave the killer a perfectly understandable motive for that murder, but you made the kidnapping seem much more real, too.'

A fatuous smile – half-relief, half-triumph – suddenly appeared on George's face. 'I've just found a big hole in your theory,' he said.

'Have you?' Blackstone asked.

'Indeed I have. According to you, we covered up our father's death to safeguard the value of our shares. Is that right?'

'Yes.'

'And yet we were prepared to fake a kidnapping, which was bound to have a similar effect. How do you explain that?'

'You've had seven years to re-jig the company so that you could protect yourselves from a fall in share prices,' Meade said. 'You told us yourselves that you signed an agreement with another company the very day your "father" was "kidnapped".'

'But you'd have had to fake it even if it ruined you,' Blackstone added. 'You had no other choice – because your father was about to be subpoenaed by the grand jury, and there wasn't any way of explaining why he couldn't appear without implicating yourselves in his murder.'

George's smile had already faded away into nothingness, but he made one last attempt to fight back.

'If Rudge didn't die in the fire, but lived here instead, where is he now?' he asked.

'He died in the woods outside this house, four days ago – just as you intended him to – and now he's in the Coney Island mortuary,' Meade said.

George looked thunderstruck.

'You didn't know we'd found the body, did you?' Blackstone asked. 'But your brother did. He realized quite a while ago that that was the only possible way we could know so much.'

They had returned to the parlour, but now, instead of occupying a sofa each, the two brothers had decided to sit side by side.

'Your path has certainly been littered with bodies,' Blackstone said, looking down at them. 'Let me see if I can remember them all. There was Fanshawe and Rudge, Turner and Cody—'

'Mad Bob and Jake the Snake,' Meade interrupted.

'Yes, it's quite true that you hired a second set of killers to rub out your first set,' Blackstone said to the brothers, 'but we'll never be able to prove that, and anyway, rubbing out Bob and the Snake was almost a public service – so you get a free pass on those two.'

'How very kind of you,' Harold said.

'And now we come to the big one – the one that started everything,' Blackstone continued. 'I mean, of course, your father's murder. Would you care to tell us about it?'

Harold smiled sardonically. 'No, if you're so smart, *you* tell *us*,' he said.

'All right, I will,' Blackstone agreed. 'I can't tell you *exactly* when he was killed, but it must have been some time between when Knox shot him and the evidence against Knox went missing.'

'You didn't expect any trouble from the powerful Holt family over the fact that the evidence had disappeared?' Blackstone asks Captain O'Shaugnessy.

'Hell, no! They knew the way things work in this city. If they wanted the case to go to court, all they had to do was pay the sergeant a bigger bribe than Knox had, and the evidence would turn up again.'

'But the Holts never did pay a bribe?'

'That's right. And that was a real surprise to me, because Big Bill was known to be one of the most vengeful men in New York City.'

'Your father couldn't pay the bribe because he was already dead,' Blackstone said. 'And you didn't *want* to pay it, because if the case ever went to court, Big Bill would have to appear as a witness – and, of course, he couldn't.'

'Why *should* we have killed him that night?' George demanded.

'Fool!' Harold spat angrily.

'What your brother means is that you've just given the game away, because I never said he *was* killed on *that* night,' Blackstone told George. 'But if you want me to give a reason why it happened then, I will.' He paused for a moment. 'According to the police report, filed by our old friend Inspector Flynn, your father wasn't alone when Knox tried to kill him. He had a woman with him.'

'He always had women with him,' George said with disgust.

'Knox thought that the woman was a common whore – but I'm guessing she wasn't. Your father – monster that he was – was known for seducing any woman he could, including the wives of close associates. And I think this time he got even closer than that – I think that this time the woman was Virginia.'

'That's a disgusting suggestion,' George said.

'Seducing your son's wife,' Blackstone mused. 'That's the supreme act of bullying, isn't it? But it was also a big mistake. When George came to his father's aid that night, and saw the two of them together, he must have been so shocked he hardly knew what he was doing. Certainly, his first act was to protect your father by disabling Knox – but that was no more than a reflex action. But later, when the shock had worn off, he found that he was in a blinding anger, because this really *was* the straw that broke the camel's back. I would guess – and again, I *am* guessing, though you have pretty much confirmed it – that you confronted your father that very same night, George, after the police had had taken Knox away, and then, in a towering rage, you killed him.'

'Of course, you'll never be able to *prove* any of this,' George said.

'Oh, George, why *are* you such a fool?' Harold asked, exasperatedly.

'Your brother's right,' Blackstone agreed. 'If you think we can't prove it, you *are* a fool. Even as we speak, your father's body is being disinterred from the grave that bears Rudge's headstone.'

'It's only bones,' George said.

'Indeed it is,' Blackstone agreed. 'And one of those bones, the scapula, will have a chip out of it which will be a perfect match with the wound your father received when Knox shot him.'

'You've no idea what it was like to have a father like ours – to go through the miserable childhood we went through,' Harold said, with unexpected vehemence. 'We'd *earned* a better life when we grew up. We were *entitled* to it. And if we had to kill our father to get it, who can blame us?'

'You may have a point,' Blackstone conceded. 'But how do you justify killing the two Pinkerton men?'

'If we were to have what we deserved, they were necessary sacrifices,' Harold said, with an indifference which was even more shocking than his sudden anger.

'There's a lot of your father in you,' Blackstone said thoughtfully. 'Probably much more of him than there is in George.'

'Do you think I don't know that?' Harold demanded. 'Do you think I don't have that brought home to me every single day, when I see just how weak my big strong brother really is?'

'Please, Harold, don't . . .' George begged, as tears began to run down his cheeks.

'I love you, George,' Harold said, and he began crying, too. 'You're the most important thing in the world to me. But you have to see that none of this would have happened if only you'd been a different man.'

THIRTY

'**N**ow haven't you just gone and made me look like some kind of prize idjit?' Inspector Flynn asked, gazing up from his hospital bed at his visitor.

'You made a valuable contribution to the investigation,' Blackstone told him.

'Sure, and what could be *more* valuable than chasing after a man who's already been under the sod for seven years?' Flynn countered, with just a flicker of a smile appearing at the corners of his mouth.

'Without the work you put in, there'd have been no investigation at all,' Blackstone pointed out.

'And I'm not sure that would have been such a bad thing,' Flynn said, growing more serious. 'If I'd have kept my nose out of it, Harold and George would have got away with doing the world a favour – and the two Pinkerton men would still be alive.' He paused. 'It could be argued that those two men's deaths are on my head.'

'You can't think about it like that,' Blackstone told him. 'You just have to do what you believe is right, and hope that people don't get hurt in the process.'

Flynn's amused grin returned for a moment. 'You're wasted in Scotland Yard, Mr Blackstone,' he said. 'You'd have made a damn fine priest.'

'Which, given your opinion of priests, is not necessarily a compliment,' Blackstone said.

'That's right enough,' Flynn agreed.

'So what are your plans when you're discharged from hospital?' Blackstone wondered. 'Will you stay on Coney Island? Or now that your reason for being there has gone, will you ask for a transfer back to Manhattan?'

'Maybe neither,' Flynn said reflectively. 'Maybe, now I've got my own personal monkey off my back, I'll go back to the old country and help my compatriots get the monkey off theirs.' He paused again. 'It's you English I'm talking about,' he amplified.

'I know it is,' Blackstone said. He flicked open his pocket watch. 'I have to go.'

'And what might you be rushing off to?' Flynn asked. 'Is Wall Street so grateful that you've proved Bill Holt is finally dead that it's throwing you a victory parade?'

'Nothing like that,' Blackstone answered. 'I have to say goodbye to a friend.'

'Goodbye? Or *au revoir*?' Flynn asked, detecting something in the other man's tone.

'I don't know,' Blackstone admitted. 'Only time will tell.' He walked over to the door, then turned on the threshold. 'You know what you said about returning to Ireland?'

'Yes?'

'I wouldn't, if I were you.'

'And why might that be?'

'There's been a lot of blood spilled there in the past – and there'll be more spilled in the future. And I wouldn't like to think that some of it might end up sticking to *your* hands.'

'You can't think about it like that,' Flynn said, mockingly throwing Blackstone's own words back at him. 'You just have to do what you believe is right, and hope that people don't get hurt in the process.'

The train was almost ready to leave the station, but Ellie Carr still seemed reluctant to board it.

'Don't worry, you'll charm Chicago just like you've charmed New York,' Blackstone said.

'Yeah, I'm a real little charmer, ain't I?' Ellie said. 'A bleedin' world champion!' She paused. 'It don't seem to 'ave much effect on you, though, does it, Sam?'

'You *do* charm me,' Blackstone said awkwardly.

'But not enough to make you get on the train with me?'

'No, not enough for that. I can't just follow you around for the rest of my life. I have to *work*, Ellie. I have to do the job I *was* born to do – because if I don't, I'm nothing.'

A serious – almost sorrowful – expression came to Ellie's face, as if she were about to say something of great significance. Then, slowly, the expression drained away, and was replaced by a cheeky grin.

'Course yer can't come wiv me,' she said. 'Yer an 'ero, ain't yer? An' 'eroes 'ave got to stay around to be admired.'

Blackstone smiled. 'I might be a hero today, but it won't last,' he said.

'Bloody right, it won't,' Ellie agreed. 'Before this train even reaches Chicago, you'll have managed to get up right up the nose of *some-body* important.'

The guard blew his whistle, and as they kissed Blackstone told himself – not for the first time – that he was probably certifiably insane. Then Ellie climbed aboard, and the train pulled away.

Blackstone walked across the station, to where Meade was waiting for him.

'You should have gone with her,' Meade said.

'I know,' Blackstone agreed.

'But since you didn't, you might consider taking an excursion to Sing Sing Prison,' Meade suggested.

'Now why would I do that?' Blackstone wondered aloud.

'Because Harold Holt wants to talk to you,' Meade told him.

The prison uniform was at least two sizes too large for him, and hung off Harold's thin shoulders like the loose skin on a chicken's neck. And yet, Blackstone thought, he did not look in the least pathetic, because the strength which he had been hiding for so long had finally been allowed to come to the surface.

'I want you to speak to the District Attorney,' he said. 'I want you to persuade him not to ask for the death penalty for my brother.'

'Nothing *I* could say would influence him,' Blackstone told him. 'But even if I could swing it, why would I?'

'Because everything was my fault. I was the leader, and George merely followed my lead.'

That wasn't what he'd said just before he and his brother had been arrested, Blackstone thought.

Back then, he'd turned to his brother with tears in his eyes, and said, '*You have to see that none of this would have happened if only you'd been a different man.*'

'Maybe a great deal of it *was* your fault,' Blackstone said to Harold, 'but it was George who started it, when he killed your father.'

'Do you *really* still think that?' Harold asked, amazed. 'Can you still believe that George could have had the nerve to kill the man who so terrified him?'

'So you're saying that *you* killed him?'

'Of course it was me! I went to see him again that night, after the police had left. I told him that of all the despicable things he'd done in his life, making his own son's wife get down on her knees to him – like a common whore – was the worst. And he laughed at me. He said he hadn't *made her* do anything. He said she'd been more than willing – that she'd appreciated being with a *real* man for once.'

'It must have been hard to take,' Blackstone said, sympathetically.

'I showed him the knife I'd brought with me – and he laughed again,' Harold continued. 'As I advanced towards him, he made no effort to defend himself. Why should he? It was only weak, nervous

Harold. But he stopped laughing when I stuck the knife in his guts
– stuck it in, and twisted it around. Then, he was screaming in agony.
Then, he was begging me – *begging me* – to stop. But I didn't stop
– not until I was absolutely certain that he'd reached the point where
he couldn't feel pain any longer.'

'And you have no regrets?' Blackstone asked.

'None,' Harold told him. 'I felt then – as I still feel now – that
that was the happiest moment of my life.'

She was standing in front of the prison, looking up at the long soulless block in which Blackstone had just visited her husband. There
was an intensity to her gaze which suggested that she thought she
might be doing some good – that, somehow, just by staring at those
blank walls, she could bring her husband a little comfort.

She was still a beautiful woman, Blackstone thought, but she had
aged at least ten years in the past few days.

He wondered whether or not he should speak to her, but as he
drew closer, she showed no signs of resenting his approach.

'How often do you come here?' he asked.

'Every day.'

'I didn't realize you were such a devoted wife.'

'Nor did I. But perhaps that is because, until recently, I never
appreciated my husband – never saw the strength that lay within
him.'

Perhaps if you had, you'd never have betrayed him with his own
father, Blackstone thought.

'Did you know that it was Harold who killed Big Bill?' Virginia
asked.

'Not until he told me, less than half an hour ago.'

'I had always assumed it was big, beefy George who had done it.
It was a great shock to learn the truth, but, almost immediately, I
began to see Harold in a new light.'

'Was that because you finally understood that he loved you so
much he was willing to kill for you?'

'He certainly killed for love, but not for the love of me,' Virginia
said, perhaps a little sadly.

'Then for who?' Blackstone wondered.

'For George, his dear brother.'

Who Harold had once blamed for their predicament, but now no
longer seemed to, Blackstone thought. But what exactly *had* he meant
when he said, '*You have to see that none of this would have happened
if only you'd been a different man*'?

'I don't understand how, when Harold killed his father, he was doing it for his brother's sake,' Blackstone admitted.

'George should have taken his own revenge on his father. But George couldn't – so Harold did it for him.'

'Revenge for what?'

'You really don't know, do you?' Virginia asked.

'No', Blackstone confessed. 'I really don't know.'

'It wasn't me on my knees before Big Bill when Knox burst into the study,' Virginia said. 'It was my sister-in-law, Elizabeth.'